Frontier

Book 2 in the The Secret War series

Copyright © Simon Haynes 2019

www.spacejock.com.au

Stay in touch!

Author's newsletter:
spacejock.com.au/ML.html

facebook.com/halspacejock
twitter.com/spacejock

Works by Simon Haynes

All of Simon's novels* are self-contained, with a beginning, a middle and a proper ending. They're not sequels, they don't end on a cliffhanger, and you can start or end your journey with any book in the series.
* *Robot vs Dragons series excepted!*

The Hal Spacejock series for teens/adults
Set in the distant future, where humanity spans the galaxy and robots are second-class citizens. Includes a large dose of humour!

Hal Spacejock 0: Origins (2019/2020)
Hal Spacejock 1: A Robot named Clunk*
Hal Spacejock 2: Second Course*
Hal Spacejock 3: Just Desserts*
Hal Spacejock 4: No Free Lunch
Hal Spacejock 5: Baker's Dough
Hal Spacejock 6: Safe Art
Hal Spacejock 7: Big Bang
Hal Spacejock 8: Double Trouble
Hal Spacejock 9: Max Damage
Hal Spacejock 10: Cold Boots

Also available:
Omnibus One, containing Hal books 1-3
Omnibus Two, containing Hal books 4-6
Omnibus Three, containing Hal books 7-9
Hal Spacejock: Visit, a short story
Hal Spacejock: Framed, a short story
Hal Spacejock: Albion, a novella
*Audiobook editions available/in progress

The Dragon and Chips Trilogy.
High fantasy meets low humour!
Each set of three books should be read in order.

1. A Portion of Dragon and Chips
2. A Butt of Heads
3. A Pair of Nuts on the Throne

Also Available:
Omnibus One, containing the first trilogy
Books 1-3 audiobook editions

The Harriet Walsh series.
Set in the same universe as Hal Spacejock. Good clean fun, written with wry humour. No cliffhangers between novels!

Harriet Walsh 1: Peace Force
Harriet Walsh 2: Alpha Minor
Harriet Walsh 3: Sierra Bravo
Harriet Walsh 4: Storm Force (TBA)

Also Available:
Omnibus One, containing books 1-3

The Hal Junior series
Written for all ages, these books are set aboard a space station in the Hal Spacejock universe, only ten years later.

1. Hal Junior: The Secret Signal
2. Hal Junior: The Missing Case
3. Hal Junior: The Gyris Mission
4. Hal Junior: The Comet Caper

Also Available:
Omnibus One, containing books 1-3
The Secret Signal Audiobook edition

The Secret War series.
Gritty space opera for adult readers.

1. Raiders
2. Frontier (2019)
3. Deadlock (2019/2020)

Collect One-Two - a collection of shorts by Simon Haynes

All titles available in ebook and paperback. Visit spacejock.com.au for details.

Bowman Press

v 1.0

This edition published 2019 by Bowman Press

Text © Simon Haynes 2019
Cover art © Bowman Press 2019
Stock cover images copyright depositphotos.com

Dedicated to you, for purchasing this book!

A squadron of ageing fighters rocketed through space, arranged in a loose V-formation. Exhausts glowed with the thrust from the powerful engines, and reflected light flickered off the fighters' polished canopies. In the vast emptiness of space the tiny ships looked like a string of lost fireflies, fragile and vulnerable.

The formation wasn't perfect, with a couple of ships slightly out of position, and the flight leader activated his comms.

'Red Two, close up. Red Five, you're drifting. Pay attention, the lot of you!'

Sam Willet was flying Red Four, slightly behind Red Two and just off his tail, and she saw the puffs from his thrusters as he altered his position. She'd anticipated him, used the same thrusters the moment he did, and the ships moved in unison. As her fighter tucked in behind Red Two, Sam cut the thrusters and adjusted her grip on the flight stick.

Thanks to an extraordinary series of events, Sam had been lucky enough to fly frontline fighters in actual combat. Now, at the controls of a slow, wallowing trainer, she felt like she'd been handed the keys to an ancient groundcar. A car which had been punished for every one of its twenty years. A car with cracked upholstery, mysterious quirks and odd smells.

Even so, Sam felt suppressed excitement coursing through her veins, because she was training to become a front-line fighter pilot. To that end, she would have flown literally anything.

'Better,' said the flight leader. 'Now, listen carefully. On my mark, I want Red Two and Red Three to break to port and starboard respectively.'

The commander wasn't much older than Sam, but he spoke with the calm drawl of someone much older. She'd heard he was being rested from the front... as if training a bunch of recruits was 'resting'. In person, he was a tall, dark-haired man who considered his words before he spoke, and he was unfailingly polite. He was also remote, and none of the trainees had been able to learn the first thing about his past, or his war record.

'Once they've gone, I want Four and Five to hunt them down. Please double-check your weapons are set to training mode, and confirm with me by return. I don't want any of you doing the Mayestrans' work for them... assuming you can hit a moving target in the first place.'

There was a pause.

'Red Two. Weapons in training mode, confirmed.'

The other pilots checked in as well, until it was Sam's turn. She reached for a dial, which was already turned to the left. Above it, a green light shone. Even so, she gave it a firm twist to be sure. 'Red Four. Training mode confirmed.'

The fighters were armed with real blasters, because in the event of a big Mayestran push, the students would be thrown headlong into battle. They wouldn't last more than a minute or two, but the theory was that while Mayestran pilots were blasting noobs in their ancient, under-powered fighters, veteran Henerians would be able to shoot *them* down.

2

All Sam had to do was turn the knob to the right, and her trainer would become a fully-armed fighter. And then, shortly after landing, she'd be thrown out of the service.

'Red Two and Three, stand by,' said the flight leader. 'On my mark...'

Out of the corner of her eye, Sam caught a flash of light. She turned to look, and saw three fighters streaking towards the formation. They were close enough to make out their shape, and with a jolt she recognised the type. Mayestrans! Thumbing her intercom, she broadcast a warning. 'Bandits at nine-o'clock high. Break, break!' Even as she was speaking, her hands and feet were busy at the controls. She hauled the stick left, to face the enemy, kicked the side thrusters to throw off their aim, and boosted the main engine to max. The engine's gentle rumble became a tortured howl, and Sam's fighter tore away from the formation before the rest of the squadron even knew what was happening.

Sam tapped the side of her helmet, focusing the HUD on the lead enemy. At the same time, with her left, she turned the fire control knob to active. A baleful red light shone from the control panel, and even as her finger tightened on the trigger, she saw incoming fire lancing from all three fighters.

The blaster fire missed, thanks to her savage manoeuvring, but her own burst hosed the leader as she flew crabwise across its path. Flickers of light danced across the ship's nose-cone, canopy, and wings, and then the fighter began to tumble in space, lifeless. Sam had destroyed enemy fighters in combat before, and they usually blew up. With a sinking feeling, she wondered whether the Mayestrans had developed new armour... or shielding.

Whatever. One enemy was down, and the other two would surely fall against five Henerians.

The remaining enemy ships split up, flying either side of her, and even though Sam turned her ship through a rapid one-eighty, she was unable to get a shot off. The Mayestrans had much better ships, though, and both swung round to fire at her as they passed. Sam reacted instinctively, hitting the lower thrusters so her ship rose like a jack-in-the-box, and she smiled grimly as the enemy fire passed harmlessly beneath her ship.

Sam and the Mayestrans were all rocketing away from each other now, although the quirk of space combat meant they were still aiming their noses at each other. There were a few bursts of fire, harmless at that distance, and then all of them were out of range of each other.

The Mayestrans rotated their ships and fired their main drives, roaring towards the rest of Sam's squadron. Meanwhile, she did likewise, trying to bring herself back to the combat. But first she had to slow to a stop, whereas the Mayestrans had the advantage of speed. Another quirk of space combat, where angular velocity meant everything.

On her HUD, Sam saw the two enemy ships fall on the Henerian training flight like a pair of sharks. The V was *still* flying in formation, minus her own ship, and she was vaguely aware of a confusion of shouting over the intercom. Finally, the squadron broke formation, but it was a right mess. Two of the trainers tangled with each other, snapping off their stubby winglets before spiralling away into space, out of control. The other trainee applied reverse thrust, losing all momentum as they tried to slow down before turning to meet the enemy. Sam watched, sickened, as the enemy fell on the dawdling ship and savaged it with long, accurate bursts. She could see the flashes even without the HUD, and she wondered which of her fellow trainees wouldn't be sitting down to dinner that night.

Then she shifted her gaze to the flight leader. He was a veteran of the wars. A survivor. He'd take out both Mayestrans, then call for help from base. They'd retrieve the body of the trainee, and more importantly, they'd scoop up all the debris for sorting and reuse.

The Mayestrans were closing on the flight leader now, and to Sam's amazement she saw him flying in a straight line. 'Flight, this is Red Four. Two bogeys inbound. Break, break!'

'*Copy you, Red Four,*' said the flight commander, in his slow drawl. '*Unfortunately, this battle is over. Stand down.*'

Then, to Sam's utter dismay, the leader continued to fly level while the two Mayestrans joined formation either side of him. Her mouth fell open, and she realised he'd just surrendered. Then she shut her mouth with a snap, and she leaned forwards into the controls, burning with anger and resentment. No wonder this damned war had gone on for decades, if veteran pilots gave up at the first sign of trouble!

Sam raced towards the three fighters, finger on the trigger. If she approached just right, raising her nose at the last moment, she could strafe both the enemy ships. Of course, the flight leader was right between them... but in her anger she decided he could take his bloody chances.

Sam's ship came rocketing in, and the three ships made a nice steady target on her HUD. At the last second she heard a shouted warning over the intercom, but by then it was far too late... for the enemy. She opened fire with a savage burst that tore into the first ship like a stream of molten lava, splashing on the hull and causing who-knew-what damage to the internals. Then she raised the nose quickly, hitting the flight leader's ship with a couple of stray shots before the burst concentrated on the second enemy.

She was closing quickly now, but Sam kept the nose pointing at the enemy as she rocketed past, her ship twisting in space as it poured a stream of blaster fire into the enemy fighter. Then, with a buzz, her power reserves were exhausted and her guns ceased their blazing fire.

As the targets shrank on her HUD, Sam set her lips in a thin line. She had no idea whether she'd just killed her flight leader, but she *had* taken out three enemy ships. On balance, she decided she'd trade one coward for three of the enemy any day.

Then her intercom squawked.

'Red Four, this is Red Leader. I ordered you to stand down, damn you. Stand down!'

Sam smiled to herself, because for once the flight leader had lost his casual, affected drawl. 'Copy, Red Leader. Are you okay... over?'

'Do you have any idea what you've done?'

'I saved your bloody hide, sir.'

'The Mayestran ships were being flown by our pilots, you gun-happy maniac. It was a test! A training mission!'

Sam looked down at her console, and the light above the fire-control knob glowed back at her with a baleful red gleam. 'Oh hell,' she muttered.

She'd just blown up three friendlies and shot up her flight leader into the bargain.

No doubt about it, they were going to throw the bloody book at her.

The three remaining fighters dropped through the atmosphere towards the waiting planet, the flight leader taking the head of the V. Boiling, super-heated air tore at the ships as they plunged towards the surface, and they left long streamers of fire in their wake. Sam's tiny cockpit shook and shuddered from the violent forces, and she fought the stick as she followed the leader in.

Despite her concentration, she managed to steal the occasional glance at the captured Mayestran fighters, which were flying in the same formation. They were bulkier than the graceful Henerian ships, with more guns and armour, but on the flip side they were less manoeuvrable. Mayestran pilots liked to attack in force, trying to hammer their enemy into submission with heavy fire. If that failed, they tended to retreat and regroup for another pass.

Sam glanced down, towards the ground. She could see a patchwork of dry-looking fields, the result of a long hot summer, and she wondered what the locals would think if they happened to look up to see friend and foe in formation. Then again, this was a frontier world, a long way from the frontline, and the locals probably wouldn't recognise a friendly fighter, let alone an enemy one.

Suddenly, there was a bellowing roar as the Mayestran ships peeled off, heading for their own landing field. Sam wasn't sorry to see them go, because most of the Mayestran fighters she'd encountered in her brief career had been doing their best to kill her, and it was unnerving to see them close up.

The three remaining fighters angled to port, following a beacon, and Sam saw a broad swathe of green ahead, nestled between twin rows of rocky hills. Most of the continent was arid, but a local species of palm tree flourished in the gentle valleys. The training base was concealed in the midst of a large plantation, with broad expanses of camouflage netting hiding bunkers, buildings and fighters alike. She knew the netting alone wouldn't conceal the base from the enemy, and there were rumoured to be electronic countermeasures as well.

Now, though, it was late afternoon, and Sam was glad. They'd yet to start on night training, and she imagined it would be ten times more difficult to set her fighter down on a small landing pad than to dock with a space station or a large carrier.

The squadron approached the base, then flew a circuit as ground staff hauled back a section of netting. Once there was enough room, the fighters approached their designated landing zones at a reduced speed, thrusters roaring as they struggled to maintain altitude. Sam's fighter slowed in mid-air, hovering several metres above the landing pad, and she jockeyed the controls as she fought its tendency to roll and yaw. At this speed her ship was highly unstable, and it took all her concentration to bring the fighter closer and closer to the ground, aiming for a nice smooth landing. She pulled a face as the forward leg touched down first, despite her efforts, then relaxed when it was followed immediately by both rears. At least she hadn't bounced the ship right off the landing pad, or scraped one leg across the hardstand until the ship toppled sideways into the dirt. She'd seen both happen before, but fortunately not to her.

The ships had barely settled when the netting was dragged into place, shading the cockpit and leaving criss-crossed shadows on Sam's flight suit. The planet was a long way from the front line, but the Mayestrans had always been keen on sneak attacks, especially against lightly-defended targets. A few well-placed bombs on a remote training base might not destroy much of value, but the damage to Henerian morale was incalculable.

Sam sat in the cockpit and listened to assorted pings and ticks as the fighter's engines cooled behind her. She wished she could stay there, or better still, take off again before the squadron leader and the base commander got hold of her. There was going to be one hell of a chewing out, and she'd probably be reduced to base duties for a week or so. Sam hoped so, because there were far worse punishments. She lay awake some nights, worried she'd mess up so badly they'd pack her off to a front-line infantry division.

There was a sudden knocking to her left, and she started, jerking her head round. The flight leader had climbed the side of her fighter, and was now frowning at her through the curved perspex canopy. His dark hair was matted in the heat, and his face was flushed as he pointed at her, then jerked his thumb towards the admin building.

Sam nodded, and began to detach the cables connecting her suit and helmet to the ship's network. Years earlier everything had been wireless, but the Mayestrans had developed jamming tech, and they'd smashed whole squadrons of helpless fighters before the Henerians reverted to an older, albeit much more secure, technology.

Secure was right, thought Sam, as she wrestled with half a dozen odd-shaped connectors. Then, frustrated, she pulled one of her thick gloves with her teeth and resorted to using her bare fingers on the finicky connectors. Once they were all loose she operated the canopy, which rose smoothly on hydraulic rams. The cockpit had already reverted to ground pressure on approach, so there was no dramatic hiss of air. Sam did get a blast of dry heat, though, and the distinctive smell of sun-baked palm trees. The canopy rose until it was vertical, pushing the loose camouflage netting higher and higher until it rose into the air like the centre of a huge tent.

After a last check behind herself, to make sure she'd disconnected every wire, Sam stepped over the side of the canopy and slid down to the ground, using the ladder's handrails to guide herself. As she stepped onto the landing pad she noticed her bare hand stinging from the touch of hot metal, and she cursed under her breath. Why hadn't they sent her to train on a snowy planet instead? Then again, she'd probably have stuck her bare hand to a patch of icy metal instead, and ended up dangling above the ground, completely helpless and in far more pain.

'That was a bit of a mess,' said a deep voice nearby.

Sam turned to see the other trainee pilot ducking under the wing of her fighter. He was short, with a broad torso and thick arms and legs, but despite his powerful build he looked nervous. His name was Piet Renford, and Sam couldn't think what he had to be worried about, because *he* hadn't disobeyed a direct order and shot up the squadron leader. 'It wasn't my finest hour,' agreed Sam.

'Oh, you did all right.' He sighed. 'At least you *did* something. The rest of us sat around like we had bulls-eyes painted on our backs.'

'You were following orders,' said Sam quickly. She glanced towards the admin building, knowing that the flight leader's mood wouldn't be getting any better. 'Listen, I–'

'If I'm ever in a real dogfight,' said Piet gravely, 'I'd rather have you covering my six than some moving target who follows all the rules.'

Sam gave him a grateful smile. 'Thanks. Now, I really–'

'When you were stationed on the Greyforth Coriolis, and the Mayestrans launched their attack–'

'I'm sorry Piet, but not right now,' said Sam, turning to leave. 'Flight's waiting for me. He's, er, not happy.'

'Oh, of course. Sorry.' The man hesitated. 'Can I buy you a drink this evening? I want to know more about Mayestran tactics, and, well, you were there.'

'Ask me later!' Sam called over her shoulder, already hurrying away. When she was posted to the training base, the other recruits had been split into two camps. The first group had pestered her for every little detail of her encounters with the Mayestran invasion fleet out near the Greyforth Coriolis, until they'd finally heard everything she had to tell them... at least three or four times. The second group were the more experienced recruits, who weren't going to demean themselves by discussing combat tactics with a raw recruit.

Sam had thought Piet was in the second group, but maybe he'd just been shy. Or, more likely, he was more interested in having a drink with her than hearing about her thrilling escapades... again.

These thoughts kept her occupied as she hurried across the hard, parched ground towards the admin block. However, as she got closer she felt a tightness in her chest and an icy cool in the pit of her stomach. By the time she pushed the doors open and entered the building, she was in a cold sweat as well.

11

'Sam Willet, sir,' she told the adjutant. 'I'm here for–'

'I know why you're here,' said the adjutant. He was a tall, grey-haired man with a severe manner, and he ran the base's admin with an iron hand. 'Sit down and wait please.'

'Yes sir.' Sam took a seat on a nearby bench, and despite the soothing quiet of the reception area she felt the pulse hammering in her throat. She wanted to pace up and down to work off the adrenaline, but forced herself to sit still, drawing in slow, deep breaths to try and calm herself.

She sat there for at least twenty minutes, until finally the adjutant looked up from his desk. 'Squadron Leader Norton will see you now. His office is down the corridor on the left.'

'Yes sir. Thank you.' Sam got up and strode down the nearby corridor, glancing at the doors. When she saw the one marked Sqn Ldr Norton, she stopped and tugged at her flight suit, trying to neaten it up. The shapeless outfit resisted her attempts, and so she gave up and knocked.

'Come,' said a grave voice.

Sam opened the door and stepped into a large, well-appointed office. Her first impression was books, awards and photos, with the Squadron Leader seated behind a large desk, reading something in a manila folder. Sam saluted, but Norton didn't look up. He just waved her towards a vacant chair.

Was he reading *her* file? Sam tried to see the name on the outside of Norton's folder, but his left hand was covering the label. He turned a page, the swish of paper loud in the quiet room, and Sam felt a shout rising in her throat. *Just tell me why I'm here!* she wanted to scream at him. *Punish me, demote me...whatever. Just put me out of my misery!*

3

There was a window behind Norton, but the outside world was hidden by the angled slats of a blind. Sam wondered if she'd still be sitting there when it got dark, and whether the Squadron Leader would mind if she nipped out to the toilet. She also wondered whether the flight leader was going to show up. Would he put in a word for her? Then she recalled the way her blaster shots had slammed into the instructor's ship, and she realised she was clutching at straws.

There was a knock at the door and David Richett, the flight leader, entered. He'd brushed his hair back, but his face was still flushed. After saluting Norton, he took the chair beside Sam, not looking in her direction.

Norton gave it a minute or two, then set the file down and eyed the pair of them across his desk. He drew in a measured breath, and then he began. 'When a recruit takes matters into their own hands, countermanding the orders of their superiors, it puts the entire squadron at risk.'

Oh hell, thought Sam. *He's sending me to the infantry for sure.*

'On the other hand, initiative and quick-thinking are needed if we're going to beat the Mayestrans.' The squadron leader tapped the file. 'Your brother is a gifted and much-decorated pilot, and I'm sure you wish to emulate him. But you must walk before you can run, Sam Willet.'

'Yes sir.'

'I know about your experience and your background. You helped save the Greyforth Coriolis. Your brother is a decorated war hero. Your parents died in the service of their nation.' Norton gestured impatiently. 'It doesn't change anything. Our job, the job of this training base, is to teach you everything you need to survive against the enemy.'

He sounded weary, and for the first time Sam could picture the weight on his shoulders. 'Yes sir. I understand.'

'Trainee Willet, you did well out there,' said Norton, 'Your reactions were fast, your tactics worked and your gunnery was on target. But that's not the point of the lesson. The exercise was meant to show that the enemy is everywhere, and space is dangerous. Never relax.'

'But sir, that's exactly what I did,' protested Sam. 'I spotted the enemy, warned the squadron and moved to engage. You can't bust me for that!'

'I'm not busting you, Sam.' Norton eyed her steadily, his gaze cool and measured. 'I'm asking you not carry the whole squadron. If the rest of them wander into an ambush, let them suffer. It's the only way they'll learn.'

The flight leader had been silent so far, but now he cleared his throat. 'Sir, can I make a suggestion?'

Norton glanced at him. 'Yes?'

'Sam's ahead of basic training. We suspected it before she got here, but today proves it.'

'Everyone has to complete basic.'

'Yes, but why not accelerate things? She can still take basic theory, but we should move her up in the practical.'

'Is that your official recommendation?'

'Yes sir. Our job is to train them up and send them out, and we'd be wasting time and resources if we put Willet though weeks of flight exercises.' The flight leader hesitated. 'There's the media aspect too. You know the top brass love a good news story, sir. *Younger sister of war hero passes training in record time*, that sort of thing. The public will lap it up.'

'I'm not letting the media put my recruit's life at risk. She has to pass every test... practical *and* theory.'

'Yes sir.'

'I'm going to make it your responsibility.'

'I can handle it, sir.'

'Very well, and bear in mind it's subject to a probationary period. One wrong step, and this experiment ends.' Norton eyed Sam. 'As for your punishment, I will leave that to your flight leader's discretion. The other recruits must understand that disobeying an order is a very serious matter. There must be consequences.' He turned to David. 'You will see to it.'

'Yes sir,' said the flight leader. He wasn't much older than Sam, but he carried himself with easy confidence.

'You will also review the setup for this particular exercise. I don't want this happening again.'

'No sir.'

Norton eyed Sam. 'From tomorrow, you will commence advanced practical training. You will start with a flight of three, taking them through standard patrols and combat manoeuvres.' He saw her look of surprise, and continued. 'We need more pilots on the front line, and we need them quickly. You already know enough to be dangerous, and before you leave this base I'm hoping you will be more of a danger to the enemy than to the rest of your squadron.'

What about learning to walk first? thought Sam, but she didn't say anything. It wasn't the first time she'd been thrown in the deep end, and she didn't mind at all. Advanced training meant she'd be fighting the Mayestrans much sooner than she expected.

'All right, both of you. Dismissed.'

Sam and the flight leader got up, saluted, and left together.

◆

'Your fellow trainees aren't going to like this,' said the flight leader, as they headed down the corridor.

'If it means I can have a go at the enemy, I don't care, sir.'

'You can cut the sir,' he said with a grin. 'If you're leading your own flight, we'll be equal rank.'

Sam stared at him. 'That's impossible.'

'Surprised, eh? It turns out that blasting my fighter wasn't the only way to get my job.' The flight leader put his hand out. 'I'm Richett, by the way. Dave Richett.'

Sam shook his hand, still in a daze. 'I didn't mean to–' she stopped. 'When I opened fire, I–'

'Relax. You would have got two of theirs for the loss of one of ours, and the brass will take those odds any day.' Richett hesitated. 'Things are bad, Sam. The Mayestrans are coming at us with everything they've got, and Fighter Command are almost at the point where they'll be dragging newbies from the simulators and shoving them straight into combat.' He gestured at the base. 'There are powerful forces in the government who see this kind of training as old-fashioned, and a waste of time. So don't be surprised at your sudden promotion. Norton needs to get batches of pilots through the system as quick as possible, or there won't *be* a system.'

16

'It sounds bad out there.'

'Just don't tell anyone else. Morale and all that.' Richett smiled. 'Listen, there's a supply ship due later, and the mess will be awash with booze. Can I buy you a drink this evening?'

Surprised, Sam looked up at him. He was a head taller than her, slim, with dark, swept-back hair and a face that spoke of intelligence and wit. She knew several recruits had crushes on the flight leader, and if she responded to him they'd have yet another reason to dislike her. Well, sod them, she thought. There was a war on and life was short. 'Sure, why not?'

They emerged from the building into the stifling heat, and they both looked round at a deep, thundering roar approaching from behind them. It was a pair of craneships flying in formation, each carrying one of the damaged fighters from the training mission. As they circled the base Sam saw fragments of metal and insulation fluttering down, the downdraft tearing them from the damaged fighters clutched beneath the ships.

'How are the pilots?' asked Sam, raising her voice over the racket.

'Still inside,' said Richett. 'They'll be as green as those palm trees by now, the way those things are swaying around.'

Sam winced. Throwing up in a fighter's tiny cockpit was unpleasant enough, but it was ten times worse if you were sealed in a spacesuit.

They watched the ships settle down, the huge claws slowly opening to release the damaged fighters. Then they both lifted off again, heading East. 'There's a base over there, right?' Sam asked Richett. 'I saw the Mayestran fighters heading that way too.'

'If there is, we're not meant to know about it,' said Richett.

'It's hardly a secret.'

17

'Tell you what, you can ask the Squadron Leader exactly where it is next time he hauls you into his office.'

'No thank you.' Sam saw he was about to leave, but there was still something she wanted to ask about. 'There's one thing I don't understand.'

'Only one?'

Sam grinned. 'One you should be able to answer, anyway. Why didn't my weapons damage anyone? Were they live or not?' She'd been puzzling over this since the dogfight, and she hadn't been able to figure it out. She'd toggled the live fire switch in her cockpit, the indicators had changed colour, and yet her weapons obviously hadn't done any harm.

'We're not dumb enough to let raw recruits fire live weapons whenever they feel like it,' said Richett, with a smile. 'I had control over all your weapons, no matter how much you flicked the switches in your own cockpits. Every flight leader has an override switch on their console.'

Sam saw the catch immediately. 'No offence, but what if we really got jumped and the enemy took you out first? The rest of us would be sitting ducks.'

'It's a dead man's switch. If the lead fighter is destroyed, the rest of the squadron's weapons automatically switch to live fire.' Still busy with the explanation, Richett continued. 'Obviously that's just for training squadrons. In real combat–' Then he stopped. 'Yeah. Well, you know about real combat.'

Sam saw a pained look cross his face, and she remembered why he was there, teaching recruits. He'd survived a couple of tough tours on the front lines, something many failed to do, and the scars obviously ran deep. 'I shouldn't ask,' she said lightly, 'but what's my punishment going to be?'

'Your what?'

'The Squadron Leader said you had to choose my punishment.'

'Oh yeah.' Richett eyed her thoughtfully. 'You did say you'd have a drink with me later, right?'

'*That's* the punishment?'

'You obviously haven't tried the booze around these parts.'

And with that, he was gone.

4

Sam was late for the afternoon lecture, and she slipped into the small room as quietly as she could, closing the door softly. There were a dozen students sitting at basic desks, the tutor up front giving a presentation on single-seater tactics.

Sam sat at an empty desk, moving the chair as quietly as possible.

'Nice of you to join us,' said the tutor sharply. Aren Grant was a short, fair-haired woman in her late twenties, and there was a jagged line of scar tissue down one side of her face, extending all the way to her neck. Rumour had it her fighter had been caught in the crossfire during a fleet encounter, and she'd been posted to the training base once the medics had patched her up. This seemed to be standard procedure for the wounded and the broken.

'I'm sorry, sir. The Squadron Leader asked to see me.'

Grant had no answer to that, and she turned on her heel to point at a diagram. 'As I was saying, this is a Mayestran single-seater, the Phase III Cygnet. They're developing a newer version, of course, but this is their primary front-line fighter for the time being.'

Piet put his hand up. 'Were those Phase III's we saw today?'

'No, they were early Phase I's, retrofitted with a few mods.'

A few students looked thoughtful. They'd already heard about the dogfight with the captured Mayestran fighters, and the ease with which they'd jumped the training squadron. Sam knew what they were thinking: If the elderly Phase I's were so capable, how much worse would the newer models be?

'We've managed to capture a few Phase Is over the years, and we have three stationed nearby for training purposes.' The tutor hesitated, as though she'd revealed a little too much. 'Keep that to yourselves, please. It might not seem like important information, but the less the enemy knows about our methods, the better. Incidentally, the Phase I might seem like a dangerous ship, but that's because you're flying outdated trainers. The Phase I is no match for our newer fighters, which is why you'll never see them in real combat.' The tutor looked around the class. 'I'm not going to lie to you. A Mayestran in a Phase III is a formidable opponent. Their fighter is powerful and heavily-armed, but they do have a couple of weaknesses.' She pointed to the diagram. 'Their extra mass means you can out-fly them, even though you'll need to hit them more often. And they also burn more fuel, which means a shorter range. More often than not they'll have to break off a fight before you do, and head for home. You will then be able to chase them down, using your superior speed against them.'

'Is it true they sometimes ram our fighters?' asked someone else.

'There have been reports, yes. We're not sure whether it was deliberate or not.'

'But their pilots survived the impact, yes?' asked Piet. 'They still got home?'

Grant nodded.

'And our pilots?'

'It's not a situation you want to be in,' said the tutor flatly. 'Now, let's discuss armament.'

The presentation went on for a couple of hours, and at the end the tutor doused the room lights before the outer doors were opened. Once Sam was outside she glanced up, but all she could see of the stars was a point of light or two gleaming through the holes in the camouflage netting. When she first arrived at the base she'd asked a fellow trainee about the low-tech defences. They'd explained that Fighter Command preferred to spend their resources defending front-line bases. That's where the early warning satellites, gun batteries and missiles went. Training bases got netting.

Then Sam realised how cold it was, and she lowered her gaze and hurried towards her quarters.

The quarters had an airlock-style arrangement, with two sets of double doors. Only one set could be opened at a time, which kept light spillage to a minimum, and Sam saw the last of her fellow students filing in as she got there. She jogged the last few metres and nodded a thank-you to Piet, who'd held the doors for her.

'Hurry up and shut the damn things,' called someone further in.

Sam obeyed, and then the short tunnel was flooded with light as the doors to the living quarters were pushed open. She was last through, and she squinted as she entered the common room. It was a large area with several desks, sofas and armchairs, and it was surrounded by doors leading to the sleeping quarters. At the rear was a double door leading to the dining area, and a separate door for the locker room, showers and toilets.

The rest of the students dispersed quickly, some flopping down on the sofas, others heading to their quarters and a few making their way towards the showers. Sam decided to clean up before heading off to meet David in the mess, so she collected a couple of things from the locker at the foot of her bunk and strode towards the showers. On the way she almost ran into Piet.

'Can we meet up in the mess later?' he asked her.

'I can't tonight.' Sam was going to tell him she was busy, but there was no point lying. He'd probably see her in the mess anyway. 'I'm already having a drink with someone.'

He looked disconcerted. 'But I really do want to talk about tactics. You must relate your experiences with the enemy.'

'Tomorrow, I promise.'

He nodded his thanks, and she walked around him and hurried to the showers. Ten minutes later she emerged again, wearing a fresh flightsuit and carrying her things. She dumped her spare gear on her bunk, then changed her mind and jammed them into her locker. It'd be just her luck if there was an inspection while she was out, even though Norton, the squadron leader, didn't seem to go in for such things. Not that the base was run like a college dorm, far from it, but Norton focused on training up pilots who could handle themselves in combat, and he didn't seem to care whether they folded their bedclothes properly.

5

The mess was five minutes' walk from her quarters, and Sam was one of several students following the narrow trail between the palm trees. It wasn't long before she encountered a low-lying building nestled in a thick grove of trees, and after passing through another airlock she ended up in the canteen. There was a bar along one wall, with several pilots sitting on stools talking to each other, their elbows resting on the scuffed wooden surface. Tables and chairs were arranged in the central area, and Sam could see a couple of her tutors relaxing with drinks. As the group of trainees arrived she saw a couple of tutors exchange a glance before moving from their table to the bar. The mess was for all ranks, but clearly they didn't feel like mingling with student pilots.

Behind the bar was a row of dispensers, and a battered green robot took orders and served drinks. Everyone paid with credit chits: little plastic squares embossed with the crest of the Henerian Navy. There was background music, of sorts, and a hubbub of voices as the crowd grew.

The lighting was low, and it was a moment or two before Sam noticed someone waving at her. It was Dave Richett, and he had another man with him. Sam knew the second man by sight, but she'd never spoken to him. With his blonde, swept-back hair, piercing blue eyes and rugged good looks, he was a perfect fit for the public's idea of a fighter pilot.

Sam made her way towards the two men, and David gestured at his companion. 'Roger Mellish, Sam Willet. Watch your six with her around. She'll blast you away soon as look at you.'

Mellish grinned at Sam's discomfort. 'I hear you got the jump on Dave. Really took him apart.'

'He was caught in a stray blast, that's all. It wasn't deliberate.'

'Don't worry about it,' said Mellish, still grinning. 'Everyone's tried to blast him before now. You just landed the first punch.' He offered Sam his hand, and they shook. 'I'm the base liaison officer, by the way.' He saw her puzzled look. 'A kind of public relations man, really. I smooth things with the locals, keep everyone happy... you know.'

Sam nodded, surprised. She'd already formed a mental image of Mellish shouting 'tally-ho, chaps' as he roared towards a squadron of enemy fighters, guns blazing. Public relations seemed a little... tame. She was still studying his face when David caught her attention.

'Hey, would you like a drink?' he asked her.

'Sure. I'll have a cider, thanks.'

David signalled to the robot, which came towards them with a groaning, wheezing sound from its motors. 'One cider, two more beers thanks.'

'Four chits, sir,' said the robot.

'For three drinks?'

'Cider is two. It's harder to source.'

'I'll have a beer instead,' said Sam quickly.

The robot waited for Dave to confirm, then went to fetch their drinks.

25

'I met your brother a couple of years back,' said Mellish suddenly. 'It was after combined raid, a big one. About three hundred fighters, dozens of heavy bombers and a couple of destroyers. They were meant to take out a Mayestran Orbiter.'

'How did it go?'

The beers arrived, and Mellish drained half his glass in one go. 'It was a complete shambles. The Mayestrans got wind of the attack and bulked up their defences. Half a dozen Triton satellites, a heavy cruiser and clouds of Mark III fighters. We lost a quarter of our fighters, nearly every bomber *and* the destroyer. Word is that Intel knew about the defences but sent them in anyway, the callous bastards.'

'Keep it down, Rog,' murmured David, glancing around the mess.

'What they going to do, make me disappear?' demanded Mellish bitterly. 'These sprogs have to be told about our failures too, not just our glorious victories... such as they are.'

'You're just trying to get us in trouble,' said David. 'The brass are big on keeping morale up, and discussing failures in public is going to put us on their hit list.'

'You know what would help with morale? Suing for peace and ending this damn war once and for all.'

There was a long silence, and Sam got the impression he was waiting for her to speak. David seemed to have tensed as well, as though he was worried about her response. 'I, er–' she began. *Smooth*, she thought. 'I really don't get much time for the bigger picture,' she said, and it felt like a cop-out. 'Point me at the enemy, and I'll shoot them down. That's pretty much it.'

Mellish drained the rest of his glass and got up. 'I'm going to turn in,' he said, then gave Sam a smile. 'Congrats on the promotion, by the way. You'll do just fine.'

With that, he was gone, and Sam saw David looking after him, a thoughtful expression on his face. 'Well, it looks like you passed,' he told Sam quietly.

'What do you mean?'

'Liaison, my arse. He's our political officer.' David glanced at her. 'It's a government appointment. He's supposed to weed out combatants who'd rather be growing vegetables than blowing up the enemy. Pacifists, dissenters and the like. You know, sensible types.'

'He was testing me?'

'Yeah, it wasn't very subtle though, and I think you put him off your trail.'

His tone was sarcastic, and Sam glanced at him. 'You don't like him, do you?'

'If he was flying fighters into battle against impossible odds, I dare say he'd be going around telling people he'd rather be gardening too. Who wouldn't?' David sipped his drink, then winced. 'I can't tell whether this is beer, cider or iced tea.'

'Don't look now, but I think that robot is spraying all of the drinks out of the same spout.' Sam spotted Piet watching her from a nearby table, then realised he wasn't the only one. Reddening, she turned away and tried her beer, which was flat, listless and about as appealing as three Mayestran Phase III fighters on her tail, all guns blazing. 'What's it really like on the front line?' she asked David.

'Grim.' He turned his glass slowly on the bar, his eyes unfocussed. 'You already know about the Mayestrans' love for surprise attacks. They'll send a small squadron far behind our lines, blast an unprotected target before we can intercept, and then fade away like a bunch of ghosts. Even if we do catch up with them, they don't seem to care about the losses.' He shrugged. 'We knock out two or three fighters, which

27

sounds good in the news, but in return they have our entire population on edge.'

'Don't we do the same to them?'

'We used to, until they came up with their Tridents. They're defensive satellites, small and well-armed, and they're pumping them out by the thousand. We've developed something similar, but their fighters are heavier, which means we have to fit bigger guns, bigger power supplies, bigger heat fins... the lot. It makes for an easy target, and they take them out as quick as we can launch them.'

Sam was silent. The Mayestrans seemed to have the upper hand in many areas, and she wondered whether it would ever be possible to defeat them.

'This is just stuff I picked up,' said David. 'Rumours, that kind of thing. I shouldn't be telling you, but you're probably hearing it from your brother anyway.'

A couple of trainees came to stand at the bar behind Sam, one of them ordering a round for their table. 'Yeah, it's true,' said a loud female voice, right behind her. 'I heard she was screwing the instructor!'

'You're kidding! But isn't that against the rules?'

'Oh, like little miss perfect cares about *rules*.'

The two of them left again, carrying trays of drinks, and seconds later Sam heard laughter from their table. Then David got up. 'Come on. Let's get out of here,' he said abruptly.

Sam hesitated. Relations between ranks were forbidden, but she was supposed to be getting a promotion. And once the others learned of *that*, they'd be pissed at her anyway. 'Sure,' she said lightly. 'Why not?'

They left the mess together, and Sam couldn't help noticing the looks they got from several of the others. The woman who'd insulted her at the bar was staring at David with an unreadable expression on her face. Piet was staring at Sam, looking as though he wanted to corner her there and then to ask about her battles with the Mayestrans. Other students were merely exchanging glances.

Outside, they made their way down the path to the base itself. Insects chirped and whirred in the darkness, and there was a chill in the air.

At the end of the path Sam half-expected David to turn left, towards the officers' quarters. Instead, he kept going, heading for a line of groundcars. They were painted with yellow and ochre camouflage, matching the tones of the desert surrounding the base, and as Sam got closer she saw they were as battered and worn as the fighters. There was a sentry posted near the vehicles, and he saluted as David approached. 'Evening sir.'

'At ease, Tim.' David nodded towards the nearest vehicle. 'Log that out, will you? We're going to scout the perimeter.'

'Yes sir. They're all ready.'

Moments later Sam and David were seated in the car, and as the motor whined up to speed it rose from the ground on its invisible cushion. Dust billowed out, sending the guard staggering backwards, coughing and spluttering. 'Give those Mayestrans hell, sir!' called the man, raising his voice over the racket, and then David turned the car in its own length and headed for the base entrance.

Here, another sentry glanced over the car and its occupants, then raised the flimsy barrier. Sam couldn't see the point of a sentry, because the base wasn't fenced and anyone could have walked straight in through the palm trees. Then again, who was going to stroll into an oasis in the middle of a vast desert?

The car picked up speed, and a tearing headwind soon blew the dust away. Sam looked back and saw they were leaving a thick plume of the stuff, shot through with red from the tail lights. Then she turned to look at David. 'Where are we going?'

'There's a spot I know. Peaceful. Good view of the night sky.'

Sam looked up. Now they were clear of the camouflage netting the stars were everywhere, scattered overhead like thousands of gleaming jewels. Taking the car seemed a bit excessive when they could have simply walked to the base entrance. On the other hand, she could feel herself relaxing as they left the base behind, and there was also a twinge of excitement as she wondered what lay ahead.

6

Once clear of the base, the powerful car leapt forward, and they soon left the oasis and the low, rolling hills behind. The rough track they were following was little more than a strip of dirt, slightly less dusty than the surrounding landscape. Now and then Sam saw a pothole or deep ruts, presumably where a heavy supply truck had bogged down, and each time she braced herself. And each time, the car slid right over them on its invisible cushion. In fact, they could have struck out in any direction, apart from the risk of running into a stray rock or a palm tree.

The road veered to the left, then started to climb. Moments later, David slowed the car and turned right, heading up the side of a hill. There were scattered palm trees, their huge fronds blotting out patches of stars, and their trunks cast long shadows in the glare of the headlights.

The engine began to struggle, and the anti-grav whined as the car went up the incline. The palms got thicker, hemming the car in, and then ended in a ragged treeline. The headlights illuminated a patch of ground, and then... nothing.

The car stopped, and David got out. 'Come on. It's quite a sight.'

'Even in the darkness?'

'Especially in the darkness. Just take it easy until your vision adjusts.'

They moved forward, walking slowly until their eyes recovered from the glare of the headlights. Gradually Sam made out more and more detail, until she realised they were on top of an impressive cliff. The ground fell away sharply, and far below she could see mounds of boulders, worn smooth with age.

David pointed out the area of trees far to their right, which hid the base. The whole thing was just a darker patch on the lighter shades of the surrounding desert, and there was no sign of life. Then he pointed to the left, where Sam could just make out a glow on the horizon.

'Is that the other base?' she asked him.

'No, the settlement. There's not much there, just a few traders and a tavern. The local farmsteads use it as a watering hole, somewhere to get offworld supplies, that kind of thing. If you get your hands on a leave pass, I'll take you there for a look around.' David sat on the edge of the cliff, and several seconds later Sam heard the stones he'd dislodged rattling on the rocks below.

'Is that safe?' she asked him.

'I've been here a few times, and it hasn't collapsed yet.'

Sam sat beside him, and admired the thick starfield that arched overhead. There was a light breeze, and apart from a faint rustle of palm leaves it was as quiet as the grave.

'I come out here to absorb the peace and quiet,' said David. 'Next time I'm stationed on an orbiter, breathing tinned air and living with noise and light all hours of the day, I'll close my eyes and imagine myself in this place.'

Sam knew exactly what he meant, and as they sat there in the darkness, not speaking, she could feel the cold immensity of the night-time desert seeping into her. The war seemed distant, remote, and the longer she sat there, the more her worries about combat training and study and her sudden promotion seemed to dissipate. She turned to look at the settlement, and as she did so, she noticed David studying her face in the near-darkness. They were sitting close, shoulder to shoulder, and for a second she thought he was going to kiss her. She wondered how she'd react, but instead he smiled and turned to look at the horizon. 'I've been fighting for three years now,' he said, in a low voice. 'Most don't make it past one, and I know the odds are against me.'

'You must be pretty good,' said Sam.

He shook his head. 'Surviving that long isn't skill, it's pure luck. And every time you climb into the cockpit you know you're overdrawn, and that luck is due to run out. It's a numbers game, after all.'

'What do you mean?'

'Say you have three dozen pilots in a squadron. A tour lasts for thirty ops, and if you lose two or three pilots every time your squadron encounters the enemy, which is likely, then none of the original pilots will survive the tour.'

Sam was silent. David had completed *two* tours, which explained why he felt his luck must run out.

'They bring in replacements, of course. Endless new faces, fresh from training, until eventually those newbies become the next crop of veterans.'

'Will the war ever end, do you think?'

'Not in our lifetimes.' David snorted. 'Which isn't saying much.'

'There's always hope.'

'Sam, everyone you and I know will die in this war. You're going to die, I'm going to die. It's a colossal waste of life and for what?' He gestured at the stars. 'The galaxy is *full* of bloody planets, and yet we're fighting over a handful of local systems. Why?'

'The Mayestrans encroached on our territory. They wanted to increase their influence in the sector, and they were prepared to trample us in the process. We had to stand up for ourselves.'

'Yes, but it's not working is it? Roger was right, you know. We should sit down with the Mayestrans and hammer out a peace treaty, even if it meant giving up a world or two. But anyone who talks about ending the war is branded a traitor, or a coward. We're too invested in winning this thing...but then so is the other side.'

Sam eyed the stars overhead. 'Why doesn't the rest of the galaxy step in? With their combined power, they could stop this war in days.'

'Vested interests. We buy supplies and arms from dozens of neutral systems, which keeps their economies going. They'd love to see us fighting forever. Further out, the rest of the galaxy just doesn't care. There are untold thousands of systems with their own problems to deal with. We're too far away to bother about.' David laughed suddenly. 'Listen to me dragging the mood down. I didn't mean to–'

'No, it's fine. You're not telling me anything I didn't already know.'

'Forget the war. Tell me about your family.'

'My brother you know about. My parents... ' Sam's voice tailed off. 'They both died,' she said at last.

David shook his head. 'I'm sorry. I was trying to lighten the mood again, but–'

'It was a long time ago. My dad worked in a factory which was hit by the Mayestrans. My mum was infantry, and she lost her life on one of the Mayestran worlds. Some big push that didn't go the way it was supposed to.' She glanced at David. 'How about you?'

'I never knew my parents. Their place was destroyed in a raid when I was a baby. Rescuers found me in the ruins, barely alive, and after that I was raised in a military orphanage.'

Sam shivered.

'Come on, I'll drive you back,' said David. 'Tomorrow's going to be pretty busy.'

7

'Move up, Green Two.' Sam checked her cockpit display, and frowned as the fighter remained in exactly the same place. 'Green Two, move up.'

'Sorry,' came the lazy reply. *'Comms problems.'*

'You will address me as Green Leader,' said Sam.

'As you wish.'

Sam glanced at her display, and she wasn't entirely shocked when Green Two maintained her previous distance. If anything, the other pilot seemed to be dropping back even more. Then Sam eyed the third ship in her flight, and her lips thinned. Green Three was there all right, but he was much too close. 'Piet, fall back ten metres.'

'Yes sir,' said Piet, and his ship dropped back until it trailed her own by at least twenty.

So that's how they're going to play it, thought Sam. She'd been sent out with two students, Piet and Anna Cherenko, with orders to hold combat drills in low orbit, covering an area stretching for thousands of kilometres in every direction. At first the two students had been silent, but once the flight reached orbit they'd started acting up. Sam knew they were unhappy with her promotion, and she guessed they wanted to put her in her place. On the other hand, promotions happened fast in a war zone, and they had to learn to obey orders from people they considered their equals. Or, in her case, beneath them.

Anna was the girl who'd commented loudly in the mess the night before, and Piet was still sullen after she'd knocked him back to spend the evening with David. That hadn't been a great start, and things had only got worse when they heard she was leading them on patrol. For a second, Sam wished Norton hadn't thrust the command onto her, and she wondered whether it was a deliberate attempt to rein her in. He'd probably give her a day or two, declare her unready to lead a flight, and then withdraw her promotion. He'd told her she had to learn to walk before she could run, and maybe this was an elaborate ploy to prove it.

Well, she wasn't giving up yet. 'Green flight, vector 280 by 120,' she called over the intercom, and angled her fighter towards the heading. The others turned more slowly, and when she increased thrust they were left in her wake. Slowly, they caught up, and once they'd rejoined in a ragged formation, Sam thumbed her mic again. 'Flight, vector 125 by 90,' she called, and immediately roared away on the new heading.

'What the hell is she doing?' grumbled Anna.

Sam knew she wasn't hearing the comment by accident, because pilots had to activate their mics to transmit. However, she decided it would be wise not to react. 'Green flight, vector 210 by 130, then 130 by 90.'

The flight swooped towards the planet, and Sam could see the desert as a huge brown scar across the planet's major continent, the edges blending into lush green lands above and below. Oceans hemmed the continent on all sides, bright blue under the glare of the local primary. Then she hauled back on the stick, rocketing back into space, and this time the other two kept up. Sam eyed her display and saw a debris marker on a slightly higher orbit. It was either a decommissioned satellite or a ruined ship, and it had been marked for destruction. David had told her about several derelicts in orbit, which were often used as practice targets. So, she decided to make use of this one. 'Sector control, this is Green Leader. Permission to engage derelict alpha niner-zero golf.'

There was a slight delay, and then a voice replied.

'Permission granted, Green Leader. Try and keep your kids out of the debris field, though. We're done with sweeping up your wrecks.'

'Copy, Sector Control. How big is the field?'

'Safety margin is three klicks in every direction.'

'Thanks. Green Leader out.' Giving the other two an intercept course, Sam angled towards the debris and increased to attack speed. 'Arm weapons. Prepare to engage my target.' She glanced at the override switch on her console, ensuring it was in the safe position. 'Weapons live, flight. I want you to destroy the target on the first pass.'

The three Henerian fighters rocketed towards the distant target, and as the range closed Sam felt her pulse rate climbing. It was easy to imagine this was a real combat, with her leading a flight into battle. Then she recalled how two of the fighters had fared during the practice dogfight the day before, and she decided to make sure these two weren't hauled back to base under a crane ship. 'Flight, stand by to fire on my mark. Green Three, at range four thousand you will break right. Green Two, you're going to starboard.'

'Copy, Green Leader,' said Piet.

Sam thumbed her mic. 'Green Two, you will respond to my transmissions or I'll have you on report. Are we clear?'

'Copy.' There was a pause. *'Sir.'*

Sam led the two fighters towards the target in a loose V formation, the pulsing light from their exhausts illuminating the ships in the darkness of space. They were flying away from the planet, and the only sign of their target was a red indicator on the HUD. Sam watched the range, saw her indicator turn green, and gave the order to fire.

As she did so, a stream of blaster fire lanced past her port wing, close enough for her to reach out and touch it. She twisted her head and saw Anna's fighter right on her tail, just a fraction above her, the nose cannon spitting blaster fire almost directly at Sam's ship. Sam's first instinct was to break right, but Piet was on the other side, firing at the target himself. He was nowhere near as close as Anna, but Sam would fly directly into his gunfire if she angled towards him. Or worse, she might smash right into his ship.

More streams of fire shot past on the left, getting even closer as Anna chanced her hand. Sam's grip tightened on the flight stick, and she fought the overwhelming urge to dive for safety. She knew Anna was baiting her, daring her to break and run, and Sam also knew that if she did, she would never earn the respect of her fellow students. So, instead of running, she thumbed the intercom. 'Green Two, your formation flying needs work,' she said, keeping her voice as calm and level as she could. 'Adjust position ten metres to port, if you please.'

Even as she spoke, blaster shots continued to streak past her cockpit, now closer than ever. With the override active, Sam knew they'd only do minor damage if they struck her ship, but the gunfire still looked dangerous enough. The ship behind her maintained a tight formation, though, and in some recess of Sam's mind she felt a sneaking admiration for Anna's skill. Then she noticed the range marker on her HUD, which showed they were closing rapidly with the target. The last thing she wanted was for one of the fighters to be testing its ageing hull against a field of debris, however small the fragments might be. 'Cease fire. Stand by to break on my mark,' she said, and she felt a rush of relief as Anna's shots stopped whizzing past her canopy. 'Break!' she called, and the fighters either side of her rocketed away in separate directions.

As she hauled back on the stick Sam spotted a glowing cloud of fragments ahead, where their shots had struck home. There was a brief glimpse of a dark, misshapen object, and then she rocketed upwards, away from the target.

'Weapons to standby. Form on my tail.'

The others obeyed, and for once they were in a reasonably tight V. 'We're going to try a combat exercise,' said Sam. 'Give me twenty seconds, then come after me.'

'Hell yeah,' came Anna's voice. *'Now you're talking.'*

Sam didn't wait. She angled her fighter down, flew a long, curved course before spinning the nose around until she was facing the other two. She was still travelling in the same direction as her pursuers, only her gun was now facing the pair of them.

The others barely waited ten or fifteen seconds before coming after her, and Sam tracked them on her HUD. Weeks earlier she'd trained in tactical operations – TacOps – which was the career the Navy's personnel system had chosen for her. She'd eventually wangled a transfer to fighters, but before that she'd been forced to study fleet tactics, and some of it had actually stuck with her. Of course, two versus one was hardly a fleet action, but the principle was the same. Take out your strongest opponent first, then mop up the weaker ones.

So, Sam fired a quick burst at Piet to keep him occupied, then twitched her fighter's nose to cover Anna. She fired, expecting to see the shots striking home, but the other fighter leapt sideways, dodging the fire easily. Then it moved down, still travelling at high speed towards her, and Sam fired several bursts in succession, trying to follow the fast-moving target on her display. Every shot went wide as the other fighter blazed across her HUD, and then Sam ducked instinctively as blaster shots came out of the darkness towards her. The shots bracketed her ship, and she ran the right-hand thrusters at full bore to escape the incoming fire, throwing the fighter to the left. Then she blazed upwards, and spun her ship to face the attacker. As she came around in a big, swooping arc, she saw the male pilot trying to turn his fighter to meet her. He presented an easy target, and so she fired a brief burst as she tore past, noting the hits with grim satisfaction. Then Sam scanned her HUD for Anna, and with a sinking feeling she realised she'd been over-confident. The other fighter had followed her, tracking her every move, and even now shots were flying past Sam's canopy. She turned her fighter, willing her guns to bear, but with growing desperation she realised she was out-matched. No matter how much she tried to dodge and weave, Anna stuck to her tail like glue. Then, as Sam tried yet another sharp turn, a series of bright flashes came rushing along the sleek nose of her ship, passed right over her canopy, and continued along the hull to the tailplane and the main drive.

In a real combat, the shots would have ripped her fighter open, torn her body apart and left her twitching remains to freeze in the vacuum of space. As it was, they only blasted her confidence.

'Nice try, Green Leader,' came Anna's voice. 'Guess you weren't quite good enough.'

'That was damn good shooting,' said Sam, recovering quickly. 'And where the hell did you learn to fly like that?'

'Aren't you supposed to use my call-sign, Green Leader?'

Okay, so that's how Anna wanted to play it. 'Green flight, form up,' said Sam, her voice businesslike. 'We're going to patrol up and down for the next hour.' Sam heard Anna groan, and she smiled to herself. Then, as they set off on the first leg of the patrol, she realised she'd be subjecting herself to the exact same punishment, and her smile slipped.

They were only ten minutes into the hour when Sam's headset crackled.

'Green Leader, this is Sector Control. I have multiple bogies converging on your position. Do you copy, over?'

'Copy, Control,' said Sam calmly. 'Thanks for the warning.' She switched channels and addressed the rest of the flight. 'Green Leader to all craft. Arm your weapons, we have enemy inbound. I repeat, arm your weapons.'

'Copy Green Leader,' said Anna. 'What vector?'

Sam had been so relieved at the interruption to the patrol that she'd forgotten to ask. However, just then she saw a group of red dots on her HUD, at extreme range, and she relayed the information. There were four enemy ships, and as green flight altered course towards them, Sam realised this was going to be one hell of a battle. Still, she felt a flash of gratitude towards whoever had sent the captured Mayestran ships up for a mock dogfight, because it sure beat flying up and down for another fifty minutes.

8

The two groups of fighters raced towards each other, and Sam ordered her flight to spread out slightly. The more experienced pilots would be expecting the trainees to scatter, she was sure of it, and she was determined to surprise the 'enemy' by meeting them head-on.

'Green Leader, Control here. Bogies are heading straight for you. You want to get out of there, fast!'

'We've got this, Control,' said Sam. 'Thanks for the warning. Over and out.'

After that it was just a matter of seconds before they closed on the enemy. Sam ensured the master override was on, because the last thing she wanted was for her pilots to damage the captured Mayestran ships. Then she toggled her mic. 'Good luck, guys. Pick your targets, and take them out in the first pass if you can.'

The enemy fighters opened up at long range, and flashes of blaster fire lanced out of the darkness ahead. The three Henerian fighters responded, their guns hurling a maelstrom of fire back at the enemy. Sam felt a familiar thrill as the battle kicked off, even though she knew it was just a training exercise.

Then she saw a bright flash to her right, and she looked back to see Piet's fighter tumbling in space, one winglet ripped off, burning fuel spewing from the shattered fuselage. She saw another burst of fire rip the tailplane right off his stricken fighter, and then she caught a flash of silvery white as a Mayestran fighter rocketed between her ship and Piet's.

What the hell?

Sam was still staring at the burning fighter, stunned, when the canopy jerked open and the squat pilot pushed himself free. Piet tumbled away from the wreck in his suit and helmet, seemingly unharmed, and then Sam's gaze flicked to the fighter which had blasted his ship. It was turning sharply, and she realised it was coming back for another pass.

'Green Leader to Mayestran fighters,' she shouted, thumbing her mic. 'Stand down! I repeat, stand down! You're firing at friendlies!'

That's when she saw something that made her blood run cold.

The Mayestran fighter was clearly illuminated by the glare of Piet's burning ship, and it wasn't a captured Phase I. No, this was a front-line fighter, a Phase III, and with a sick feeling of despair Sam realised there was a *real* Mayestran at the controls. This wasn't a practice dogfight, it was for real!

Worse, the enemy had already taken Piet out, and now there were four modern fighters against two patched-up trainers. With a shaking finger she flipped the master switch on her console, activating the flight's lethal weapons, and then she used her mic. 'Red Two, engage at will. This is not a drill, I repeat, this is *not* a drill!'

'You just figured that out?' snapped Anna. She sounded strained, and Sam could see the reason why. Three fighters were pursuing her, firing repeatedly, and the smaller Henerian ship was darting all over the place as it tried to shake them off.

The fighter which had damaged Piet's ship was still coming in fast, and it blew the wreckage apart with one burst from its nose guns. Sam was already turning to meet it, and she fired off a burst even as the other ship darted sideways to avoid the spreading cloud of debris. Her shots went wild, but the return fire, when it came, was all too accurate. The shots skimmed her cockpit, and Sam felt her craft shudder as they struck the angled tailplane at the rear of her ship. Fortunately it was only needed for atmospheric flight, and that was the last of Sam's worries at that moment.

'*I can't hold them off!*' shouted Anna. '*Sam, help me!*'

Sam knew she'd be offering herself as an easy target if she turned away from the lone Mayestran fighter, but she couldn't leave Anna to fight three of the enemy single-handed. So, she turned her ship and streaked towards the distant flashes, tagging one of the Phase IIIs on her HUD. As she got closer she saw Anna pulling wild manoeuvres, the pilot desperately tried to get away while the three Mayestrans took turns to blast away at her. Fortunately the tutor had been right: the heavier Phase IIIs were having trouble matching Anna's turning circle, and were forced to swoop round in much wider arcs every time she threw an evasive move. They were all trying to get on her tail when Sam arrived, and she managed to catch the rear ship with a quick burst of fire. She saw one of its tail planes disintegrate, and then the enemy fighter reversed direction, still pursuing Anna but now flying backwards. Sam threw her fighter to the right just as the enemy opened up, and blaster fire shot past her ship from *both* directions. She'd almost forgotten the lone Mayestran, who'd followed her towards the dogfight, and if she hadn't moved suddenly that burst of fire would have torn her ship apart.

Sam kept moving right while spinning her nose to the left,

loosing off a wild arc of fire towards both fighters. She didn't care if she hit anything, she just wanted to get one or more of the enemy off Anna's tail, so the other pilot could stop evading them and start fighting back.

'*Green Leader, this is Control. Hold on as long as you can. We've got a squadron on the way, over.*'

Sam was too busy to respond, since she was hurling her fighter around in tight turns and firing bursts whenever the enemy flashed across her sights.

Then, all of a sudden, the four enemy fighters turned and streaked away.

'*Green Flight, this is Jackal Squadron,*' said a lazy voice. '*You kids can head for home now. We've got this covered.*'

Six fighters rocketed past Sam and Anna, pursuing the distant Mayestrans, and despite the pilot's arrogance she couldn't help admiring the sleek, powerful lines of their ships. They were Kestrels, the newest fighters in the Henerian Navy, and they should have no trouble seeing off the Phase IIIs.

Enemy and friendly were soon specks in the distance, and Sam turned away and slowly flew back to the spot where Piet's ship had been destroyed. She could see a cloud of fragments on her HUD, and a proximity warning buzzed in her ear as she got close. Unfortunately, she couldn't distinguish Piet from the many bits and pieces of his fighter. 'Piet, do you read me?'

'*I see you, Green Leader,*' said Piet, his voice strong in her headphones.

'Can you direct me?'

'*Nose up ten degrees, starboard forty or so.*'

Sam angled her fighter to the heading, then followed his directions until she was pointing directly towards him. While she was busy Anna flew up, bringing her ship to a halt nearby. 'Stay clear,' said Sam. 'I'm going to pick him up.'

'*I don't think so,*' said Anna.

Sam frowned. Her fighter had storage space behind the pilot's seat, and there was plenty of room for Piet. 'This isn't the time for rules and regulations,' she snapped. 'He can't stay out here. His air might not last.'

'*Yeah, I agree with you, but your ship isn't going anywhere near the planet. Half your tail is missing.*'

Sam remembered the Mayestran shots hitting her fighter, and she swore. She could hardly rescue Piet when she was going to need someone to pick her up as well.

Meanwhile, Anna continued. '*Piet, direct me towards you. I'll give you a lift back.*'

'*Nose up five, port ten,*' replied Piet.

Sam watched the fighter picking its way through the debris, and then she saw a distant puff of vapour as the canopy opened. A tiny figure, barely visible against the darkness of space, clambered into the ship, and then the canopy closed again. 'All okay?' asked Sam.

'*Bit of a squeeze, but we'll make it.*'

'I'll track you until orbital insertion, then wait for pickup. Good luck.'

'*You'll need it more than us,*' said Anna. '*It could be a while before they risk a craneship, what with a squadron of Mayestrans in the system.*'

They set off towards the planet, and on the way Sam called Control to report on the combat.

'*One destroyed, pilot saved,*' Control repeated. '*Plus one fighter damaged, unable to land. Is that correct?*'

Sam's lips thinned. Stated like that, her first patrol sounded like a complete shambles. 'Affirmative, Control.'

'*Okay, park the damaged fighter in low orbit and sit tight. Green Two, you have clearance to land.*' There was a pause. '*What the hell were you trainees doing, taking on those Mayestrans? Didn't you copy my warning?'*

'There was a bit of a misunderstanding,' Sam replied.

'Well, you're bloody lucky to be alive. Control out.'

Sam glanced to her right, towards Anna's fighter. She could see the other pilot's helmet through the plexiglass, and then she saw the visor turn to face her. 'Sorry about that,' said Sam. 'I didn't realise...I mean, I thought they were the captured fighters. You know, a mock dogfight.'

'Yeah, you could have got us both killed,' replied Anna. Then she laughed. *'But hey, anything's better than a boring old patrol.'*

'Speak for yourself,' muttered Piet, from his cramped position behind her seat.

Sam watched them go, then shut off her engines and switched to low power mode. She could do nothing but wait...that, and hope like hell the crane ship got to her before the Mayestrans did.

9

The crane ship showed up promptly, and it wasn't long before Sam's damaged fighter was securely held by its massive claws. Then the descent began, and she had a front-row seat as the crane ship dropped through the atmosphere, its nosecone glowing cherry red and streamers of flame flickering and twisting directly above Sam's canopy. She could feel the radiated heat, but although it was uncomfortable it wasn't unbearable.

Then, as the crane ship sank lower, it started to sway. Throw in the occasional bump and shudder, and Sam was soon gritting her teeth and trying not to be sick. She remembered how green the two pilots had looked the day before, when they too had to be rescued, and she began to understand why.

The swaying stopped as the crane ship came swooping in above the desert, and Sam saw the familiar swathe of green palm trees ahead. Knowing it was there, she was able to pick out the more regular shape of the camouflage netting, but she was surprised at how effective it was.

Then, remembering the fleeing enemy squadron, she wondered whether the countermeasures would be of any use. The Mayestrans now knew the Henerians had one or more bases in the system, and they would surely send more ships to investigate. If small groups of fighters found nothing, the enemy would send a bigger force with more powerful scanners. After all, that seemed to be their standard procedure.

Sam was feeling less queasy by the time the crane ship set her fighter down, and she opened the canopy as soon as the big hauler roared away. She clambered down to the ground, slightly unsteady on her legs, then spotted Piet and Anna approaching. 'Are you both okay?' she asked them.

'Wow, you're as green as those palm trees,' remarked Anna.

Sam turned to Piet. 'Listen, I'm going to buy *you* a drink. It's the least I can do.'

He looked surprised, then smiled weakly. 'Thank you.'

'What about me?' demanded Anna.

'Sure, you too.'

Anna looked happy enough, but Sam couldn't help noticing Piet's shell-shocked expression. It wasn't really surprising, given he'd barely escaped with his life, but there seemed to be something more. 'What's up?' she asked him.

'I lasted no more than ten seconds,' he said morosely. 'I did not know which way to turn, I could not see the enemy, I got blown up.' He shrugged. 'I might as well be fodder for the cannons, with a big target on my back.'

'Hey, I got my arse handed to me as well,' said Sam, gesturing at her damaged fighter. 'We're all learning.'

'Yes, but you survived longer.'

'I can see that chiselled on my headstone.'

He looked at her, puzzled.

'Tombstone,' she explained. 'On the grave.'

'We are space pilots,' he said quietly. 'We do not get graves.'

Chilled by his fatalism, Sam could think of nothing to say. Then she felt Anna's hand on her shoulder. 'I think the squadron leader wants to see you,' murmured the other woman.

Sam looked towards the admin building, where the adjutant was standing just outside the entrance, staring in her direction. When he saw he had Sam's attention, he crooked his finger.

'Oh crap,' muttered Sam. Then, for the second time in two days, she made her way towards the admin block for a difficult meeting with the squadron leader.

◆

Squadron Leader Norton was sitting at his desk, reading a report. Sam and David sat opposite, and to Sam it felt like a carbon copy of the day before. Everything was the same, although if anything the expression on Norton's face was even more forbidding. He looked up as he turned a page, his eyes boring into Sam's, and she felt small and cowed as she perched on the hard wooden chair.

'What an absolute shambles,' said Norton at last, as he closed the file. 'A rolled gold, grade-A mess. Another fighter destroyed, more pilots lives at risk, and to cap it all off I've got the enemy sending squadrons into my system.'

Sam frowned. She'd wear the blame for the damaged fighters and Piet's unplanned space walk, but Mayestran visitors were hardly *her* fault. She opened her mouth to object, but David immediately nudged her with his knee.

Norton didn't notice, and he continued unabated. 'I get all sorts of students through my base. Many have an exaggerated idea of their competence.' He frowned at Sam. 'Some think they're a match for decorated veterans before they've even seen combat. Well, my job is to grind them back to their smooth, inner selves, and then build on that. I'm the sandpaper, and they're the rough-hewn wood. One cannot apply the finishing touches, the coat of fine lacquer, until every rough spot has been removed from these imperfect specimens.'

David nudged her again, just in case.

'You're not just running before you can walk, Sam Willet. You're sprinting and hurdling and trying to perform cartwheels.' Norton tapped the file on his desk. 'When Commander Tosell of the Greyforth Coriolis sent you here, she felt the need to include a personal note about your behaviour. From the way she described you, I could see you'd have more rough edges than most. Insubordination, refusal to obey orders, unauthorised rescue missions...' He paused for breath. 'Well, you've had a taste of command, and perhaps now you understand just how unready you are. You're going to learn to walk, and it's going to be one baby step at a time. As of right now, you're back in basic training. This nonsense about promoting you to flight leader is over.'

Sam was surprised. She'd expected worse, a lot worse, and getting busted back to basic didn't seem like much of a punishment. She guessed Norton had bigger things to worry about... things like Mayestrans in Phase III fighters, for example, and the odds of a full-blown enemy assault. 'Yes sir. I understand.'

'Good. Dismissed.'

Outside, David turned to her. 'I'm sorry, Sam. It wasn't your fault, we both know that.'

'Yes sir,' said Sam evenly.

He stared at her, then nodded briefly. 'Very well. Carry on.'

As Sam walked away from him she felt a stab of regret, mixed with anger at herself. Apart from the Mayestrans showing up in the first place, it *was* all her fault. She'd been so keen to prove herself she'd ignored all the clues and led her flight straight into deadly combat, pitting them against a vastly superior force. The previous day, her tutor had told the entire class that there were only *three* captured Phase Is on the planet, but today there had been *four* enemy fighters on Sam's HUD. Next, the Mayestrans had approached from the far reaches of the system, which meant they'd either sat around out there waiting for her to happen by, which was highly unlikely, or they'd only just arrived from enemy space and were heading towards the planet. And finally, to cap it all off, Control had tried to warn her about the enemy, and she'd ignored them. She remembered her flippant remark – *we've got this* – and prayed the transcript never made its way to Norton's desk.

Her mind was churning over these thoughts and more as she made her way towards the lecture room. She pushed the door open, then stopped as Aren Grant, the tutor, gave her an arch look.

'Don't tell me,' said Grant. 'Visiting the Squadron Leader once more?'

'We had a bit to discuss,' admitted Sam.

'I'll bet.' Grant nodded towards an empty desk. 'Take a seat, please. We're discussing dynamics of space flight, chapter one.'

10

'Hey, I heard about your little set-to with the enemy.'

Sam was halfway to her quarters, and she turned to see who'd spoken. It was Mellish, the political officer, and he was hurrying to catch up with her. 'It didn't quite go to plan,' she said shortly.

'Well, at least you tried.'

'Sounds like my school reports,' muttered Sam.

Mellish hesitated. 'Listen, I'm heading into the settlement later. Do you want to come along, take a look around?'

Surprised, Sam stared at him. 'Why, so you can trap me into saying something I shouldn't?' She hadn't forgotten the way Mellish had spouted a load of anti-war rhetoric the night before, in an attempt to sound her out, and if this was another trick–

'Dave never could keep his trap shut,' said Mellish cheerfully. 'Look, I don't arrest people, or brainwash them. My job is to find out each recruit's thinking, as regards the war. Are they going around telling everyone it's a waste of time, encouraging others to desert, that kind of thing. It's just precautionary.'

Sam came to a halt and faced him. 'Has it occurred to you that maybe, when you spout a load of nonsense in public, other people might be too polite to call you out? Oh, they'll nod and smile and look like they're agreeing with you, when secretly they can't wait to get away from the raving lunatic.'

For a second, Mellish was taken aback. 'Steady on.'

'You tried to entrap me last night, pure and simple.' She prodded him in the chest. 'I don't need your bullshit, and you can shove your little expedition to the settlement.' With that she turned and strode away, leaving him speechless. Sam felt good, and she felt even better when she emerged from a long hot shower. She dressed quickly, and was heading towards the room she shared with five others when she stopped dead. Mellish was sitting in a nearby armchair, leafing through a training manual. 'What the hell?' she demanded.

'You got the sandpaper speech from Norton, didn't you.'

'Yeah. So what?'

'He pisses everyone off, but you'll get over it.' Mellish got up, tossing the manual aside. 'The offer stands. If you want to see the settlement, meet me at the car pool in thirty minutes. I've organised a leave pass for you.'

He didn't wait for an answer, just turned and left, and Sam was conflicted as she watched him go. On the one hand he was far too sure of himself, and he seemed to think she'd join him on his little road trip without a second thought. On the other hand he didn't seem to take anything seriously, despite his job, and she found the contradiction intriguing. Finally, there was no way David would be taking her to the settlement, and even less chance of Norton issuing her with a leave pass. Not this side of a peace treaty with the Mayestrans, anyway.

So, after thinking about it for a few minutes, Sam found a warm jacket to protect against the night air, dug out her meagre stash of credit chits and made her way to the car pool. Now the Mayestrans had put in an appearance, she figured it might not be long before the entire system was under siege. This could be her last chance of a break for some time.

◆

Sam felt a growing excitement as she approached the row of battered groundcars. Until recently, she'd been stationed aboard the Greyforth Coriolis, a huge orbiter near the front lines. After the Coriolis was attacked by a Mayestran fleet, and all but destroyed in the desperate battle, there had been no time for leave. First came the funerals and memorial services, sombre and rehearsed. Next came the repairs, involving weeks of hard work for everyone on board. Finally there was the system testing, and assignment of new duties.

Only then had Commander Tosell let Sam go, and with bad grace at that.

So, Sam was more than keen to leave the base and relax in a new environment, even if it was just for a few short hours. She had a few credits in her pocket, and she was looking forward to picking up a few luxuries. A reader with a few local books, maybe, or something nice to eat. For that, she'd even put up with Roger Mellish.

'Good evening. Glad you could make it.'

Sam spotted Mellish leaning against one of the cars. He was wearing a scruffy pair of jeans and a T-shirt that had seen better days, and as she approached he held the door open for her. Once she was seated he closed the door, and then he vaulted into the back, stepped over the driver's seat and settled himself with a thump. 'Right, let's go,' he said, and he fired up the motor.

Seconds later they swept past the sentry at the entrance, the flimsy pole across the road barely rising in time. Mellish waved casually as they sped past, and then he floored it. 'I probably should have told you about the dress standards,' he shouted, eyeing her flight suit. 'Still, it's not too bad. Looks like a pair of overalls, if a bit too clean.'

'Is that why you're done up like a tramp?' she asked him.

He grinned. 'My attempt to fit in with the locals. Sometimes works, mostly doesn't.'

They tore through the darkness, and Sam gripped the armrest beside her. The car was on manual, and Mellish kept taking his hand from the control as he told her about a previous visit. She could barely hear him over the rushing headwind, and was barely listening anyway. Palm trees whipped by, and just when it seemed they were going to smash into one, he'd avoid it at the last second with a casual flick of his wrist.

David was right, she thought. Mellish should have been a fighter pilot. The guy had the touch for it, plus a total disregard for his own life.

'When we get there, I've got some business to attend to,' shouted Mellish, narrowly avoiding a rocky outcrop. 'If you're happy to wait for me, I'll show you round afterwards.'

'I thought fraternising with officers was against the rules?'

'Fraternising? How old-fashioned!' He gestured dismissively. 'Anyway, I'm a civilian, so you don't have to worry on that score.'

Sam decided to wait until she saw the settlement... assuming they got there in one piece. She'd hardly need a guide if there were three ratty old buildings and a water tank. Anyway, the more she replied to Mellish, the less attention he paid to where they were going.

The groundcar rocketed onwards, eating up the miles, until eventually the faint glow on the horizon grew to a visible patch of light, and then a ragged assortment of buildings. Most were low domes, just one or two storeys high, and the spaces between them were lit with spotlights mounted on poles. There were maybe three dozen domes in total, and Sam could see a handful of people going about their business. Most stopped to eye the newcomers.

Mellish brought the groundcar to a shuddering halt near a row of similar vehicles, and the car sank to the ground with a sigh. The dust cloud kicked up by their arrival washed over them, making Sam cough, and she got out quickly, flapping at her face. She saw the cloud dispersing under the lights, before it vanished altogether. Meanwhile, the people she'd seen had lost interest and turned away.

Sam eyed the domes, which were stained with rust and covered in metal patches, all riveted on with little regard for the finished appearance. She realised she'd been a little optimistic when she dreamt of buying a few luxuries.

'Yeah, it's not much,' said Mellish. 'This place is really just a hub for the surrounding farmsteads. Fuel, spare parts, machinery, that kind of thing. They do have a general store and a tavern, though.' He eyed her. 'I'm guessing you don't have any currency yet.'

'I have some credit chits.'

'They'll take 'em, but they won't like it. You'll get a lousy rate, too.' Mellish dug in his pocket and took out a few metal disks. He handed them over, and Sam inspected them in the glare of the overhead lights. There were several denominations, the coins small but heavy, with a hologram on either side.

'Thanks,' she said. 'What do I owe you for these?'

'We'll sort that out later, if you manage to spend any.' He gestured at the domes. 'The tavern's that way, and I should be there in thirty minutes or so. The general store is over the other side, and they close up soon so you might want to look around there first.'

'Anything I should know?'

'They tolerate us because we're their only defence against the Mayestrans, but we're not popular. Some of them think we're only going to bring the enemy here sooner.' He hesitated. 'I wouldn't mention today's events. Those fighters you encountered.'

'We're not going to tell them the Mayestrans are here?'

'Sure, but let me handle it my way. I'm going to break the news to some of their leaders, and they'll make an official announcement. These people are pretty solid. There won't be any panic.'

They split up then, with Mellish heading for the tavern and Sam making her way towards the store. On the way, she realised Mellish's boyish, life-of-the-party manner was just an act. He'd been deadly serious when talking about the settlement, and he seemed to know exactly what he was doing. Shouldn't have been surprised, she thought, because you didn't get appointed as political officer unless you were halfway competent.

Sam passed several people, all dressed in work clothes, but apart from a brief nod and a curious look or two, nobody paid her much attention. When she arrived at the store, Sam found it was mostly stocked with dried goods: large bins containing flour, beans, spices and the like. There was a man behind the counter, tall and elderly, but he ignored Sam once he realised she was from the base.

One wall was given over to tools and hardware, half of which Sam didn't recognise. Unfortunately, there was no sign of any book readers, or anything remotely interesting to eat. Rapidly losing interest, Sam took a last look around, then headed for the exit.

'I hear you lot ran into the Mayestrans today.'

Sam paused in the doorway. Some instinct told her to keep going, to pretend she hadn't heard, but the old man's voice was clear and it carried easily. 'Sorry, I can't talk about that,' she said. It sounded weak, but on the spur of the moment it was all she could come up with.

'Should I be worried?' asked the old man. 'I've got family, and if there's any chance of an attack–'

'If we see them coming, you'll get plenty of warning.'

'If you see them coming it's already too late,' said the old man.

With his words ringing in her ears, Sam left the store and walked along the main street between the ramshackle domes. Up close, she could see just how fragile they were, and the locals would have no chance if the Mayestrans launched a raid. Then again, would the Mayestrans hit a civilian target? Out here, on the frontier, they'd probably aim to take the system for themselves, and that would be ten times harder if they had the civilian population up in arms too.

A few minutes later she reached a bigger dome, the front wide open with light and music spilling out. There were a dozen people inside, and she spotted Mellish to one side, where he was sitting at a small table with a couple of older men. He was facing the street, and as he caught sight of her he gave a quick shake of the head, indicating he was still busy. Then he returned to the conversation.

Sam kept walking until the main thoroughfare petered out. Here, she found an area set aside for flyers, with a couple of odd-looking craft parked next to the fuel stations. One was a 'copter, which was little more than a seat with a large rotor blade up top, while the other was an enclosed flyer with seating for six or so. A faded sign along the side identified the craft as 'luxury transport' belonging to Presidential Airways 'exclusive fleet'. Maybe once, thought Sam, but now the thing looked like it was used to haul bulk fertiliser.

Moments later she heard footsteps, and she turned to see Mellish approaching. 'Sorry,' he said. 'Things are a bit delicate right now.'

'They already knew about the Mayestrans,' said Sam.

'Yeah. It seems news travels fast. There are civilian contractors on the base... one of them might have overheard something and passed it on.' He gestured at the tavern. 'Come on, I'll get you that drink.'

11

On the way, Sam passed Mellish the coins he'd given her earlier. 'Here. Thanks for the loan.'

He took them with a grin. 'Didn't fancy a few kilos of flour or a bag of nails, eh?'

'Yeah. Not quite what I was after.'

'Life's pretty tough around here. They don't have much time for luxuries.'

They reached the tavern, and Mellish led her to an empty table. He signalled to the barman, who brought over a couple of glasses brimming with amber liquid. Mellish drained his in one gulp, then banged his glass down. Sam did likewise, and for a second it felt like she'd swallowed a slug of jet fuel. When she could breathe again, she put the glass down and eased it towards the middle of the table.

'Another?' Mellish asked her.

Sam nodded. If she couldn't have chocolate and a few books, this was the next best thing.

The drinks arrived, and this time she tackled hers with a lot more caution. 'Someone's been asking about us,' said Mellish, in a low voice.

'Us?'

'The training base, amongst other things. Couple of

strangers showed up a day or so back. They claimed to be seed merchants, but they knew less about crops than I do, and that's saying something.' He examined his glass. 'It can't be a coincidence. The Mayestrans are showing too much interest in this system for my liking.'

Sam spotted a couple of men at the bar. They were leaning against the worn timber, untouched drinks at their elbows, and several times she'd noticed them looking towards her table. Were these the enemy agents? They looked like any of the locals, dressed in work gear with unkempt hair and five-o'clock shadows, and Sam decided she was being paranoid. Then one of the men caught her glance, and frowned. 'What are you looking at?' he called out.

Sam raised one hand, apologising, then focused on Mellish. Out the corner of her eye she saw the two men coming towards her, and her heart sank. From their reddish eyes and slightly unsteady progress she could tell they'd been drinking heavily, but they were sober enough to cause trouble. She'd seen bar fights before, and these were the sort of guys who started them.

'I said, what are you looking at?' demanded the man again.

Mellish turned to look at him. 'What's the problem?'

'She was staring at me.' The man frowned at Sam. 'See something funny, did you?'

'Let me get you a drink,' said Mellish disarmingly. 'Come on, have a round on me.'

'You can't buy us off, fly boy,' said the man thickly.

Sam could see where the encounter was heading, and she moved her hands off the table and into her lap. Out of sight of the two men, she began clenching and un-clenching her fists, rolling her wrists and flexing the muscles in her forearms as she prepared to take the pair of them down. Mellish was

63

only a civilian, and she had no idea whether he'd be any use, but she wouldn't need his help to deal with a pair of drunks. Quickly, she glanced around the tavern, but everyone else seemed to be minding their own business and it didn't look like she and Mellish would be jumped. Sam started to ease her chair back, giving herself room to move, but then the two aggressors glanced towards the tavern entrance, saw something they really didn't like, and they faded back to the bar in a hurry.

Curious, Sam looked round, and her eyebrows rose as she saw half a dozen Henerian military personnel in fatigues. From the insignia they were pilots, and they looked like a tough, no-nonsense bunch. She guessed they were from the other base, the one everybody was cagey about, and her interest was piqued. A conversation with the newcomers could be very illuminating indeed.

One of the pilots, a man with cropped blond hair, spotted Mellish, and the group came over to Sam's table, surrounding the pair of them. There was a round of introductions, but with so many people Sam barely managed to attach a single name to any of the newcomers. Then the pilots grabbed spare seats, and within moments there was a large crowd around the small table.

The blond-haired pilot nodded at Sam's drink. 'Can I get you another of those?'

'Sure. Thanks.'

Another round arrived, and Sam heard fragments of conversation all around her.

'–we got them, but not before they took out a couple of rookies–'

'–flew right through the middle, like they didn't care. Flanks almost crapped himself!'

'–not my problem. When the firing starts, I always say–'

The blond pilot handed Sam her drink. 'You're from Mellish's base, right?'

'Yeah.'

'What are you guys *doing* over there? Yesterday one of your gun-happy kids catches our Phase Is on the hop, and starts blasting away like they've won the ammo lottery. And today, some lunatic of a flight leader takes a pair of sprogs and leads them straight into battle against a squadron of Mayestran Phase IIIs.'

'Actually, that was me,' confessed Sam.

'Which?'

'Er, both.'

'*You're* a flight leader?'

'Not any more,' she said.

'I'm not bloody surprised. They must have chucked the book at you.' The man sipped his drink.

'The squadron leader did share a few choice words,' said Sam, with a rueful grin.

'Sandpaper Norton? Fun.'

'Did I hear you got all the Mayestrans?' Sam asked him.

He hesitated. 'Sorry, but that's classified.'

Sam leaned forwards. 'I missed your name.'

'Tim Davis.'

'Well, Tim. You should tell the rest of your crew to keep their voices down. I think there's one guy at the bar who didn't quite catch the intel.'

Davis winced. 'Don't you start. I get enough grief from Mellish.'

Lively conversations were going on all around them, with some pilots acting out dogfights with their hands, while others made pithy comments about their flying. In the middle of it,

Tim managed to get their attention, particularly a serious-looking pilot with dark hair, and the tough-looking woman sitting beside him. 'You remember that rookie who blasted you both yesterday?'

'You're never going to let me forget that, are you?' said the man.

'Of course we remember,' snapped the woman. 'Damn near wrecked my offside engine. The CO went nuts at me.'

With a shock, Sam realised they were the pilots who'd been flying the Mayestran Phase Is the day before. Then she realised what was coming next, and she suppressed a groan.

Smiling, Tim indicated Sam with his thumb. 'Meet your nemesis, Sam Willet.'

Everyone fell silent, and all of a sudden Sam was the centre of attention.

'You're the rookie?' demanded the woman.

'Yeah.'

'And get this,' continued Davis, before Sam could say anything. 'Norton promoted her on the spot, and she took her first command and led them right at those Phase IIIs today.'

'That's insane,' muttered someone.

'Hang on, did you say Willet?' asked the dark-haired man. 'Are you any relation to Lim Willet?'

'He's my brother,' said Sam.

'Really?' The man whistled. 'I heard he fought off a bunch of raiders and saved the Greyforth Coriolis. Took out a Mayestran cruiser all by himself.'

Sam nodded. The cruiser had actually been her doing, but she held her tongue. Commander Tosell had filed the official report, giving all the credit to Sam's brother, and Sam had no choice but to accept her version. Lim had been disgusted by the whole thing, but the top brass wanted a decorated war hero for the press, not some rookie who'd disobeyed a bunch of orders.

'What's he like?' someone asked Sam.

She thought for a minute. 'Kind. Polite. A bit shy, sometimes.'

They all burst out laughing, not realising she meant it, and after a moment Sam laughed along with them. The media had turned her brother into an almost-mythical figure, a valiant warrior who blasted a dozen Mayestrans before breakfast, then went back for seconds after lunch. It wasn't her place to reveal the truth behind the mask.

'Another round!' shouted someone, and as the drinks flowed and the evening wore on, Sam answered questions from all sides until her voice was hoarse from shouting over the din.

◆

It was late at night, and Mellish was driving Sam back to the base. The car was on auto, which was just as well because Sam was already seeing double, and she reckoned Mellish had downed twice as many drinks.

'What a great bunch,' said Mellish. 'Good people.'

Sam nodded, and instantly regretted it. 'Oh, my head!'

'Those two pilots forgave you for shooting at them yesterday.'

'Should have got out my way,' muttered Sam. 'And flying a Mastra–' She tried again, more slowly. 'A matestan ship. No, a–'

'An enemy,' suggested Mellish.

'Yeah. Flying an enemy ship around *me*. Big mistake.' Sam leaned across the car. 'I blew up the Ma–' She swallowed. 'I got the enemy cruiser, not Lim. They took it from me after, and made him the hero.'

Mellish stared at her.

'Don't tell anyone,' said Sam, putting a finger to her lips. 'Hush shush.'

'You bet I won't,' muttered Mellish.

Sam sat back, suddenly tired. It had been a long day, and her head was spinning from the drinks. She wanted to curl up and fall asleep, and was about to close her eyes for a quick nap when she saw a bright glow streak across the night sky. 'Pretty,' she said.

'What is?'

Sam pointed. 'Shooting star.' She spotted two more flares, then blinked. The last one had gone in the opposite direction from the first two, travelling left to right.

Mellish spotted them too, and he brought the car to a standstill and turned the lights off. They sat there in pitch darkness, staring up, and then another bright star flared across the sky, leaving a broad streak before fading all too soon.

Moments later, they heard a distant rumble.

'I don't think they're shooting stars,' said Mellish slowly. 'That's–'

'Combat,' said Sam, sitting up in a hurry. They weren't watching pieces of rock burning up in the atmosphere, they were watching the last gasps of stricken fighters. There was no way to tell friendly from foe, but one thing was certain.

The Mayestrans had arrived in force.

'Base. Quick!' shouted Sam, her mind suddenly clearer. Mellish needed no second bidding, and the headlights blazed as he grabbed the controls, sending the groundcar hurtling along the desert track at full speed.

They were still miles from the base when a squadron of fighters roared directly overhead, the flight announcing its presence with an ear-shattering howl. The ships were so close Sam could pick out every detail, and then they were gone. The wash from their engines hurled the groundcar around, almost sending the vehicle spearing off the road in a raging dust storm. Mellish fought the controls, and as he managed to settle the vehicle Sam raised a shaking finger towards the departing ships. 'Mayestrans!' she shouted, her ears still ringing from the unbelievable noise of their passing. 'Phase IIIs!'

There was a series of bright flashes ahead, a continuous rippling barrage which lit up the sky like daytime. Then darkness, and deep, ominous silence. Mellish urged the car onwards, and as they got closer to the base Sam noticed a dull red glow in the sky. She could hear sirens too, even over the sound of the groundcar. As the pitiful sounds wailed into the night, she realised the Mayestrans had just hit the training base, and with a growing feeling of dread she wondered what horrors she and Mellish were about to encounter.

12

The groundcar rocketed between the palm trees, then came to a juddering halt near the base entrance. The ground was ripped up where the sentry post had been, and Sam could see scattered bits and pieces of the hut and barrier. The long scar in the road was still smouldering, and Mellish drove on, skirting the deep hole.

They accelerated, and seconds later they came across a scene of total devastation. The sleeping quarters had no roof, and sheets of crackling flame blazed through the doors and windows. Sam could see several bodies on the ground outside, and even from this distance she knew it was hopeless. Further on they saw the admin block, now a blasted shell, and the blazing remains of the officers' quarters. Shattered palm trees were everywhere, with pieces of blasted trunk covering the area like a scattering of snow.

The mess was still standing, but the walls were full of gaping holes and the roof had fallen in. There was no fire, not here at least, and in the darkness Sam saw a few bloodstained survivors stumbling out of the ruins. She leapt out of the groundcar and ran to help, even as a nearby explosion hurled metal fragments far and wide. Through the remaining trees Sam could just make out the landing pads with their rows of fighters. Now, the machines were so much twisted wreckage, and even as she watched another of the ships blew up. Sam ducked as pieces of metal fell all around her, then put her head down and ran for the mess. She helped someone to cover, unable to make out their face in the darkness, then ran back for someone else. Once the wounded were clear she made to enter the building, but someone – David – called out to her. 'Don't, Sam. There's nobody else.'

'There might be survivors!' cried Sam.

'Trust me, there aren't.'

Sam stared at the mess, unwilling to let it go. Then, with a creak and a groan, the damaged walls gave up the struggle and toppled over, sending a cloud of dust across the clearing. As she stared at the rubble, Sam realised she would have been inside if David hadn't stopped her.

'Where's Norton?' she demanded. 'Did he make it?'

'This time of night? He'd have been in the officers' quarters. There, or maybe his office.'

Sam eyed both buildings, or what was left of them. 'Did they have bunkers underneath them?'

David shook his head. 'Even if there was, we got absolutely no warning.'

Mellish ran up, and he started checking the survivors. 'Any of you badly injured?' he called, as he checked a cut on David's forehead.

The others shook their heads, and as flames began to lick at the remains of the mess, Sam recognised several faces in the glare. Piet was there, and Aren Grant, the tutor with the scarred face and neck. Anna Cherenko was sitting against a palm tree, head back, her face pale. There were a couple of mechanics, still wearing their stained overalls, and David was sitting next to three admin staff Sam didn't recognise.

There were fewer than a dozen survivors in all, out of a base with maybe a hundred personnel. The Mayestrans had struck hard, turning the thriving base into a graveyard in a matter of seconds.

Mellish was just finishing his inspection, and he signalled to Sam. 'Go and check the car pool. We're going to need two more vehicles to get everyone out of here.'

'Hold on there,' said David, getting to his feet. 'I'm the ranking officer now.'

'This isn't the time,' said Mellish urgently. 'You can play soldiers later. Right now we've got to get these people to safety.'

'And where's that exactly?'

'The settlement is closest.'

'And then what? Wait for the Mayestrans to show up there... if they haven't already?' David pointed to the East. 'We should head for the other base. They'll have ships, and–'

'We're not going to make it that far in groundcars,' said Mellish. 'It's hundreds of kilometres away, and most of that is desert.'

Anna sat up. 'Shouldn't we call someone? Tell them what happened?'

'Definitely not,' said Mellish. 'If the Mayestrans have a task force in this system they'll be intercepting every communication. Send any kind of signal, and they'll come straight back to finish us off.' He gestured at Sam. 'Go check the cars, please. The quicker we leave this place, the safer we'll be.'

Sam jogged through the palm trees towards the car pool, clambering over fallen trunks and almost falling headlong several times. The Mayestran attack had all but razed the plantation, shredding trees wholesale and turning the whole area into a churned-up mess.

She lost her way a couple of times, the path having been blasted to oblivion, but as she left the area immediately surrounding the base there were more trees and the path was still visible. That's when she heard footsteps ahead of her, and she took cover quickly in case it was the Mayestrans.

When the person came into view, though, it wasn't the enemy. It was the sentry from the car pool. He was carrying a blast rifle, and Sam remained behind the tree as she called out to him. 'Don't shoot,' she said quickly. 'It's Sam, from the base. Friendly.'

'Come out where I can see you.'

Sam obeyed, and when the sentry saw her he lowered his weapon. 'What the bloody hell is going on?' he demanded.

'The base has been hit.'

'I guessed that, but where is everyone?' The sentry gestured behind himself. 'I stayed at my post to start with, tried to get through to admin on the blower. Nobody answered, so I came to find out for myself.'

'Any damage to the cars?' asked Sam.

'None.'

'Good. Follow me.' Sam turned and led him back to the others, where he was quickly brought up to speed.

'They slaughtered us,' said the sentry, his voice hollow. He turned to look at the burning mess hall, the flames reflected in his eyes. 'Those poor bastards didn't stand a chance.'

'We'll avenge them another time,' said Mellish matter-of-factly. 'Right now it's us I'm worried about. Let's get to the cars and put some distance between us and any more attacks.'

— 13 —

As they made their way towards the cars Sam noticed some of the others freezing at every sound. Unfortunately, if the Mayestrans *had* sent ground troops to finish off any survivors the battle would be short and one-sided. Apart from the sentry and his blast rifle, none of the group were armed.

They made it without incident, and they split up with two to a vehicle. There were eleven of them across five cars, with Piet choosing to ride with Sam and one of the mechanics rather than taking a sixth car on his own. Before they left, David eyed the remaining vehicles. 'I'm tempted to blow them up,' he said. 'If the Mayestrans get troops on the ground, they could follow us.'

'Best leave them be,' said Mellish. 'The Mayestrans don't need them, not with troop carriers to hand. And if any of our people survived we don't want to strand them here.'

His points were reasonable, but David still looked like he was going to argue. Anyone could see he was unhappy at the way Mellish – a mere civilian – was taking charge. Then, abruptly, he shrugged and turned away.

The convoy set off for the main gates, skirting the shallow crater and the scattered wreckage. As the car slid past, motors whining, Sam heard a faint shout to her right. She glanced round, and saw the gate sentry limping from cover, one trouser leg ripped and bloodstained. He had a blast rifle slung over his shoulder, and his face was creased with pain as he struggled towards her. Sam brought her car to a halt, while the other four vehicles purred off down the track without her. 'Help him in,' she told Piet.

The gate sentry passed his weapon up first, and then Piet leaned over the side of the hovering groundcar and hauled the man bodily into the vehicle. 'Thanks,' grunted the sentry. 'I didn't think you'd heard me.'

'How's the leg?'

'A big splinter slashed my calf. Nothing broken.'

'Piet, check it will you?' asked Sam, as she pulled away. Then, briefly, she told the sentry about their plan.

He was silent. 'Are all of them dead?' he said at last.

'Nobody left in the buildings, that's for certain. There may be others like you, taking cover, but we left several cars for them.' Sam eyed the road ahead, but apart from a dust trail slowly drifting away there was no sign of the others. She sped up, driving into the choking dust, and was relieved when she eventually spotted the convoy ahead. They'd switched off all their lights, and she saw someone looking back at her from the rearmost car, gesturing. Quickly, she cut her own lights, and the five cars motored along the track in darkness. It was dangerous, but the alternative was even more so, because five sets of headlights blazing across the desert would be like a beacon to any Mayestrans patrolling the skies above.

They were about halfway to the settlement when Sam heard a growling roar, barely audible over the sound of the car at first, but rapidly getting louder. It was approaching from behind, and as she glanced over her shoulder she saw a flight of Mayestran fighters racing towards her, flying parallel to the track. They were three abreast, and were almost casual in their approach to the fleeing convoy. In the back seat the sentry raised his weapon, preparing to fight back, but before he could open fire the ships swept past and were gone, the thunder of their exhausts the only sign they'd been there.

Sam guessed the enemy had missed the convoy of groundcars in the darkness, with the mottled desert camouflage doing its job perfectly. Her relief was short-lived though, because it was obvious the Mayestrans were heading towards the settlement.

David pulled over, and the convoy came to a halt under a stand of palm trees. Everyone got out, gathering around him. 'Well, they've cut us off,' he said. 'I know the settlement was a long shot, but it seems they're planning on sticking around.'

One of the civilian contractors put his hand up. 'Why don't we surrender? I mean, I don't want to live out my days in a prison camp, but I'd rather that than... well, you know.' he glanced down the track, towards the faint glow on the horizon where the base was still burning.

David shook his head. 'They're attacking in fighters. How are they going to pick up a dozen prisoners?'

'They might have ground troops on the way. Assault vehicles.' The contractor swallowed. 'I was caught in a firefight once before. I–I'm not going through that again.'

'Fine. Take a car and head for the Mayestrans. Everyone who agrees with him can go too.'

'No, that's a lousy idea,' said Mellish. 'First, the Mayestrans are liable to shoot them out of hand. And second, we don't want to divide our forces.'

'I'm not a force,' said the contractor. 'I'm just a cleaner.' He gestured at the other two. 'They take care of the grounds. None of us can fight.'

'Doesn't matter. You'd front up to the Mayestrans driving a military vehicle. They'd blast you before you could get within speaking range.'

David nodded. 'He's right. I'd do the same.'

'I have a suggestion,' said Sam. 'When I visited the settlement earlier, I saw a couple of flyers. One wasn't much good, just a single-seat 'copter, but the other was a transport. If we could get our hands on that–'

'We could fly to the other base,' finished David. 'Sounds like a plan. Where were these ships parked up?'

'On the far side of the settlement, beside a fuel station.' Sam hesitated. 'Of course, there's no guarantee they're still there. The locals might have fled in them, or those Mayestran fighters might have blown them apart.'

'We'll have to take that chance.' David picked up a fallen palm frond and snapped off a length. He drew a circle in the dirt, barely visible in the starlight, then scratched a cross on the far side. 'We'll have to go cross-country,' he said. 'Give the settlement a wide berth, and approach from the other side. We'll stop about a kilometre out and approach on foot to assess the situation. If the flyers are still there, one of us will go in and check them out properly.'

'What about the enemy?' someone asked.

'We don't even know if the Mayestrans have landed there. They might have flown a couple of passes over the settlement to make sure it wasn't another of our bases, then left.' He gestured at the cars. 'If we keep the speed down and travel in darkness, they won't spot us. Come on, let's get moving.'

The group returned to the cars, and soon the convoy was back on the road, heading for the settlement once more. Sam brought up the rear, feeling a lot happier now they had a plan of sorts. If they could get hold of a flyer and avoid the enemy fighters, they might be able to join up with the rest of the Henerian forces.

Then they could set about kicking the Mayestrans out of the system.

14

When they got closer to the settlement David slowed the convoy and led them off the road, into the scrub. They were about two kilometers from the cluster of domes, and Sam could see lights glowing in the distance. Swirling dust from the cars made it hard to see any detail, though, and she couldn't tell whether the Mayestrans had landed a troop carrier at the settlement.

They drove carefully, avoiding rocky outcrops, clumps of dry-looking brush and sudden dips in the ground. The cars could travel right over smaller obstacles, but sailing into a deep ditch would have them crash-landing on their noses, or even flipping right over.

They drove in a big semi-circle by keeping the lights to their left and maintaining the same approximate distance from the domes. Eventually the convoy arrived at the rear of the settlement, and then they aimed their cars at the lights and drove straight ahead for a few hundred metres. They encountered a dried-up riverbed slashed across the terrain like a scar, and they managed to find a spot where the gully was shallow enough to drive the cars in. Then they parked up and clambered out.

'You three stay here,' said David, indicating the civilians.

'We're going in for a closer look. If you hear shooting, take one of the cars and do your best to get away.'

'To where?' muttered one of the civilians, but there was no answer to that. The three of them just seemed relieved they could stay out of sight in relative safety.

There was a roar from the direction of the settlement, and Sam clambered up the other side of the gully to find out what was happening. Several others joined her, and they all watched, dismayed, as they saw three Mayestran fighters circling the settlement. They were loud, even at this distance, and the deep rumble of their engines caused several cascades of sand and stones in the gully.

'At least they're not attacking,' said Sam.

David snorted. 'Yet.'

Then Sam pointed. 'There's the flyer I mentioned.' She could just make it out, gleaming dully in the light from the nearby streetlamps. It looked smaller than she remembered, and she wondered whether they'd be able to get everyone aboard.

Then there was a roar from behind them, and David shouted a warning. 'Everyone freeze! Lie still!'

They obeyed, burying their faces in their arms. The roar grew louder, and Sam heard the screaming whistle of heavy thrusters. It wasn't a fighter, that was for sure, and with a sinking feeling she realised the Mayestrans were landing a bigger craft – a transport, or a troop carrier.

The craft flew directly overhead, the wash blasting clouds of dust high into the air, and sending small stones flying like shrapnel. Sam felt the heat from its thrusters as the ship passed over them, and she protected her head with her arms, trying to ward off the intense noise.

Then it was gone, and she shook her head, scattering stone chips and coughing in the thick choking dust. Everyone was coated from head to toe, and as they moved it was like the desert itself was coming to life. Sam raised her head and stared after the ship, but she couldn't see a thing.

'Get up!' said David urgently, as he clambered to his feet. 'We'll follow them in while we have cover!'

'It's not worth the risk,' said Mellish. 'If they spot you, we're *all* dead.'

David indicated the dust, which had dropped visibility to about ten metres. 'Spot us in *this?*'

The others scrambled up, and once they were free of the gully they crouched double and ran for it, following the sound of roaring engines. The sound was quieter now, and Sam guessed the ship had set down. Then she saw light ahead, and she realised the dust was thinning. 'Better find cover,' she said quickly.

Mellish pointed. 'There's a ruined wall or something over there,' he said, pointing to a darker line.

The wall wasn't very high, and they were forced to lie full-length. Then Sam raised her head, and she saw a big slab-sided vessel about twenty metres away. It was sitting on its thick landing legs, the ramp at the back already dropping to meet the ground. Two dozen troops in dark combat armour emerged from the craft, moving swiftly and with well-drilled ease. Each carried a blast rifle at the ready, and with their combat helmets and equipment packs they looked nigh-on invincible.

'Shit,' growled David, echoing all of their thoughts. It was one thing to sneak past a couple of guards to steal an old flyer, but this was a whole new game. 'Maybe they'll take a look around and leave again.'

'They certainly won't be doing any shopping,' remarked Sam, as she remembered the general store with its basic goods.

David glared at her. 'You find this funny, do you?'

'Sorry sir,' mumbled Sam.

'She's right in a way,' said Mellish. 'They'll probably ask the locals a few questions about the base, then go. They've got no reason to stick around.'

David glanced at the sky. 'If it gets light we're going to be sitting ducks.'

'We've got a few hours yet.'

Sam had no idea what the time was, but she guessed one or two in the morning. Then the troop ship lifted off again, flying away with a sound like endless peals of thunder. As the night finally grew quiet, they could hear shouted orders as the Mayestran troops formed up. Sounds carried easily, and Sam knew anything above a whisper would reveal her position. The dust and sand were settling again, and visibility was improving too.

She risked a look, and she saw a senior officer, a female, leading the combat troops into the settlement. They rounded up locals efficiently, dragging them out of the domes and herding them together with shouted commands and gestures from their blast rifles. Then Sam saw a couple of the troops dragging a uniformed figure into the light, and she swore under her breath. It was one of the pilots she'd met on her first visit, from the other Henerian base. The Mayestrans shouted at her, then one of them hit her with his rifle, knocking her off her feet.

David rose to his feet immediately, but Mellish and one of the sentries dragged him down again. 'We've got to help her,' said David urgently.

'We can't do a bloody thing, and you know it,' hissed Mellish.

The woman was dragged upright, clutching the side of

her face, and soon she was joined by three more Henerian pilots. They all looked like they'd been mistreated, with ripped uniforms caked with dust. 'There were more of our people when I was here earlier,' muttered Sam. 'Maybe some got away.'

There was a large group of civilians outside the tavern, and they looked sullen and scared as a dozen troops covered them with levelled blast rifles. The four Henerian pilots stood apart, guarded by several wary Mayestrans, while the rest of the troops finished searching the domes with their leader.

Finally, satisfied they'd got everyone, the leader returned to the group of civilians. She put her hands on her hips and faced them, just as three Mayestran fighters roared overhead. They banked sharply, circling the settlement, then tore away again.

'There's no way we're getting to that flyer without them spotting us,' whispered Mellish.

'Never mind getting away, we've got to save our people!' David eyed the sentry lying beside him, and Sam wondered whether he was going to grab the man's blast rifle and charge the enemy. Then, with a muttered curse, David turned away.

'The Imperial Mayestran Navy wishes you no harm!'

The female officer's voice carried across the open ground, every word as clear as day.

'However, you should know that we offer our enemies no such mercy,' said the officer. She indicated the Henerian pilots, who were staring down the dozen or so Mayestrans facing them. 'These terrorists have slaughtered our families and murdered our children, and they continue to fight this senseless war against our peace-loving kind.'

Sam's eyebrows rose. 'She's laying it on a bit thick.'

'I don't like this,' said Mellish. 'I don't like this one bit.'

'Therefore, I sentence these bloodthirsty criminals to death.'

Suddenly, Sam realised what was happening. 'No! They're going to–'

There was a ripple of blaster fire and the Henerian pilots went down like rag dolls, dead before they hit the ground. Sam turned away, sickened, and was scarcely able to believe what she'd just witnessed.

'Look upon their corpses,' shouted the officer. '*All* enemies of the Mayestran empire will be treated thus!'

15

The sentry next to David gripped his weapon, his face set, and Mellish laid a hand on his arm. 'Don't be a hero, son. You can't do anything for them now.'

Sam was still in a daze, could still picture the Henerian pilots twisting and falling in the murderous gunfire, but then she heard a noise behind her. She turned, looking up, and saw two shadowy figures approaching fast. It was their boots on the gritty soil that she'd heard, but before she could utter a warning the newcomers flopped down into cover beside her, raising a small cloud of dust. That's when she realised they were wearing Henerian uniforms, and she recognised the new arrivals instantly, having met them in the tavern earlier.

'Did the others get out?' one of them whispered.

Sam could only shake her head. 'They… they just shot them.'

The pilot swore savagely. 'I'm going to kill every one of those murdering bastards,' he vowed.

'Join the queue,' said Mellish, and he glanced up as the Mayestran fighters flew another pass. 'This place is getting too hot for comfort. We've got to move soon.'

'How long have they been flying around?' asked the second pilot.

'At least half an hour.'

'They'll be getting low on fuel, then. Those things are thirsty as hell.'

'There's a fuel depot by the flyer,' said Sam.

'No chance. They'll never put that civilian crap in their nice shiny fighters.'

As if on cue, the three enemy fighters raised their noses and blasted straight up, rapidly vanishing from sight. In the sudden quiet, Mellish explained the plan to the newcomers. When he got to the part about meeting up with the rest of the Henerian forces at the pilot's home base, the man looked doubtful.

'They probably hit ours first. No offence, but we're a much bigger threat than a bunch of rookies.' He glanced at Sam. 'Even if they're trigger-happy nut-jobs like her.'

'It's our only chance, unless you know of some other way off this planet,' said Mellish.

The pilot shook his head, and his gaze rested on the huddled bodies of his comrades. The Mayestrans had left them right were they'd fallen, and were now shepherding the local residents past them, taking them back to the domes. 'You need a distraction,' he said quietly.

'What do you have in mind?'

'Revenge.' The pilot turned to the sentry. 'I'll need your weapon.'

David shook his head. 'You can't just throw your life away.'

Sam remembered the way David had leapt up from cover when the Mayestrans knocked the female pilot down, desperate to charge in and help despite the odds, but she kept quiet.

The pilot, however, wasn't keeping quiet about anything. 'They just killed four members of my squadron,' he hissed. 'I don't need some glorified flight instructor telling me what I can and can't do.'

'Flight instructor?' David eyed him steadily. 'They only assigned me to the training base after I completed my second tour of duty.'

The pilot looked at him with new respect. 'I'm sorry, sir. I didn't know.'

'They're withdrawing to the tavern,' whispered Sam. Peering over the low wall, she'd spotted the Mayestrans returning to the centre of the settlement, leaving a guard or two behind to cover the domes. They obviously didn't expect any trouble from the locals, and Sam guessed that was why they'd slaughtered the pilots in cold blood. A swift, bloody demonstration was more effective than any spoken threat.

There was only one sentry near the flyer, and he had his back to them. Problem was, the whole lot would come running the moment they started the flyer's engines...assuming it was capable of starting in the first place. Sam remembered the rust streaks and patched hull from her earlier visit, and her lips tightened as she realised they were pinning all their hopes of survival on an old heap that might not have flown for some years. Then, as she studied the layout of the settlement, she had an idea. 'We can use the groundcars,' she said.

Everyone stared at her in surprise. 'What are you talking about?' demanded David.

'We could have used the groundcars back at the base,' whispered Mellish. 'Why the hell did we drive all the way out here, if–'

'No, not to get away,' said Sam urgently. 'We can use them to distract the Mayestrans!'

There were a few raised eyebrows as she explained, and

then Mellish laughed, shaking his head. 'It's great! They won't know what hit 'em.'

The whole group returned to the groundcars, where they found the civilians behind a large rock, peering out nervously as they waited for signs of friend... or foe. They were relieved to see the others, but slightly less happy when they learned they'd have to board the flyer under enemy fire, then sit on board while someone tried to start the engines. 'Does it have armour?' one of them asked.

'Er, sure,' said Sam, lying through her teeth. 'Lots.'

'Oh. I guess that sounds all right then.'

Several of the others gathered round, and together they pushed and pulled one of the groundcars until they'd forced it up the far side of the shallow gully. Sam enlisted the help of the two mechanics, who jury-rigged the controls in a matter of moments. Then, when they were ready, David jumped in and started the engine.

The car rose with a whine, blowing clouds of dust, and David immediately turned for the settlement. He lined the car up on the sentry, and the tavern beyond, then stepped out, leaving the door open. He reached inside, and with a quick push he forced the throttle to full, throwing himself backwards as the car leapt forwards.

The sentry was already looking towards them, having heard the distant whining noise. Now he stared as the groundcar shot towards him at top speed, covering the hundred metres or so in just a couple of seconds. He raised his blast rifle, but only got two wild shots off before he was forced to dive for cover. The car blasted by, then skimmed the side of a dome, scattering bright sparks.

Sam's heart was in her mouth as she watched the groundcar roaring towards the open front doors of the tavern. She saw the sentry raise his gun, but there were people just inside the tavern and shooting at the car would have put them in danger.

Not as much danger as the speeding car, though. At top speed the groundcar could hit three hundred, and it was doing two thirds of that when it smashed through the front of the tavern. There was an ear-splitting bang as the vehicle took out the front wall and most of the people inside, and another as it tore through the rear wall, still travelling fast.

The guard ran after it, stopped, ran a few paces, then froze at the scenes of destruction.

'Let's go,' said Sam.

They ran for the flyer, all of them, and as they pounded across the open ground Sam heard screams from inside the tavern. The guard was still frozen, about forty metres ahead of them, but then he heard the footsteps as a dozen or more Henerians thundered towards him. He turned, fumbling with his weapon, but the Henerian sentry stopped, took aim and coolly shot him down before the Mayestran could fire at them. Anna ran forward and grabbed the Mayestran's weapon, then dived into a doorway for cover.

A couple of troopers staggered out of the tavern, bleeding and dazed. They'd barely taken three paces before Anna aimed her weapon, shooting them both down. 'Plenty more where that came from, you murdering bastards!' she shouted. 'Come out and get it!'

Meanwhile, Sam, David and the pilots ran to the flyer. They hauled the cockpit door open, and there was an indrawn breath as they saw the state of the controls. 'What did they use it for, a chicken coop?' growled one of the pilots.

David climbed into the pilot's seat and examined the console, then started flipping switches and levers. A few lights flickered on, which was promising, and while he was busy

Sam went to the side and yanked the passenger door open. Inside there were six tatty chairs, just bare metal frames with fragments of ancient fabric clinging to them. The floor was knee-deep in straw, and she could have sworn she spotted a rat scurrying away. Then she paused. There were thirteen of them now, and the flyer was meant for two up front and six in the back. They could fit the others in, just about, but would it lift off?

16

David fired up the flyer's engines, the jets whirring and groaning as they wakened from their long slumber. Grit and black smoke belched from the exhausts, but after a few seconds they settled down to a steady roar.

'Check number three!' shouted David from the cockpit. 'Back right.'

Sam put her head out the door and looked along the fuselage. She could see vapour jetting from the side of the engine, and she pulled her head in and made a throat cutting motion. David cut the throttles, and the engines rumbled away to silence. 'Fuel leak,' she called. 'I could see the stuff spraying out.'

'Get hold of those mechanics. See if they can plug it.'

'Will it fly on three engines?'

'With this old wreck, even four might not be enough.'

Sam jumped down and ran to the 'copter, where the rest of the group were taking cover. The landing area was exposed, and she knew it wouldn't be long before the surviving Mayestrans got themselves organised and mounted a counter-attack. As she ducked behind the slender vehicle she saw Anna and the two sentries firing occasional shots at the tavern, the blasts helping to keep the occupants' heads down. Unfortunately, despite the spectacular crash when the groundcar flew into the building, Sam was pretty sure most of the Mayestrans had survived. They'd doused the lights, leaving the interior of the tavern in darkness, but even now she could see shadows flitting across the doorway as the enemy got themselves organised.

Anna fired a burst into the tavern, and the glare showed several armoured troops approaching the door, weapons ready. They began firing back, and with their greater numbers Anna was forced to retreat, firing wild shots as she ran. The two Henerian sentries opened up, covering her, but the flashes of their weapons revealed their position, and the enemy began firing at them instead.

Swearing under her breath, Sam knew they wouldn't be able to hold a determined enemy off for long. She turned to the others, and caught the attention of the two mechanics. 'The right rear engine is leaking fuel. Any chance you can patch it up?'

'Sure, if we had tools.'

'Just do what you can. It's only got to hold until we're clear.'

The female mechanic nodded. 'We'll fix it.'

They ran towards the flyer, and Sam heard a wrench of metal as they pulled the cowling right off the engine, tossing it aside like so much scrap. Then they went to work, tracing the fuel lines to find the leak.

A blaster shot skimmed by, and Sam ducked her head. She turned towards the tavern, and saw several Mayestrans out front, fanning out. They'd left two or three casualties behind, lying motionless in the dirt, but the four or five soldiers who'd managed to leave the tavern were already moving to flank Anna and the two sentries. The Henerians had no combat training, not when it came to close quarters fighting, and

Sam knew the well-drilled Mayestrans were going to have no trouble silencing them.

A couple more shots flew past, stray blasts which tore down the street and zipped past the flyer, leaving a searing after-image in Sam's vision. In the sudden glare from the shots she saw the mechanics struggling with the engine's internals, and she wondered if they'd manage to fix it. She was hoping it was just a split hose, something they could undo and fold double, clamping it to stop any fuel leaking out. It meant the flyer would have to lift off on three engines, which would leave no margin for error, but they were running out of time and the old wreck was their only hope.

The male mechanic left his companion and ran back to Sam, squatting in the dust and keeping his head down. 'It's not too bad. A loose clamp and a split hose.'

'Can you block it off?'

'Better. She's cut off the end, and now she's refitting it. If we're lucky, the engine will run.'

'Okay, great. Go and tell David, and–' Sam ducked as something slammed into the 'copter, showering her with sparks. 'They've made us,' she said, raising her voice as much as she dared. 'Everyone on board, now!'

The group ran for the flyer, and she saw them scrambling through the doors. More shots followed them, some punching holes in the rusty old bodywork. 'Anna! You two!' shouted Sam, getting the sentries' attention. 'Covering fire, everything you've got.'

Behind her, the flyer roared into life again, and she glanced round to see flames jetting from the damaged engine's exhaust. There were flames on the ground too, where the fuel had sprayed earlier, but the wash from the jets kept blowing them out. David gestured at her from the cockpit, and Sam stood up, cupping her hands to her mouth. 'Henerians!' she shouted. 'To me!'

Anna and the sentries began to fall back, still firing at the unseen enemy, but mostly dodging and weaving. In return, many more shots came blasting out of the darkness, slamming into buildings and tearing furrows in the dirt road.

Sam's mouth was dry as she watched the three of them trying to retreat. She wished she had a gun, to provide covering fire, but like most of the Henerians she was unarmed. Then she eyed the 'copter, which was providing her with cover. It was in better condition than the flyer, although that wasn't saying much, and when she reached inside and turned the ignition on she was relieved to see a glow from the instruments. She found the starter, which had the blades whirling around overhead in seconds, and then located a switch for the headlights. Twin beams came on, shining along the street, and Sam slid the throttle to full and rolled away from the little machine before it could take to the air with her dangling from the side. With no weight on board it took off like a rocket, weaving and diving as the control stick yawed aimlessly. Then it rolled on its side and plunged to the ground, hitting with a solid crunch. It hadn't been airborne long, but it distracted the Mayestrans for a few seconds, and that was enough for Anna and the two sentries to beat a hasty retreat. They ran past Sam, jumped into the flyer and reappeared in the doorway, all three of them firing down the street to keep the Mayestrans busy.

Sam ran towards them, keeping her head well down as the shots flew overhead, and when she was close enough she took a flying leap through the open door. Willing hands grabbed her, dragging her into the stale-smelling straw, and then the engines howled and the floor tilted as the ancient flyer rose from the landing pad.

17

Sam rolled over and sat up, and as the flyer banked she saw three or four Mayestran troops below, firing up at the slow-moving target. Anna and the two sentries blazed back at them, and neither side gave up firing until they were well out of range.

'How's she flying?' Sam shouted at David.

'We're up and we're moving.'

'Keep an eye out for the Mayestran fighters. If those Phase IIIs come back...' Sam didn't finish the sentence. There was no chance of out-flying or outrunning them, and the guns on the enemy fighters would tear the old flyer to pieces in seconds. Then she looked round, and she saw one of the civilians poking his finger through a jagged hole in the hull where a Mayestran blaster had hit it.

'You told us this thing was armoured,' he shouted.

'It set your mind at rest, didn't it?'

'Not now, it hasn't!'.

Sam moved to the door and hauled it to, cutting off the howling gale. It was still noisy, but at least it stopped the years of accumulated filth and straw blowing all over them. Then she moved to the cockpit, where she found one of the pilots from the main base giving David directions. 'How far?' she shouted, raising her voice over the roar of the thrusters.

'About eight hundred kilometres.'

'Really?' She stared at him. 'How did your people get to the settlement? I didn't see any military vehicles.'

'Dropped off earlier for some R&R. We were due to be picked up tomorrow morning, but I guess the schedule got disrupted a little.' He indicated a display, and David altered course a touch.

They were flying low, not much higher than the palm trees, but even so Sam was sure they'd be a big, slow-moving target if the Mayestran fighters returned. 'How long until we get there?' Sam asked.

The pilot checked another display. 'At this speed, just under two hours.'

'Can we go any faster?'

David shook his head. 'Not unless you want more bits and pieces falling off.'

'More?'

'Don't look back,' he advised her. 'I know I'm not.'

They flew on for ten or fifteen minutes, with Sam scanning the sky through the cracked windshield. She was looking for any sign of the enemy fighters, because while they couldn't defend themselves in the junky old flyer, they might still be able to set down and run for cover. Of course, a whole squadron of fighters could be right on her tail, fingers curled around their triggers, but she couldn't do anything about that. Anyway, they were flying a civilian ship, and the Mayestrans would probably circle them once or twice before they decided to attack.

'Smoke!' said David, gesturing through the screen.

It was a thin vertical line in the distance, the base shot

through with red. At first Sam thought it was the ruined training base, but as they approached she saw it was much smaller. David throttled back, and as he banked the flyer they looked down to see wreckage scattered across a wide area, with the largest part in the middle still burning fiercely. 'There's a winglet,' said Sam, pointing at the crumpled piece of metal.

'It's one of ours,' said David. 'Was, I mean.'

'Poor bastard,' said the pilot sitting beside him.

Without another word, David returned to their original course and sped up. Since escaping the settlement they'd all been feeling more positive, but the sight of the crashed fighter had given them a nasty dose of reality. What if every Henerian fighter on the planet had been blasted to pieces? thought Sam. What if the handful of survivors aboard the rickety old flyer were all that remained from the two bases? She gripped David's shoulder, getting his attention. 'When we reach the other base, don't fly over it. If there's anyone left, they might think we're attacking and shoot us down.'

David gave her a look. 'I have done this before, you know.'

'Sorry, sir. Just thinking aloud.' She realised they would also have considered her other sudden thought... that the Mayestrans could have overrun the second facility, and that the place might even now be swarming with their fighters, troops and dropships.

'We already planned to set down nearby. It'll mean another hike, but that's better than the alternative.' He nodded towards the rear compartment. 'Maybe you should let them know how long we're going to be. Some of them might want to grab a few winks.'

Sam took the hint, and returned to the rear of the ship. Once she imparted the news, she settled down in the rancid straw and put her head on her arm. She'd been awake at least eighteen hours, and even a few minutes rest would be welcome.

◆

Sam woke with a start, instinctively knowing something was different. Despite the steady roar from the engines she'd been out for an hour, maybe a little longer, and it was a change in that noise which had just dragged her from a restless sleep. There was no doubt about it, the engines were throttling back and the thrusters were firing, which meant they were about to set down.

She sat up, shaking her groggy head to clear it, then got to her feet.

'Everyone hold on back there,' called David from the cockpit. 'We're coming in now.'

Sam took hold of a seat back, her fingers gripping the slick, worn metal. Nearby, Anna was checking and re-checking her captured Mayestran gun, and Sam saw Piet eyeing it thoughtfully. She'd hardly spoken to the stocky pilot since everything kicked off, and she leaned across and touched him on the shoulder. 'We should be able to get weapons here. It's an active base, not a training facility.'

'I hope so,' said Piet gravely. 'Like this, I feel useless. It's like flying into combat naked.'

She gave him a smile, then hung on as she felt a gentle bump. The ship rocked once or twice, and there was a loud whine as the engines spooled down. The sudden quiet was unnerving, and even normal voices sounded like shouts. 'We're a kilometre from the base,' said David, twisting in his seat to face the passenger compartment. 'We saw smoke and damaged buildings coming in, so the enemy has definitely been here. There's nothing moving out there, but they might be keeping their heads down.'

'How close did you get?' Sam asked him.

'Not very,' admitted David. 'They've got defences here... or at least, they did have.' He glanced at the others. 'We're going to approach on foot. Non-combatants will remain here for the time being. The rest of you form up outside.'

Mellish looked like he was going to argue, then closed his mouth again.

Sam crossed to the door and hauled it open, wincing as it grated on the runners. It was still dark outside but she could see a faint flush on the horizon, and she knew dawn wasn't far off. They'd have to get moving if they wanted to reach the base under cover of darkness, that was for sure.

She jumped down, standing aside while the others joined her. A quick glance told her the area was very different to the one they'd just left, with thick vegetation that would give them some very useful cover. Sometime during the flight they must have emerged from the desert, and from the look of the greenery Sam assumed there was a decent-sized river nearby, or at least plenty of groundwater.

Then the two pilots from the nearby base gathered everyone together to explain the layout. 'The main base lies in that direction,' said one, pointing towards a stand of trees. 'From the air it looked like it was hit pretty bad, but there's a secondary dispersal area over that way.' He pointed again, this time slightly to the left. 'That's where we house the Phase

Is, along with the spare fighters and the repair facilities. It looked intact, so we might be able to find enough ships to get off this rock.'

Everyone brightened at that news, and after a quick briefing on the perimeter fencing and possible defences, they set off. It was chilly, but the terrain was rough and they soon warmed up. After half an hour Sam detected a smell of burning, and then she noticed her eyes and throat stinging. Then they rounded a low mound, and stopped. There was a scene of devastation on the other side, where a Henerian fighter appeared to have speared into the ground at full throttle. There was wreckage everywhere, twisted and blackened, and even though the fires had long since burnt out the acrid fumes from the crash site made it hard to breathe.

They detoured around the wreckage, moving through the undergrowth in silence. So far they'd not seen any evidence of Mayestran losses, and it was sobering to think the enemy could attack a Henerian base like this without warning, wreaking havoc with such impunity. Recruits were taught plenty about grand victories and heroic battles, but attacks like this one were rarely discussed.

Ten minutes later one of the pilots stopped ahead of them. He raised his hand and the group froze. 'We're getting close,' he murmured. 'Stay here and keep quiet. I'll scout ahead.'

He'd only been gone a few seconds when there was a faint shout, followed by the distinctive burst of fire from an energy weapon. Everyone ducked as shots blazed overhead, and in between the firing they heard a louder shout, close by. 'I'm a friendly, you bloody idiots. Stop shooting at me!'

Sam advanced through the bushes, followed by several others, and she saw the pilot standing behind a medium-sized tree. Beyond was an open area which looked like it had been levelled with heavy equipment, creating a fire zone around the base. And beyond that was a wooded area with the familiar camouflage netting draped between the trees. From her angle she could see beneath it, and there were several darker shadows which looked like fighters...intact, and ready to fly.

That brought a grin to her face, because now, at last, they might have a chance of getting away!

18

Sam glanced to her right as the group crossed the broad expanse of compacted earth. It was definitely getting lighter, and she could see columns of smoke about three or four hundred metres away, rising into the sky from the ruins of the main base. She couldn't see any buildings, but that wasn't surprising since David had told her the whole place had been comprehensively smashed. What she *could* see was the spindly silhouette of a comms tower, leaning over drunkenly with the upper section completely missing. There were fragments of satellite dish still dangling from the wreckage, and she wondered whether the base had got any kind of signal out before their comms were completely cut off. Judging by the speed of the attacks, she doubted it.

Still, *someone* had fired at them from the dispersal area, and that meant some of the base staff had survived. She turned to look at the pilot who'd been shot at, and saw him forging ahead of the group, accompanied by the second pilot from the nearby base. It was a smart move, because the two of them would be known to the survivors, and they could then vouch for Sam, David and the other new arrivals.

'All right, this is close enough,' said David, calling a halt. 'Those guys over there are jumpy as hell, and we don't want to spook them.'

Sam glanced up at the sky, then at the treeline they'd just left. The group had stopped in the middle of the open expanse, with no cover at all, and if the Mayestrans happened by there could only be one outcome. The sky was getting much lighter now, and the Henerian group would be easily spotted from the cockpit of a fighter.

The light also revealed more details beneath the camouflage netting, and Sam made out three Mayestran Phase Is on landing pads. Nearby there were several Kestrel fighters, all of them intact and seemingly in working order. The two pilots they'd arrived with were standing in front, talking to a man and a woman, both in fatigues. One of the pilots turned and beckoned, and David gave the order to move.

As they got closer, Sam eyed the fighters. Why hadn't they flown into battle, to defend the planet? Then her face cleared. Six pilots had been absent during the attack, having been stranded at the settlement. That had to be the reason some of the fighters hadn't even taken off.

Sam's group were introduced to the survivors, about six in total. Four were ground staff who'd been working on the fighters when the main base was hit. One was the adjutant, who'd witnessed the base commander's death in the attack, and the final member of the survivors was a squadron leader. Farren was an older man, mid-fifties, and Sam guessed it was many years since he'd flown anything more challenging than a desk. He sized up the new arrivals, and once he realised he was the ranking officer he quickly took charge.

'We have to get off this planet,' he said, speaking fast. 'The enemy will be back in daylight, and they'll destroy anything they missed the first time around.'

'Sir, we have your two pilots, myself and Grant,' said David.

'In addition to that, there are five recruits, but they're not familiar with these ships.'

'I've flown that type in combat,' said Sam, nodding towards the Henerian Kestrel fighter standing nearby.

'Whether we have four pilots or five, it makes no difference,' said David shortly. He turned to Farren. 'We don't have enough space to save everyone, sir. With your people and mine together, we're going to need more than a dozen places.'

Squadron Leader Farren stared at him. 'If we can't get everyone away at once, we'll have to make several trips.'

'Excuse me sir, but trips to where? The nearest friendly orbiter is three systems from here, and we don't have the range.'

This was news to Sam. She'd been concentrating so much on fleeing the Mayestrans and leaving the planet that she hadn't considered their eventual destination. She'd arrived on the planet by transport, which had a much greater range than a fighter, and she kicked herself as she realised they weren't out of the woods yet.

'Dammit, man. We can't sit around here waiting to be captured.'

'I know, sir. And...you should know the Mayestrans aren't taking prisoners. We witnessed them shooting four of your pilots in cold blood.'

Farren turned to one of the two pilots who'd survived the attack. 'Is that true, Latner?'

'Yes sir. It was unprovoked. They shot them out of hand.'

'I see.' Farren was silent, but then he drew himself up. 'Well, if we can't escape and surrender is off the table, our only option is to attack. We must throw together a fighting force using every means at our disposal, and together we'll drive these devils back into the depths of space.'

Sam felt a stirring of excitement at the impromptu speech. After all the defeats, the running away and the hiding, it would be incredible if they could organise a defence, and maybe fight back for once. The Mayestrans were known for their quick attacks on soft targets, and if the Henerians bared their teeth, it was possible the enemy would take flight.

Meanwhile, Farren gestured at the fighters standing nearby. 'I'm current, you know. I can still pilot one of those birds.'

The adjutant spoke up. 'Sir, it might be best if you organised the defence, rather than participating in it.'

'No, Standish. We need a show of force, and every available gun must be brought to bear.'

Sam felt a stab of admiration for the squadron leader. He was prepared to go into battle against the dreaded Phase IIIs, even though he was unlikely to survive the encounter. He was right, though. They needed to get as many fighters into the air as possible, hopefully convincing the Mayestrans that reinforcements had arrived.

Farren turned to David. 'Richett, can you walk your trainees through the Kestrel's controls? I know they're not familiar with the type, but we're going to need every pilot.'

'I don't know, sir. Sending them into combat with no training... it could turn into a slaughter.'

Piet spoke up. 'Sir, I am willing to take any risk. I will give my life for this cause.'

'Same goes for me sir,' said Anna. 'I'd give a years' pay to fly a Kestrel against the enemy.'

'Hopefully those sacrifices won't be necessary... for either of you,' said Farren, eyeing the tall, intense woman and the powerfully-built man. 'But your fighting spirit does you credit, trainees.'

'All right,' said David. 'Sam, since you know the Kestrel

backwards, you can fetch Mellish and the rest of the civilians. The rest of you, come with Grant and me. It's time for lesson number one.'

19

On the way back to the base, Sam walked beside Mellish, telling him about the plan to fight back. He wasn't impressed.

'That all sounds very heroic, but what intel do you have?'

'Intel?'

Mellish pointed at the sky. 'What kind of force do the Mayestrans have up there? Did they bring a lone destroyer or a whole carrier group?'

'We don't know.'

'Then perhaps you ought to find out.'

Sam fell silent. She was pretty sure the squadron leader would have considered it, but perhaps he had his own reasons for saying nothing. For example, maybe the old warhorse wanted to go out in a final blaze of glory.

When they reached the training base the trainees were sitting in the cockpits of the Kestrel fighters, familiarising themselves with the controls while Aren Grant and David moved from one ship to another, making sure their students were up to speed. Sam knew the sleek fighters weren't much different from the elderly trainers they were used to, but they did have more power in the engines and weapons. A *lot* more power.

David spotted her and came over, giving Mellish a brief nod

before leading Sam aside. 'I'm sorry about earlier. I didn't realise Farren would be here, and–'

'It's fine, sir. I could see you didn't like giving up command.'

He winced at the sir. 'Yeah, all right, you got me. I'm sure he's great at admin work, and I admire his courage, but this is going to get dirty. We need to hit the Mayestrans hard, and if he baulks at the last second they'll crush us.'

'So, it's a quick mutiny, then? Put him up against the nearest wall?'

David gave her a startled look. 'I hope you're joking.'

'Of course I am,' muttered Sam. 'Look, Farren didn't make squadron leader because someone liked the way he filed his reports. He's hungry for revenge, and he's prepared to lead from the front. Things could be a lot worse.'

'You're right,' said David, suddenly businesslike. 'I don't even know why we're discussing this. Now, I know you've flown the Kestrels before, but if you want a quick refresher...'

'Yes thanks,' said Sam. 'It was weeks ago now, and only for a couple of hours.'

David led her towards the nearest fighter, which stood empty. 'The first thing you have to remember is that these things have more power than you're used to. A *lot* more.'

'Do they really?' asked Sam.

He glanced at her, and they both laughed. 'All right,' said David, 'I'll give you a refresher, not a sales pitch. Come on, up to the cockpit. I'll show you a few tricks you *won't* know about these birds.'

They climbed into the nearby fighter, where Sam took the pilot's seat while David crouched behind her, pointing out controls over her shoulder. Eagerly, his face animated, the flight leader explained the Kestel's quirks, and Sam saw flashes of his boyish charm. He was close, and when he reached across to tap a display, he got closer still. At that moment he turned towards her, their faces just inches apart, and Sam felt a warmth inside her. If they got through this alive, she thought, then maybe, just maybe...

She could tell David felt it too, because he turned away, suddenly stumbling over his words. He recovered swiftly, and from then on was all business as he covered the rest of the Kestrel's systems.

◆

'Okay, settle down everyone. Settle down.'

The entire group of survivors was gathered under the camouflage netting in the shadow of the Kestrels and Phase I fighters. The sun was up, and Sam could already feel the heat in the air as Squadron Leader Farren briefed them.

'Our intention is to hit back at the Mayestrans by intercepting their patrol and destroying every one of their fighters. To this end, our surviving technical personnel have gone to the main base, to see whether they can transmit a signal. If they can rig something up, we should be able to attract the enemy to this location. Failing that, we'll transmit a weaker signal from the fighters and hope it tempts the enemy to investigate.'

Several people exchanged glances. They'd expected to fly off and blast the Mayestrans from the sky, not sit around waiting to get attacked once more.

'All our fighters will already be up when the signal goes out,' continued Farren, 'Two will act as bait by flying circuits

111

around the base, while the bulk of our force will be stationed at a much higher altitude.'

'That's suicide,' muttered Anna. 'Those two pilots won't stand a chance. They'll be destroyed before those waiting above can reach the battle.'

'I agree that's likely,' said the squadron leader. 'I don't expect any of you to take risks that I wouldn't face myself, and so I will fly one of the two decoys.'

There was a chorus of protest, especially from the elderly adjutant, but Farren motioned them to silence. 'I haven't flown a combat mission for years,' said the squadron leader. 'However, while I may be of limited use in a dogfight, I can still fly a circuit or two.'

Sam felt a surge of respect for the older man. He was a good sort, a true leader, and he was making an incredible sacrifice. Then she looked around the other pilots, because someone was still needed to fly the second decoy ship. One by one, they avoided her gaze. Even Anna looked uncomfortable, and she was usually combative to a fault. Like the rest, she knew the decoys sent up to bait the Mayestrans would be flying a suicide mission. Then Sam pictured the squadron leader valiantly holding off three Mayestran Phase IIIs on his own, and she opened her mouth to volunteer.

But, before she could speak, someone else got in first.

'I offer to fly the second ship.'

Everyone looked at Piet. The broad-shouldered trainee was standing under the wing of a fighter, and his gaze was resolute and unwavering.

'No, I'll do it,' said Sam, hardly realising she was speaking aloud.

'Sam, you know I make an excellent target,' said Piet quietly. 'It is what I do best.'

'I'll fight you for it.'

There was a ripple of laughter, breaking the tense moment. With his powerful frame and thick arms, Piet could have snapped Sam in two with his bare hands. Then David spoke up. 'He's right, Sam. We'll need you up above, waiting to attack.'

Sam frowned. Piet would stand no chance, and she felt like she was sentencing him to death. On the other hand, she knew deep down that David was right. She *was* a better combat pilot than Piet, at least for now, and it would only harm their chances if she gave her life as a decoy.

Piet saw her expression, and when he realised she wasn't going to object further he nodded his thanks. 'I will carry out my duty with honour,' he rumbled.

'I'm certain you will,' said Farren, with an encouraging smile. 'Now, those above will be running in stealth mode, and when the Mayestrans show up you must fall on them with fury and passion. You must give no quarter. None!'

'Would you just *listen* to yourselves for a minute?' Mellish strode into the centre of the group. 'You've all gone crazy! Suicide missions and pointless sacrifices? What's next, heroic speeches?'

'Who the hell are you?' demanded Farren.

'I'm a political officer, appointed to this planet by–'

'Oh, a *civilian*.' The squadron leader drew himself up. 'Listen, son. When I need advice from a pencil-pusher, I'll call my local member of parliament. In the meantime, keep your opinions to yourself.'

'You don't even know what you're fighting!' shouted Mellish, more worked up than Sam had ever seen him. 'Just because you've seen three enemy fighters flying around... it means nothing! There could be a carrier group up there with

113

dozens of fighters. They could be holding back until they've gauged your strength, and once they realise there's just a handful of you left they'll come down and erase every living being off this planet.'

'You're not a fighting man, are you?' asked Farren mildly.

Mellish reddened. 'I don't go around shooting at the enemy, but I've saved more of our people than you can possibly imagine.'

'How? By destroying their morale before a major battle? By convincing them not to fight?' Farren frowned at him, all traces of the kindly older man suddenly gone. 'You will stop talking now, or I'll have you arrested for sowing dissent. Is that clear?'

Sam almost laughed. The previous day Mellish had tried to trick her into making unwise comments about the war, as part of his job to weed out dissenters. Now, here he was facing the same threat.

Defeated, Mellish could only nod, and after a few more stirring words from Farren the pilots dispersed, heading for their fighters. The remaining personnel, with the help of the civilians, began drawing back the camouflage netting.

Sam climbed into her fighter and donned the helmet, fastening the connectors and data cables. Then, at a signal from Farren, all the pilots fired up their engines. Flames jetted from thrusters as the powerful ships roared into life, and the very air trembled as one fighter after another lifted off, with all but two arrowing straight up into the sky. Those two, piloted by Piet and Squadron Leader Farren, levelled off and began to fly a broad circuit around the base.

Tearing into the sky, Sam grinned as she felt the Kestrel's near-unlimited power. The ship was agile and fast, and as she pictured the nose-mounted blasters waiting to unleash death on the Mayestran invaders, she felt a fierce surge of pride. The enemy had struck a savage blow, but payback was going to be swift and brutal.

Then she looked down, and drew in a sharp breath. The main base was spread out below, and the scenes of destruction were incredible. Entire buildings had been flattened, destroyed fighters lay in ruins where they'd been blown apart, and worst of all she could just make out the huddled forms of casualties, dozens of them still lying where they'd fallen.

Her lips pressed together in a firm line, Sam gripped the flight stick and vowed to make the Mayestrans pay.

20

At such a high altitude the sky outside Sam's cockpit was a deep blue, with just a thin band of lighter colour on the horizon separating it from the planet's surface. It was an awe-inspiring sight, and if the situation hadn't been so fraught she would have spent more time admiring the view.

They had a job to do, though, and Sam glanced left and right to see the other Kestrels close by, plumes jetting from their thrusters as they maintained position.

David had led the flight straight up, and they were now in position high above the decoys piloted by Piet and Farren. They couldn't see them, not from their height, and David was relying on the two pilots to sound the alarm. As soon as the Mayestran Phase IIIs were spotted they were to transmit a signal, and at that point David would lead the flight in a vertical dive, the half-dozen waiting fighters spreading out to cut off the enemy's retreat. The hunters would become the hunted, and Sam felt a grim satisfaction as she imagined shattered and twisted wreckage from the Majestran fighters strewn across the landscape.

David banked his fighter to the right, sunlight gleaming off his canopy as he brought the ship round in a gentle turn. The squadron followed, maintaining their position above the base, and as Sam completed the turn and centered the controls she itched for the signal to go. There wasn't even any chatter to keep her occupied, because Farren had ordered complete radio silence until the Mayestrans were sighted. Or, in the event the enemy didn't show up, to abort the operation and order the squadron back to base.

'Base, this is scoutship one. No sign of the enemy. I repeat, no sign of the enemy.'

Sam jumped as Farren's voice crackled in her headset, and then she felt a surge of excitement. The innocent-sounding signal had been pre-arranged, in case the enemy had managed to crack the Henerian encryption. In truth, it meant the Mayestrans had been sighted. They'd taken the bait!

Still the squadron maintained silence, since they didn't want to give the Mayestrans any inkling of the doom that was about to befall them. Instead, Sam saw David's fighter waggling its wings, before he put its nose down and streaked for the ground. In a matter of seconds the entire squadron was following him down, the thin whistle of disturbed atmosphere becoming a roar as the fighters blasted their way through denser and denser air.

They were still high, far too high, and Sam couldn't make out anything bar the blotchy greens and browns of the planet's surface. She checked her HUD, but with no TacOps to guide her, and no anti-jamming tech at her disposal, she couldn't even see the friendlies, let alone the enemy.

Their dive steepened until Sam could imagine the Kestrel's stubby winglets ripping themselves right off the sleek fuselage. That's when she had a disconcerting thought. She'd flown space battles before, but she'd never met the enemy inside a planet's atmosphere. The fighter would react like a plane, not a spaceship, and she'd have to allow for drag, and manoeuvring, and gravity, and a hundred other variables. Her usual tactics wouldn't work. The tricks she'd pulled in the past to surprise the enemy would be useless. In fact, as she raced closer and closer to the enemy, it dawned on her that she was going to be totally outclassed.

Then Sam spotted movement below, a series of white specks moving against the darker surface, and she put the doubts out of her mind. She could see the base clearly, could see the two specks representing Piet and the squadron leader which were already heading towards the enemy. And she could see the enemy, too: a v-shaped formation which was rapidly growing from tiny dots into white smudges, and then individual ships as the Kestrels plummeted towards them. Then she stared in shock. They'd expected *three* enemy fighters, but there were half a dozen in the formation!

Instead of a one-sided battle it was going to be very, very close. Mellish had been right. The Mayestrans had been holding back, and now they had an ace up their sleeve.

'Red flight, engage the enemy,' said David, his voice calm in her headset. *'Pick your targets and make sure of them. We don't let any get away.'*

He said nothing about the extra ships, but that Sam could understand. There was nothing they could do about it now, not unless they turned tail and ran, abandoning Piet and the squadron leader to their fate.

They were still several hundred metres from the unsuspecting Mayestrans, travelling fast, when she saw gunfire flickering from the lead fighters. The enemy flight had divided, three ships going after each of the decoys, and Sam saw Piet and Farren weaving and twisting as they tried to avoid the murderous fire. Then she saw one of the ships coming around in a tight turn, heading straight for the enemy.

Guns blazed, the energy bolts searing bright as they sought out one of the Phase IIIs. It was hopeless, though, and the end came quickly. The enemy ship avoided the incoming fire easily, and then all three blasted away the lone fighter. Sam saw fragments ripped from the Kestrel, sparkling in the sunshine as they tumbled towards the ground. Then a streamer of flame, and at the head the fighter itself, no longer a graceful machine but instead a ball of scrap which was already falling away in a long, slow arc.

There was no time to watch its final flight, because Red flight was finally onto the Mayestrans. There were targets galore, and Sam fastened onto the nearest Phase III and willed it into her sights. She fired a burst, saw it miss by the tiniest of margins, and then she was past and hurtling straight towards the ground. Hauling back on the stick, she felt the pull of gravity despite the ship's dampers, and as the horizon vanished and she raced skywards, she noted blaster fire zinging past. One of the enemy had already fastened onto her tail, and she threw the fighter into a tight turn and pulled back on the stick, intending to flip it end-over-end as she had in so many battles before.

Instead of reacting as she expected, the fighter rolled onto its back and stalled, dropping from the sky like a tumbling leaf. Sam saw ground and sky wheeling past, and she forced the stick into the spin and applied full power, desperately trying to regain control before she scattered the Kestrel – and herself – all over the landscape.

The horizon righted itself, and Sam glanced around for the enemy. Not only had the Phase III disappeared, she couldn't even see the rest of her flight. In fact, she couldn't see any ships at all. Then she saw a spark out the corner of her eye, and she turned to see another streamer of flame plunging towards the ground. Friend or foe, she had no idea, but at least now she had a heading. Turning the ship she rocketed towards the battle, and as she arrived she was met with a scene of complete chaos.

The orderly formations were gone, and the sky was filled with whirling, squabbling fighters. Kestrels and Phase IIIs battled ferociously, and she saw bright streams of gunfire everywhere she looked. Then a Kestrel flashed past her nose, two Phase IIIs in hot pursuit, and Sam rolled her fighter and set off after them. The two ships were firing continuously, and she saw shots striking the Kestrel even as she gave chase. One winglet came off in a shower of sparks, and the ship moved left just as a lethal burst threatened to tear the fuselage in two.

The Phase IIIs never saw her coming. Sam lined one up in her sights and fired a long burst, and even as the tail disintegrated, shedding fragments, Sam adjusted her aim to the second ship and fired again. This time she missed, and the ship turned with frightening speed, coming at her before she could react. She hit the upper thrusters, sending her fighter plunging downwards, and the enemy's fire streaked past, narrowly missing her canopy. Then it was gone, and when she looked back she spotted it giving chase to another Kestrel.

There were fewer ships around now, and Sam noticed several burning wrecks dotting the landscape, their smoke rising like blackened, twisting funeral pyres. Then she was set upon by a pair of Phase IIIs, and she fought like crazy to get them off her tail. No matter what she tried, the Mayestrans anticipated her and followed, their deadly blasts of gunfire getting closer and closer. Then, suddenly, they were gone. Free of their pursuit, Sam turned to see the two enemy ships being pursued by three Kestrels, and even as she watched both enemies were hit. One tumbled out of the sky, shedding bodywork and vitals and thousands of fragments, while the other just blew up. One second it was there, twisting and dodging, and the next a burst of fire struck it directly between the twin exhausts. There was a vivid flash, brighter than the midday sun, and when Sam's eyes recovered she saw bits and pieces of the Phase III hitting the ground, raising a succession of dust-clouds.

She looked around, seeking more enemies, but apart from four other Kestrels there were no ships in sight. 'Red leader, did we get them all?'

There was no reply.

'Red leader, do you copy?'

'Sam,' said a low voice. *'I saw David going down. I'm sorry.'*

Shocked, Sam recalled the plume of flame she'd seen plunging from the sky, and the smoking wreckage dotted across the ground. David couldn't have been shot down. He was the veteran of two tours! He couldn't have lost his life on a miserable backwater planet like this, fighting an enemy that shouldn't have even been there! 'Are you sure about that?'

'It was his ship, Sam.'

She recognised Anna's voice, but the normally chipper pilot sounded flat. 'Did you see it hit?'

'Negative.'

'What about the Squadron Leader? And Piet?'

There was no reply, and she felt sick to her stomach. They couldn't all be gone!

'Red Flight, cease the chatter,' said a new voice, which Sam recognised as flight sergeant Aren Grant, her lecturer. With David and the squadron leader gone, she now had seniority. *'Half of you will stay up while the rest land and refuel. Then we'll switch.'* She got the names of the surviving pilots, and by the

time she'd finished Sam realised the two pilots from the base –
Latner and his colleague – were also missing.

The squadron split, and Sam remained aloft with two others
while the rest landed to refuel. As she followed the other
Kestrels in a wide, circular pattern, Sam tried to focus on
spotting fresh enemy ships. Every time she scanned the
horizon, though, she saw David's face, or Piet's, or the
squadron leader's. Unwillingly, she looked down at the
columns of smoke rising from the wreckage of half a dozen
ships. They might have won the battle, but they'd lost too
many colleagues.

Then came a call which turned the blood in her veins to ice.

'Red flight, bogies inbound,' shouted Anna. *'I see at least a dozen
Phase IIIs, vector 125 by 45 and closing fast.'*

21

Sam angled her fighter towards the enemy, another Kestrel on either side, and she picked out the cluster of enemy ships immediately. There were four flights of three fighters coming right at her, and the Phase IIIs looked serene and invincible as they dived on the vastly outnumbered Henerians.

'Red Leader, this is Sam. Any chance you can assist?'

'*We're doing what we can,*' said Aren Grant, sounding rushed. '*We'll be up there in five, no more.*'

Sam knew it would be too late, but there was no point running from the fight. The Mayestrans would destroy every ship on the ground as they flew over the base, and then they'd hunt down the Kestrels and shoot every last one of them out of the sky. 'Okay, Red flight,' said Sam, keeping her voice level. 'Let's deal with these guys.'

'*Right with you, Sam,*' called Anna. '*Trust me, they don't stand a chance.*'

Despite the certain death which was rushing towards her, Sam managed a smile. 'It's only four each. How hard can it be?'

They closed rapidly, and then something odd happened. She saw the enemy ships spreading out, and at first she thought they were widening the net, ensuring they'd get all three

Henerian fighters. But then the Mayestrans kept spreading out, further and further, and Sam realised they weren't switching to some carefully-rehearsed formation. They were scattering!

'*Red flight, this is Phantom squadron. Do you copy, over?*'

Hearing the new voice, Sam looked up to scan the sky overhead.

'*Copy you, Phantom,*' said Grant. '*Who are you, exactly?*'

'*I'll explain later. Now sit tight while we pluck those Phase IIIs for you.*'

Beyond the Phase IIIs, much higher up, Sam saw a sight that almost brought tears to her eyes. There was a large cluster of tiny dots, black against the sky, and they quickly resolved into a force of two dozen Henerian Kestrels. The Phase IIIs were still climbing away from the planet, and the enemy ships poured on the thrust to flee the large group of Henerian fighters.

Sam willed the friendlies on, hoping they could catch the enemy and blast the whole lot out of the sky. She imagined the Mayestran fighters cut down before her eyes, with enemy ships tumbling out of the sky like so many spent fireworks. Maybe one last Phase III would remain, twisting this way and that as the terrified pilot fled for their life. Then the Kestrels would tear the enemy ship apart, the wreckage falling, falling, falling until it exploded on the unyielding ground far below.

Unfortunately, it wasn't to be. Disappointed, Sam saw the Mayestran squadron getting further and further away, until the Kestrels gave up the pursuit and turned back towards her. Puzzled, she activated her radio. 'Aren, I thought our Kestrels were faster than the Phase IIIs?'

'*That's what they told me.*'

Sam eyed the enemy fighters, now tiny specks in the distance. Maybe the Mayestrans had upgraded their ships, or perhaps they had some kind of emergency boost. Either way, the infamous Phase IIIs seemed like they were going to be more of a challenge than she'd been told.

But then she put the enemy out of her mind, because she was suddenly surrounded by two dozen friendlies, the newcomers' ships stretching out on either side of her in an overwhelming show of force. She breathed out, and for the first time that day she realised they were actually going to make it. 'Okay, Phantom Leader,' she said, so relieved at the sight she completely ignored radio protocol. 'Where the hell did you guys come from?'

'Not over comms. Fall in, and we'll escort you up.'

'Negative. We still have personnel on the ground,' said Grant.

'We'll take care of that.' Phantom Leader issued several commands, and half the force broke off and swept down towards the surface. The rest turned for the skies, and Aren led Sam and Anna after them, higher and higher. Blue turned to deep violet and then the blackness of space. Sam felt her weight shifting as the fighter's dampers took over, and then she saw an angular grey shape in the distance. As she got closer, she began to recognise certain details, and she realised it was an elderly battleship. She knew the type, having served on such a vessel when she first entered the Navy. She smiled as she remembered the Golden Lyre, and the months she'd spend on board learning about tactical operations under the strict, no-nonsense tutelage of one Monitor Pretin.

They got closer and closer, and then Sam stared in disbelief. There was a repaired section near the massive ship's engine cluster, and she recognised the irregular patch immediately. The ship wasn't just the same class as the *Golden Lyre*. It *was* the *Golden Lyre!* Pretin, Commander Hayden, Thea Broad and the others... it was like she was coming home!

'Phantom Leader, bring your guests to docking bay three. I repeat, use docking bay three.'

'Confirmed, traffic control. Bay three, over.'

As Sam flew towards the specified docking port, she noticed the *Golden Lyre* had fresh scars alongside the older, patched ones. A section of hull near the bridge had been ripped clean away, the surrounding edges blackened and raw, and one of the big gun batteries was completely missing. She was surprised at the signs of battle damage, because the *Lyre* was a training vessel, and was usually kept in reserve far from the front lines. But it seemed the old ship had been called up, and had fought a pitched battle at some stage.

By the time Sam set her fighter down, the *Golden Lyre's* hangar was more crowded than she'd ever seen it. When she'd been stationed aboard the old ship there had been three or four ageing fighters at most, unarmed and all but unused. Now there were two full squadrons of Kestrels, but she noticed there were very few ground staff tending to them. Were they in the other hangars, preparing more fighters for battle, or was the *Golden Lyre* very short of crew?

Sam removed her helmet, popped the canopy and climbed down to the deck. The familiar smell hit her first, taking her back several weeks to the moment she'd been told her brother Lim had been killed. Then she felt the throb of the battleship's engines, and the distant sounds that carried right through the bulkheads, and she paused to take it all in.

'Name and rank?'

Sam glanced round and saw an officious-looking petty officer with a thinscreen. 'Sam Willet, sir. Trainee pilot.'

'Where were you based?'

'At the training facility, on the planet below.'

'Wait there for processing, trainee.' The man indicated an area to one side, with a bench seat and rows of lockers. Aren Grant was already seated, and Sam saw Anna heading there as well. It wasn't quite the welcome she'd expected, but the *Lyre's* crew hadn't expected the influx of survivors, and were probably working out where to put them. She fell in beside Anna, and the two of them joined Grant on the bench. As she sat down, Sam heard the thunder of the battleship's main drives. She stared towards the hangar entrance, where a gleaming force field kept the atmosphere in, but there was no sign of the survivors from the planetary surface. 'Where are we going?' she asked. 'They others haven't docked! We can't leave yet!'

'It seems the rest of our group will have to catch up,' said Grant.

'What do you mean, sir?'

Grant looked at her, clearly unsure how much she ought to share. 'I just spoke with my opposite number. The top brass discovered a Mayestran raider was heading for these parts, and the *Golden Lyre* was sent to intercept. Now the commander has their scent, he's not going to wait around.'

Sam knew it made sense. Once the Kestrels picked up the survivors from the planet below, they'd soon catch up with the *Lyre*.

'They tell me the commander is ambitious,' continued Grant. 'He's keen to make a name for himself, and he's determined to catch and destroy this Mayestran raider.'

Sam frowned. She knew Commander Hayden, and he was

a veteran officer, patient and measured in his approach to war. Ambitious was the last word she'd use to describe him. 'We *are* talking about Commander Hayden, sir?'

Grant shook her head. 'Commander Tyler is the new guy, and from what I hear he's a tough nut. Step out of line and he'll throw the book at you.'

Great, thought Sam. Just when she thought she'd be getting a warm welcome, too. She pictured the survivors from the planet below, heading towards the ship and safety, only to watch it power away from them. What kind of commander did that to his people? She glanced around the bay, at the handful of men and women working on the ships, and she realised Grant wasn't exaggerating about Tyler's style of command. The people she could see were working efficiently, sure, but they looked sullen and they kept their voices down as though unwilling to draw attention to themselves. She also saw two petty officers stationed in the hangar, watching the handful of workers closely. Each was armed with a thinscreen, and even as she studied them she saw one of the officers taking notes.

'All hands, this is your captain speaking. Pay attention.'

The voice from the tannoy was dry, emotionless. In the hangar, the ground crew immediately stopped what they were doing and stood to attention. Someone dropped a tool on the deck, the loud clang echoing around the big open area, and one of the petty officers immediately made a note on his screen.

'We're tracking a valuable target, and will engage within minutes. I expect you to perform your duty with skill and precision, and I want it known that I will personally deal with anyone who lets me down. Commander Tyler out.'

'Wow,' muttered Sam. 'You weren't wrong.' Then she saw one of the petty officers coming towards them, and she hoped like hell he hadn't heard her.

Fortunately, the man wasn't interested in Sam. 'Flight sergeant Aren Grant? Would you come with me please?'

Grant followed the petty officer to a bank of lifts, leaving Sam and Anna by themselves. 'I don't know about you,' muttered Sam, 'but I could use something to eat.'

Anna glanced around. 'You know somewhere?'

'Yeah. There's a mess on the next deck.' Sam hesitated. 'The petty officer said to wait here, though.'

'So? We'll grab something and come back.'

Even so, Sam and Anna waited until they weren't being observed before getting up and heading for the nearest stairwell. Technically, they were disobeying orders, and from what they've heard about the new commander, that wasn't exactly a smart move. On the other hand, they'd survived several enemy attacks plus dogfights at close quarters, and Sam reckoned nobody could begrudge her a sandwich and a mug of hot coffee.

They made the mess in no time, and found it deserted. It was a large area with canteen-style tables, and the far wall was studded with narrow portholes that looked straight out into space. Sam used the machines to get food for herself and Anna, then grabbed two mugs of coffee and made for a table near the portholes. They sat, and Sam was about to tuck in when Anna raised her mug. 'To Piet, David, and the rest of our fallen colleagues. They fought bravely.'

Sam nodded, moved by the gesture, and then they wolfed down the food, the first they'd laid hands on since the previous evening. Once they'd drained their mugs of coffee, they took their cups and plates and loaded up with seconds.

'That's better,' said Anna, once she'd cleared her plate. 'I couldn't believe how hungry I was.'

'I won't need to eat for a week,' groaned Sam. 'Why didn't you stop me?'

'After the fourth sandwich you mean? Or was it the fifth?'

Sam took a sip of her coffee, luxuriating in the strong, sweet taste. She still couldn't believe they'd escaped the attack on the planet below, and even though Commander Tyler sounded like a strict disciplinarian, it wasn't like she would be aboard the *Lyre* for long.

She noticed Anna looked tired, and she watched as the other pilot raised her coffee to her lips and took a decent swig. Anna was looking out of the porthole, lost in thought, and Sam wondered whether she was remembering the colleagues they'd lost. Then Anna's expression changed, and she leaned forward to stare through the porthole, eyes wide with shock. 'What the hell?' she breathed.

Sam leaned back to look through the next porthole, but could only see empty space in every direction. 'Yeah, it's dark out. Why the surprise?'

'I just saw a Phase III go by.'

Sam laughed and gestured at Anna's mug. 'You've had too much of that coffee. Funny, because it tasted as weak as–'

'I'm serious,' said Anna, keeping her voice low. 'I'd know those tail fins anywhere.'

'Maybe it was a captured Phase I. You know, from the base. They wouldn't leave them behind, would they?'

Anna looked unconvinced. 'It's possible, but I've seen plenty of Phase IIIs lately. I'm not going to forget them in a hurry.'

Sam drained her coffee. 'Come on.'

'Where are we going?'

'Docking bay two is just down the corridor. We'll look in so you can see the Phase Is for yourself.'

'Are you sure? We've been gone a while, and they're going to be looking for us soon.'

'So what? I'll tell 'em this was my old ship, and I was showing you around.'

22

They ditched their mugs and plates, and then Sam led the way down the corridor to a large airlock. The indicator was green, and after cycling the matched doors they emerged into a large hangar. It was a twin to the one they'd landed in earlier, but there was one important difference.

As Sam and Anna stood there, the sight that met their eyes was enough to shock them beyond words. A dozen Mayestran Phase IIIs were sitting on the landing pads, the air shimmering above their super-heated exhausts. Pilots were climbing out of the cockpits, and Sam gaped as she saw the deep red uniforms of the Mayestran Imperial Navy. Ground crew hurried forward to service the ships, attaching fuel lines and data cables, and could only stare at the ordinary, everyday scene. Ordinary, that was, except for the enemy ships and the enemy pilots.

Beyond the Mayestran fighters she saw half a dozen troop carriers, the hulking ships dwarfing the smaller fighters.

Then, as she eyed the enemy ships, she realised the danger. She and Anna were going to be spotted any second, challenged, and having seen the Mayestran ships in the hangar their lives wouldn't be worth a Henerian credit chit. Thinking quickly, Sam snatched up a thinscreen from a nearby workbench and gripped it in one shaking hand, holding the display out to Anna and pointing to something at random. Anna played along, nodding and touching the display, and they were still acting like a pair of techs on a routine inspection as they backed into the airlock and closed the door.

'Are you shitting me?' breathed Anna. 'Did Commander Tyler switch sides or something?'

'Talk later,' said Sam urgently. 'Right now we've got to hide until we can figure out what's going on.' She opened the inner door, and they hurried away from the hangar, the thinscreen still gripped in her hand. Sam's heart was pounding, and she expected a shout or a challenge at any second. If the Mayestrans were using the *Golden Lyre* as a base, then anyone they met could be an enemy. Anyone... or *everyone?* Was Commander Tyler a Mayestran? Were the petty officers and the ground crew? What about Phantom squadron, who'd saved her, Anna and Grant from the Phase IIIs? Then she remembered Aren being led away from the hangar, and she wondered whether they were interrogating the lecturer at that moment... with Anna and Sam next in line.

They passed a couple of techs in the corridor, who were kneeling next to an open panel, the cavity beyond packed with cables and ducting. There was a drum of cable and a red box on the ground, the latter the size of a small suitcase, and the techs were checking the wiring inside the cavity with a probe. Sam kept her gaze on the thinscreen as she and Anna hurried past, but the techs were engrossed and didn't look up.

As they continued down the corridor Sam recalled how puzzled she'd been when the Phase IIIs had turned and fled, easily outpacing the Kestrels. Well, of *course* they'd been quick enough to get away, if both sets of fighters had been piloted by Mayestrans. As for the Kestrels, if the *Lyre* had surrendered, then her squadron of Henerian fighters would have ended up in enemy hands. Phantom squadron, the pilots who'd saved her life, had been nothing but Mayestrans masquerading as friendlies.

Sam remembered the damage she'd spotted as she docked with the battleship. The big rip in the hull, and the missing gun battery! What if the Lyre had fought a battle, and lost? What if Commander Hayden, Pretin and the others had surrendered, and the entire crew had been imprisoned... or executed? It was the only explanation she could think of, and it meant the entire ship had to be in the hands of the enemy.

Then Sam remembered the others they'd left behind, and her blood ran cold. Mellish and the other civilians, the pilots who'd gone back to refuel, the adjutant and more. She thought they were being picked up and brought to safety, but the Mayestrans might have executed the lot without a second thought.

Her mind racing, Sam led Anna down a smaller corridor, leading the way automatically.

Now she turned to the biggest *why* of all. Why had the Mayestrans 'rescued' her, Anna and Grant? They could have shot them down in seconds and been on their way, and nobody would have been any the wiser. Instead, they'd staged that mock encounter between the two forces, wasting who knew how much fuel in the process.

Did they think their prisoners would have valuable information? If so, Sam was going to be a massive disappointment, because she knew nothing of interest. Anna was a trainee as well, and as for Grant... she was a front-line pilot who was being rested from combat. None of them had any value whatsoever, outside the cockpit of a fighter.

Suddenly it all seemed too fanciful... too far-fetched. She

skidded to a halt, and Anna stopped to look at her. 'What?'

'Is it possible the Mayestrans have captured the *Golden Lyre*?'

'Sure looks like it.'

'So why did they save us?'

Anna shrugged. 'If the Mayestrans were logical people they wouldn't be fighting a war against us, would they?'

'But–'

'Maybe they've heard of your brother, and they want you for leverage.'

'He's a fighter pilot, not the Henerian Premier.'

'It would be a big propaganda win for them.'

'I'm sorry, but it doesn't fit. In the past twenty-four hours I could have been killed a dozen times. It's pure chance that I'm standing here now instead of Piet, or David, or any of the others.'

Anna nodded. 'You're right. There has to be another explanation.'

'If I knew why they'd captured the Lyre it would help.'

'Maybe we should ask the Commander.'

Sam laughed, and then she realised Anna was serious. 'You mean...force it out of him?'

'Sure. You know this ship, and we easily can blend with the rest of the crew. We find weapons, you get us into his cabin and then *we* run an interrogation.'

'He'd call for help.'

'So?' Anna regarded her steadily. 'He is a high-ranking Mayestran. I would give my own life to kill him, and the exchange would be in our favour. We could kill many others as they came to his aid.'

'Yeah, well let's not be too hasty. I'd rather defeat the Mayestrans and live to tell people about it afterwards, if that's all right with you.' They turned another corner, and Sam led Anna into a locker room.

'Are there weapons here?' Anna asked her.

'No, but it's time we got out of these flight suits. They might look like overalls in the hangars, but we'll stand out like sore thumbs on the upper decks.' Sam opened several lockers until she found what she was looking for: uniform shirts and trousers in dark Henerian green.

'The upper levels could be full of Mayestrans in red uniforms,' Anna pointed out.

'Those petty officers were wearing green in the hangar.' Sam hesitated. 'If they've taken the Lyre for some kind of sneak attack, they'll all be dressed as Henerians. Otherwise the first time someone saw the bridge crew on a comms channel the game would be up.'

'I hope you're right, or this is going to be the shortest assault in history,' murmured Anna.

They got dressed quickly, stuffing their flight suits into a pair of empty lockers before placing spare clothes on top and closing the doors. They were both wearing the insignia of petty officers, which they hoped would be enough to stop anyone questioning them. The petty officers in the hangar had certainly commanded obedience, and Sam guessed that would apply throughout the ship.

They searched the other lockers, but unfortunately there were no weapons. 'There's an armoury three decks up,' she told Anna. 'It's risky, though. I mean, why would we need guns?'

'To shoot the commander,' said Anna promptly.

'No, I meant what excuse could we give,' said Sam patiently.

'Maybe we overpower the guards and take as many weapons as we like.'

Sam felt Anna might be getting a little too enthusiastic. Then she glanced at the other pilot, and she realised she was being teased. 'All right, forget the guns. You can slice Tyler in two with your wit.'

They left the locker room, feeling stiff and unnatural in the uniforms. Further down the hall they passed a couple of techs, who kept their gaze firmly on the deck as they hurried by. For the first time, Sam felt like their plan might actually work. . . such as it was.

They passed the mess, where they saw a dozen pilots in flight suits grabbing a quick meal. One of them, a man with cropped black hair and an open, honest face, caught Sam's eye, and she averted her gaze and kept moving. If these *were* Mayestrans, she thought, they certainly didn't look like cold-blooded killers.

The passage curved, following the lines of the hull, and as they rounded the bend they encountered a large group coming towards them. There were a dozen troops in combat armour, marching fast, and they were accompanying more than a dozen weary-looking men and women. Sam stood aside to let the group go by, and as they hurried past she happened to glance at a few faces. There, amongst the armed troops, she saw the familiar stocky figure of Piet Renford, his flight suit torn and his head bowed. He'd survived! She glanced at the others, moving from face to face, scarcely daring to hope. There was Mellish, looking cool and composed, and the two sentries from the training base, now without their blast rifles for once. Latner, the flight sergeant, had survived his wreck too, and the elderly adjutant stumbled along beside him, looking exhausted. All the civilians she'd helped to rescue were there, as well as the ground staff from the base below. Then, with a wrench inside her chest, she spotted

David Richett limping behind the others, his face twisted in pain. As the group headed down the passageway Sam saw that one sleeve of his uniform was soaked with blood. He'd made it, but at what cost?

Sam glanced at Anna, and she knew the other woman had seen their comrades too. Her face was set, angry, Sam prayed the impulsive pilot didn't try to intercept the troops, or shout out to their captives. If she did, the narrow corridor would likely turn into a slaughterhouse.

Then the group turned the next corner and vanished from sight.

'Right. Change of plan,' said Sam. 'The commander can wait. We're going to free our people.'

23

'I'm always happy to hit the enemy, but have you thought this through?'

Sam was glad Anna was up for the rescue, but she understood her concerns. They were following the armed troops and their captives, hanging back enough to avoid attention, but still remaining close enough to see where the larger group went. Now and then they passed people coming the other way, and each time Sam would busy herself with the thinscreen, pretending to examine some riveting piece of information. It worked, because nobody spared them a second glance.

She knew it couldn't last though. Someone in the hangar would raise the alarm, and then everyone on board the huge ship would be looking for them. The only solution was to overcome a dozen heavily-armed troops and share the weapons out amongst their Henerian prisoners. Unfortunately, the first part of that solution was going to be damn near impossible. They'd need flash grenades, or maybe a dozen armed troops of their own.

'Maybe we can get them all into an airlock, then space them,' muttered Anna.

'Yes, and maybe we can convince them the war is a waste

of time, and get them to surrender,' snapped Sam. 'We need a workable plan, not a party trick.'

Anna was unfazed by Sam's outburst. 'The airlock idea is a good one. Once inside, they couldn't shoot their way out.'

'What about their weapons? Those would vanish right along with them.'

They walked on in silence, and Sam realised they were approaching the crew quarters. There was a sentry further along the corridor, leaning against the wall with a blast rifle cradled against his chest. He saluted the newcomers, then glanced towards Sam and Anna.

They'd just passed an elevator, and there was nowhere else to go but straight ahead, past the sentry. Sam knew they were trapped, so she did the only thing possible. She stopped, showed the thinscreen to Anna, then gestured at the lift.

'Idiot,' said Anna, playing along. 'I told you deck three.'

They beat a retreat, then waited for the lift to arrive. Sam felt a prickling between her shoulder blades, and she knew the sentry was watching them. Would he come over? Challenge them? Very slowly, she began to clench and unclench her fists, mentally preparing herself for a swift physical response.

Then the lift pinged, and she and Anna hurried inside while the doors were still opening. They exited on the deck above, and then Sam led the way down the corridor to a nearby stairwell. She pulled the door open and they slipped through, taking the stairs two at a time. At the bottom she eased the door open a fraction and looked out, and when she saw an empty corridor in both directions she motioned Anna out ahead of her. They were back in the original corridor, having bypassed the sentry, but Sam knew there would be another if the Mayestrans were keeping their captives in this section of the crew quarters. They were passing doors now, leading to individual sleeping quarters, and she noticed some had red indicators on their control panels. That meant the doors were sealed, and it could also mean each room held one or more prisoners. She'd been worried the Mayestrans might have spaced the entire crew, and she was relieved to think they might be locked up instead.

She was tempted to open a few doors and check inside, but if the troops were leaving their prisoners here, then very soon they'd be marching straight back up this very corridor. If they saw prisoners in the corridor, they were likely to open fire, and that wasn't the kind of rescue Sam had in mind.

The corridor curved to the right, and as they rounded the corner they ran slap-bang into a sentry. He was less than ten metres away, standing to attention with a blast rifle at his hip, hanging from a shoulder strap.

Heart pounding, Sam didn't break stride. She kept on walking as though she had every right to be there, keeping her gaze firmly on the thinscreen.

'Hold on,' said the guard, stepping away from the wall.

'Huh?' Sam looked up, feigning surprise. 'What is it?'

'This section is restricted. What's your business?'

'I've got an update on the prisoner backgrounds,' said Sam, thinking quickly. 'The new arrivals. One of them talked.'

He studied her for a second, then looked down at the thinscreen. 'Show me.'

Sam held it out, and as the sentry reached for it Anna grabbed his arm and hauled him forwards, towards herself. Off-balance, he started to fall, and Anna lashed out with her free hand. There was a thud as her fist connected, and the man went down as though shot. Anna crouched, tugging the blast rifle free, then stood up to see Sam staring at her in shock. 'What?'

'Is he dead?'

'If he is, the Henerian Navy should demand a refund.'

'What?'

'They pay a fortune to train us in unarmed combat.' Unconcerned, Anna examined the blast rifle, then worked the safety and sighted down the barrel. 'It's just a stun weapon, but it'll do,' she remarked. 'Now we just need another.'

She started to move off, and Sam stood over the unconscious guard, hands on hips. 'We can't just leave him here.'

'Why not? He doesn't care.'

Speaking slowly, Sam gestured at her with both hands. 'Because those troops will be coming back any second, Anna, and that gun is going to be useless against so many.'

Reluctantly, Anna came back. 'In there?' she said, indicating a nearby door.

'Sure, why not.' Sam activated the panel, and the door slid open. Inside was a room with six bunks, all empty. She helped Anna to move the guard inside, and then they closed the door again.

They set off again, fortunately without running into any more sentries, and then they slowed as they approached another canteen. From her position, Sam could just see the troops inside, sitting at tables with their helmets off, their weapons leaning against nearby chairs and tables. Sam realised there was a good chance she and Anna might sneak past, and perhaps find out where David and the others were being held.

Unfortunately, Anna had other ideas.

They were about ten metres from the canteen, and it took Anna three seconds to reach the doorway at a dead run. The blast rifle came up, and she'd already shot three of the troops inside before Sam even knew what was happening. Flashes of blaster fire lit the corridor as Anna stood right there in the doorway, shifting her aim and firing repeatedly, her face completely emotionless as she shot one enemy after another.

None of the troops got anywhere near their weapons, and when the firing stopped, haze drifting gently down the corridor. Sam was relieved the gun was only a stun weapon. The way Anna had handled the thing, they'd have had a dozen enemy deaths on their hands, and the Mayestrans would have had no compunction in executing them both if they managed to get their hands on them.

Meanwhile, Anna disappeared into the canteen, emerging moments later with a second weapon. 'Have you fired one of these before?' Anna asked her.

Sam examined the gun. 'Not this exact model, no.'

'Set that dial halfway. It'll stun your target for a couple of hours instead of five or six.'

Sam cradled the weapon in both hands, and together they set off along the corridor. As they hurried further into the restricted area, Sam wondered how long it would be before the troops in the canteen were discovered. Once the alarm was raised, she and Anna were going to find it next to impossible to move around the ship.

24

Sam was standing with her back pressed to the smooth wall, Anna to her left. To the right, just out of sight around the curved corridor, their way was barred by a set of thick doors. They formed an airlock, designed to seal off the rest of the section in the case of a hull breach, and Sam knew they'd have to go through it to continue onwards.

Normally that wouldn't be a problem, but there was a sentry on this side of the doors, alert and ready. And, through the big plexiglass panel in each door, Sam could see a second sentry on the other side of the airlock. He had his back to her, but the doors were airtight, not soundproof. If she took out the nearest Mayestran, the other would be able to raise the alarm before Sam managed to cycle the airlock and get to him.

'We could chance it,' muttered Anna. 'Shoot this one, chase the other down.'

'He might have a commset.'

'Unless he speaks fast, it won't help him.'

Sam risked another look, then motioned Anna to silence. Coming towards the airlock from the far side was an officer, accompanied by a medic wearing light green scrubs. The outfit was streaked with blood, and the man was carrying a large medical bag over one shoulder. Sam recalled David's injury, and she guessed the Mayestrans might have been fixing him up. If so, they must want him alive, perhaps for interrogation or propaganda. Or both.

'The doors are going to open,' she whispered. 'When I give the word, we start firing. Two sentries, one officer, one medic.'

Anna nodded, and Sam double-checked the setting on her gun. Then she peered round the corner until she saw the new arrivals enter the airlock. The far door closed, sealing them in, and then, as the inner door started to open, she cried 'Now!' and sprang into the middle of the corridor, gun raised.

She went for the sentry first, the sudden burst of fire taking him completely by surprise. He was thrown backwards by the impact, slamming into the wall, and he was still dropping to the floor when Anna shot the officer. She shifted aim to the medic, who stood completely shocked with both hands towards her, palms outwards, and was about to fire when Sam knocked her gun up. The blasts tore into the corridor ceiling, bringing down insulation and paneling before the firing stopped.

'Leave him,' shouted Sam. 'Get the other sentry!'

They ran towards the medic, and Sam pushed him against the wall, muzzle of her rifle under his chin. 'Don't move a muscle,' she hissed.

Meanwhile, Anna slammed her palm on the airlock controls. Just the other side of the door, the guard had been staring at events with a stunned expression. Now she started to back away, raising one hand to the commset at her shoulder.

The outer door started to open, and Anna poked her gun though the gap and fired down the corridor, hitting the guard with the third or fourth shot. The woman was bowled over, and she fell with one arm outstretched, still reaching for help.

Sam addressed the medic. 'The prisoners that just came

through here, where did they take them?' She pressed the muzzle of the blast rifle into his neck, hard. 'Quick, I'm not messing around.'

'D-down the corridor.'

'And the injured one? David? Is he all right?'

'I had to stitch his wound, but he'll survive.'

'Take us to them. Quick!'

Before they left Anna searched the man and his bag, checking for weapons. Sam studied him as she did so, and she felt a stab of pity. He was in his mid-twenties, with dark hair and brown eyes, and he looked scared. At first, she wondered whether it was an act, but the sweat on his brow said otherwise. From the look of him this was his first posting, and he'd probably grown up believing the Mayestran propaganda... that his people were invincible, and mighty, and all-conquering. 'If you behave yourself, you'll walk out of this,' she told him.

He nodded, but when he glanced at Anna she could see the doubt in his eyes. 'Anna?' said Sam.

'What?'

'We'll let him go after he's helped us, right?'

'Oh. Sure.'

Anna's response wasn't the ringing endorsement Sam had been hoping for, but it would have to do. They left the airlock with the medic, skirting the fallen guard in the hallway. On the way past, Anna scooped up the woman's gun and slung it over her shoulder before continuing. 'Where are you holding the prisoners?' Sam asked the medic. He had a name badge that read 'Greg Barrow', and when he didn't answer she tried again. 'Look Greg, we just want to find our people. Do you understand?'

'If I help you, they're going to kill me.'

'Why would we do that?' asked Sam. 'I've already told you–'

'Not *your* people,' said Barrow, in a low voice. 'If I help you, my people will shoot me as a traitor.'

'Maybe they will and maybe they won't,' said Anna conversationally. 'But if you don't answer her question, I swear I will end you right now.'

'Down here on the right,' said the medic.

'Any guards?'

After a moment's hesitation, Barrow shook his head. Then he changed his mind. 'There might be one.'

Then Sam asked him a question that she dreaded the answer to. 'What about the *Golden Lyre's* crew? Are they still on board?'

'Some, but most were shuttled over to the *Scimitar* after we captured the *Lyre*.'

'What sort of ship is this *Scimitar*?'

'I'm just a medic, not–'

'What type of ship,' hissed Sam.

'Cruiser. Modern and fast.'

'Any other vessels travelling with it?'

'No. It's a raider, sent to cause trouble deep behind your lines.'

'And what about the rest of the *Lyre's* crew? How many are still on board, and where are they held?'

'There's about a dozen or so, mostly support crew and civilians. They're in docking bay one. Before he left them there, Captain Tyler…'

'Go on.'

'He threatened to space them if they resisted.'

Sam pictured the dozen or so crew members sitting in the hangar with only a force field between them and the vacuum of space. She knew how easy it would be to turn off that force field, because she'd seen the same tactic used aboard an enemy ship. In the maelstrom of escaping air the crew in the hangar wouldn't stand a chance.

Then she had a nasty thought. If this Captain Tyler wanted to stop Sam and Anna in their tracks, ending their escape bid, all he had to do was threaten to switch off that force field.

They continued down the corridor, and all of a sudden Sam heard the noise she'd been dreading. A loud siren, wailing up and down the corridor, followed by an urgent, breathless announcement.

'Red alert, red alert. Escaped prisoners on deck twenty-four, armed and dangerous. Security personnel to deck twenty-four immediately. Lethal force is authorised. I repeat, lethal force is authorised!'

25

Anna swore volubly as they stood there in the corridor, surrounded by flashing hazard lights and the wail of emergency sirens. Her words were lost in the racket, and she raised her voice to make herself heard. 'We have to find somewhere to hide!'

Sam glanced over her shoulder, back the way they'd come. They'd left a trail of unconscious Mayestrans all the way back to the elevator, and the discovery of any one of them was probably the reason for the alarm. That meant they could only go forward. 'There's no point locking ourselves into a cabin,' she shouted back. 'They'll search the whole ship, and we'll end up trapping ourselves.' She also knew there was little chance of finding David and the others, freeing them and getting them to safety. She'd had a vague plan that involved getting everyone to the hangar, where they could take ships and escape, but the alarm had put paid to that.

Sam gripped the medic's arm and ushered him forwards again, with Anna close behind. The medic had been as surprised as the two Henerians when the alarm sounded, but now he seemed even more worried than he had when they'd taken him captive. He probably thought the Mayestrans would gun all three of them down, with no regard for friend or foe.

'How far?' shouted Sam.

'Round the corner, go past the elevators, and it's the first door on the left.'

Sam wondered why the Mayestrans hadn't thrown the new arrivals into hangar number one with the rest of the Lyre's crew, but figured they probably wanted to keep them apart until they'd had a chance to interrogate them. Then she thought of a question she should have asked earlier. 'How many Mayestrans aboard this ship?'

'I don't know. They didn't tell me.'

She suspected he was flannelling because he would have boarded with the rest, but short of stopping to torture the medic right there in the hallway, Sam had no way to find out what he really knew.

'Look out!' shouted Anna suddenly. 'They're behind us!'

Blaster shots streaked past, skimming off the curved walls ahead. If the corridor had been straight they'd have been easy targets, but the bend meant the pursuing troops couldn't draw a bead on them. Sam ran even faster, almost dragging the medic along by his arm. She heard Anna firing back, her blast rifle just audible above the sirens.

Then they rounded the next corner, and Sam skidded to a halt. Just ahead, a dozen troops were pouring out of an open elevator. Sam raised her gun, intending to fight, then lowered it quickly when she saw the odds. Instead, she raised her hands, and beside her Anna did likewise.

The siren volume lessened, which was a relief, but it was still there in the background. And over the wailing noise of the alarm, Sam heard more boots thundering down the corridor behind her. She dropped to her knees, putting her hands behind her head. She had no idea whether these Mayestrans had stun guns or the real thing, and had no intention of finding out. 'We surrender,' she said loudly. 'You've got us. There's no need to shoot.'

A row of troops advanced on them, weapons raised, and she could see their fingers tightening on the triggers. Fortunately, firing was impossible with more of the enemy coming up behind the two Henerians, and instead of being shot down Sam and Anna were roughly dragged to their feet, their arms quickly secured behind their backs.

Then, without a word, they were marched towards the lifts.

◆

Sam and Anna were ushered into the lift and whisked away to the *Lyre's* situation room, several decks above, where a group of officers were gathered around the plotting table. Sam identified Captain Tyler immediately, partly because of his uniform, but mostly because it was obvious he was in charge. A big man, with short grey hair and a craggy, handsome face, he didn't need the epaulettes or the rings on his sleeve to command respect.

There were several officers around the captain, and he was using a pointer to outline their course. '–no, we'll take this route,' he was saying in a deep voice, as Sam waited near the door with Anna and about a dozen armed guards. 'Go around Hester, and between these two systems. That way we'll blend in with their regular traffic.'

'Yes sir,' murmured one of the officers, and he crossed to a console to pass on the orders.

A guard standing next to Sam cleared his throat. 'Sir, I've brought the Henerians, as you commanded.'

The captain turned, giving Sam and Anna an appraising look. He had a blaster at his hip, and Sam wondered whether he was about to draw it and shoot them where they stood. Instead, he approached her, hand outstretched. 'A pleasure to meet you both,' he said, as he shook their hands. 'I trust you've been well treated?'

'Er, yes,' muttered Sam, taken aback. She'd met a couple of Mayestran commanders in the past, and they'd almost been parodies of the evil jackbooted thug featured in Henerian news stories. In comparison, Captain Tyler could have been running a children's hospital. 'Sir, can I ask what you intend to do with the *Golden Lyre's* crew?'

'Let's see how our operation pans out first, shall we?' The Captain studied them both. 'Which of you is Sam Willet?'

Sam gestured. 'I am.'

'I read the report on the Greyforth Coriolis incident, and I have to ask... did you really destroy one of our capital ships in single-handed combat?'

'I had plenty of help.'

'And yet your people gave the credit to your infamous brother. I bet that rankled.'

'I'm here to fight the enemy, not collect medals,' said Sam evenly. 'And just for the record, we destroyed your entire fleet, not just the flagship.'

Sam saw several officers at the plotting table exchanging glances, and she allowed herself a grim smile. It seemed that particular fact wasn't widely known, and she had a few more to share if they cared to listen.

Captain Tyler seemed unfazed by the revelation. 'Yes, that little incident caused a bit of a stir back home, as you can imagine. Our top brass has been stewing over a suitable response ever since.' He gestured, encompassing the *Golden Lyre's* flight deck. 'The capture of this sad old specimen is the result.'

'They're not very ambitious, are they?' Sam eyed the taller man. 'I can tell you now, the Henerian Navy would be willing to trade one old battleship for a Mayestran fleet any day. You'd lose the war in weeks, instead of months.' For the first time, Sam saw a flicker of emotion cross the Captain's face. It was quickly suppressed, but for a split second he'd seemed ruthless and calculating.

'If you think capturing this rust bucket is the extent of our plans, you're sadly mistaken,' he said, with a trace of steel in his voice.

'Sir,' began one of the officers standing at the table. 'Perhaps it would be best not to–'

Tyler gestured, silencing them instantly. He seemed to be on the point of saying more to Sam, then turned away. 'Put these two with the others and double the guards. And at the first sign of trouble, shoot every one of her companions.'

26

Sam and Anna were shown into a large room with rows of desks and chairs. Sam suspected she might have sat in that very room at some stage, back in her *Golden Lyre* days, dreaming about being a fighter pilot as she listened to a lecture on TacOps. How her circumstances had changed!

David, Piet and a dozen others were all present, casually leaning against the tables and giving the guards dark looks. They looked like they were ready to spring, to make a bid for freedom, but the guards were well-armed and none of the Henerians was foolish enough to rush them.

Once the doors closed, David limped towards Sam and Anna, his haggard face creasing into a smile as he met Sam's eyes. 'I didn't think I'd ever see you again. Are you all right?'

'Better than you, from the looks of it.' Sam glanced around the others. 'Piet, I saw you going down in flames. How the hell did you survive that?'

'My ship still had power, and the dampers cushioned the impact.'

'Offering yourself as bait was incredibly brave.'

Piet gestured at the room. 'And yet here we are.'

'Where's Mellish?' Sam asked them.

David shrugged. 'They took him away. For some reason they thought he was a high-value prisoner.'

She heard the bitterness in his voice, and she thought she knew why. Looking around the room, she couldn't help noticing that all the remaining Henerians were trainees or civilians. In other words, not worth capturing. David had been abandoned with the rest of them, and, crazy though it seemed, she guessed he was annoyed that the enemy hadn't valued him highly enough to take him with the rest. 'Hey, without that injury I'm sure they'd be torturing you for information with the others.'

'Never mind us, did you find out what happened to the *Lyre's* crew?'

'Most of them were taken off in shuttles after Hayden surrendered. The *Lyre* were attacked by a Mayestran raider called the *Scimitar*. She's a modern cruiser sent to stir up trouble behind our lines.'

'Pretty successfully, I'd say.'

Sam gestured at Anna. 'They took the pair of us to the Mayestran Commander, Captain Tyler.' She closed her eyes and tried to recall every detail of the brief conversation. 'He said they were going to circle around Hester and fly between two other systems. I couldn't get anything else, though.'

'Any idea what they're planning for us?' asked David.

'They're Mayestrans,' said Piet. 'What do *you* think?'

'They've got the rest of the *Golden Lyre's* crew in hangar bay one,' said Anna. 'About a dozen or so. They threatened to eject them into space if they caused any trouble.'

'That's bad,' muttered David. 'With that many hostages, our hands are tied.'

The elderly adjutant overheard him. 'The enemy has control of the *Golden Lyre*. If they've managed to take her over without alerting our people, they can use this ship as a stealth weapon. They can wreak havoc on cargo ships, disrupt our supply lines, and get close to our defensive positions before blasting them to ash. Nobody would suspect a thing until it was too late, and under those circumstances, I'm afraid the hostages – and the rest of us – come a distant second. We have to take back this ship, or failing that, we must destroy her.'

Everyone was quiet as they digested the enormity of the task, and then David snorted and indicated the doors. 'Okay, lead the way. I'm sure we'll have the *Lyre* back in our hands in no time.'

'I'm not a fighting man–'

'I've noticed.'

'–but I *can* read a situation. I'm telling you, the *Golden Lyre* represents a huge danger to Henerian interests. Compared to that, the rest of us are expendable.'

'Let's not throw our lives away just yet,' said Sam. 'We might be able to break out, get to the hostages–'

'You must forget about the hostages,' said the adjutant firmly.

Sam turned to David for support, but to her surprise he nodded. 'I don't like it either, but he's right. We'll save the *Lyre's* crew if we can, but they're not a priority.' David glanced around, then lowered his voice. 'The Mayestrans might be listening, so let's keep it down. Anyone got any ideas?'

Anna spoke up. 'If we can make it to the hangar and launch a couple of fighters, we could circle back and blast the battleship's engines before they realised what was happening.'

'They'll blast *us* with the defensive turrets. We'll never get close.'

'They don't have enough people to man all the defences,' said Sam. 'Think about it. After the *Golden Lyre* surrendered, the Mayestrans put a prize crew on board. They'll have a navigator, and a systems tech, and troops, but the only way they could crew every position on the *Lyre* would be to send across most of the crew from this *Scimitar*. That would leave their own ship helpless, and they wouldn't risk a modern cruiser for the sake of the *Golden Lyre*, no matter what their ultimate plan is.'

'I think I know what they're doing,' said the Adjutant suddenly. 'When you mentioned Hester it rang a bell, but I couldn't remember why. Now it's come to me.'

'And?' demanded David.

'Our Second Fleet is based out of a dockyard in the Cromwell sector, and that's only two jumps from Hester. What if they're planning to hit the Second? If they could get the *Lyre* in close and detonate her, it would probably take out several of our biggest ships. The damage would be immense if they caught the Fleet napping, and the effect on morale would be even worse.'

Sam felt a sudden twisting sensation, and the overhead lights seemed to recede before coming back into focus.

'That was a jump,' said David. 'We've just left the Handley system.'

'How far to Hester?' Sam asked the Adjutant.

He shook his head. 'I only recall that piece of intel, not every detail on the star chart.'

While they were talking, Piet had been examining the entrance doors. Sam had watched him trying to get his fingers between the two doors, in a failed attempt to force them, and now he was testing the strength of the doors with his shoulder. There was a solid thump as he drove his body against them, and Sam winced at the sound. Piet was a strong bloke, but he was likely to injure himself if he kept hitting the doors like that. 'Piet, you'll bring the guards in.'

'Good,' he said. 'Then I won't have to break these doors down.'

He wasn't the only one trying to get out. Nearby, a couple of Henerian techs had the cover off the lecturer's terminal at the front of the classroom, and they were yanking out circuits and cables while a third looked on, giving advice. Further away, the mechanics were taking apart a couple of desks, setting aside the metal legs. Someone else was collecting the legs and distributing them, arming those with the most experience at hand-to-hand combat.

In the middle of all the activity Sam felt the familiar twisting sensation as the *Golden Lyre* performed another jump. 'Dammit,' she muttered. 'We've got to get a move on. It might only take another couple of jumps to reach that naval base!'

27

The mechanics finished taking the desks apart, and David held up one of the metal legs, inspecting the end. Then he eyed the entrance doors. 'If we can flatten a couple of these, they'd make decent levers.' He put the leg down and tried stepping on the end, but it was too strong and his weight had no effect.

'Give it here,' said Piet, who'd abandoned his attempts to force the door.

'I don't think jumping on it will do anything,' said David.

Piet ignored him, and he laid one leg on the ground before balancing another at right angles across the very tip. He stepped on the second leg, holding it in place, then indicated the others. 'Join me please. Our combined weight will be enough I think.'

Sure enough, when they added their weight to his the tip of the first tube was crushed under the second. Piet shifted the second leg and got them to stand on it again, and then he switched the tubes and got them to crush the end of the second one as well.

Now they had two metal table legs with flattened ends, and by levering them back and forth they managed to get the tips into the gap between the doors. Anna and Sam took one table leg, while Piet took the second. On three, each pair pulled with all their might, and as the gap between the doors opened up David shoved the end of a third leg into the gap.

Sam put her eye to the gap. She couldn't see anyone just outside, but there was a pair of doors about twenty metres away, and through the clear panels she could make out two guards beyond. It was a smart move, because the doors formed a natural barrier and the guards would call for reinforcements if they spotted an escape attempt.

'They'll see us the second we get through these doors,' she told the others.

'Not if we douse the lights.' David strode over to the techs, who were still poking around in the guts of the terminal. 'Can you do anything with the power?'

'Not from here, sir. This thing's only used to update weapons training hours. Everything else is locked down.'

'Can't you cross a few wires or something?'

'No. Everything aboard these ships is driven by data cables and power relays. It cuts the amount of wiring down, but–'

'Yes, yes. Spare me the details. Just find a way to cut the lights.'

'Have you tried the switch?' said the woman sarcastically.

David gave her an angry look and walked off.

Piet, meanwhile, had his hands between the doors, and was testing their strength. 'I can open these,' he said.

'I guess we *could* rush the guards,' said David doubtfully. 'They might get some of us, but–'

Without waiting for the rest of the sentence, Piet wrenched the doors apart. They groaned and creaked, drowning out David's cry of surprise, and then the squat pilot grabbed one of the metal legs and took off down the corridor, his boots thudding on the deck. Sam and David exchanged a glance, and then all the Henerians squeezed between the doors and ran after Piet, carrying lengths of metal tube as makeshift weapons.

Piet reached the doors first, and he didn't stop. He took a flying leap, and just before he slammed into the clear panel he drove the metal leg forwards with all his strength. The panel crazed, bowing under his weight, then shattered. The guards had been minding their own business, lounging with their backs to the wall, and the sudden arrival shocked them into immobility. Piet executed a forward roll, bounced up and swept one man right off his feet with the metal table leg.

The other was trying to bring his weapon to bear when Sam slammed her table leg across his midriff, winding him. He went down in a huddle, and was quickly subdued.

The guards were relieved of their guns, with Piet taking one and David the other. 'These are just stun weapons,' said Piet, as he examined the blast rifle. He sounded disappointed, and Sam guessed the pilot was thirsting for revenge on those who'd shot his fighter out of the sky earlier.

'Why are they using stun weapons?' asked a pilot standing nearby.

'This better not be some kind of elaborate training exercise,' muttered a woman next to him.

Sam remembered Squadron Leader Farren getting blown apart in mid-air, and the four Henerians she'd seen executed at the settlement on Handley. 'Trust me, this is for real.'

'It's not an exercise,' confirmed David. 'Stun weapons are often used for assaults on other ships, especially if you're trying to capture them. The last thing you want to do is blow holes in the wiring, or destroy a vital flight system.'

Sam remembered the ceiling tiles raining down when Anna shot them. 'These things still pack a punch though.'

'Of course. This is war, not sport.' David checked the

Mayestrans were secure, then turned to Sam. 'You know this ship. Where are the enemy likely to be?'

'The senior officers were in the situation room. There are Mayestran fighters and transports in hangar two, and a few ground crew with a couple of petty officers in hangar one.'

David thought for a moment. 'If we're going to stop the ship we should try and launch the fighters.'

'But if we can get to the officers...' began Sam.

'Either way, we need more guns first.'

'The canteen,' said Anna. 'It's not far, and I left a dozen rifles lying around.'

'She shot the troops that brought you in,' explained Sam, and she saw David's eyebrows rise in surprise.

They moved off at speed, with the military personnel taking point while the civilian contingent followed further behind. On the way they saw a couple of Mayestran techs with their heads inside one of the maintenance hatches. There was a red box on the floor, similar to the one Sam had seen before, and they seemed to be tinkering with the wiring in the same way too.

By the time the techs heard footsteps it was too late. They were dragged out of the maintenance hatch backwards, and when they realised they were surrounded by vengeful Henerians they put their hands up, fast. 'What are you doing in there, and what the hell is this for?' David asked them, tapping the red box with the toe of his boot.

The men winced. 'Don't... don't kick that. Please.'

Sam peered in the box, then drew back hurriedly. 'It's full of *explosives*,' she muttered. Then, as she saw the drum of cable and the half-finished work inside the hatch, she realised what they were up to. 'They're rigging the whole ship to blow!'

28

Sam grabbed the nearest Mayestran, taking a handful of shirt and driving him backwards against the wall. 'Speak,' she growled, her face just inches from his. 'Why are you setting the charges? Why blow the ship now?'

'I–I don't know, I swear! They wouldn't t–tell us something like that!'

'What are your orders?'

The tech looked askance. 'I c–can't tell you. Captain Tyler will have me killed.'

Sam's grip tightened. 'Trust me, Tyler is the least of your worries right now.'

'Okay, okay! We're planting explosives at critical points around the ship. Combined, they're enough to rupture the hull.'

'Come on, I guessed that already,' said Sam. 'What's the *plan?*'

'I–I really don't know.'

Frustrated, Sam released the man. He'd been kept in the dark, which wasn't surprising. She could hardly expect Tyler to sit everyone down and explain every detail of the Mayestran plans. 'Tie them up,' she said over her shoulder. 'Stick them behind the maintenance hatch with their handiwork.'

The techs were quickly secured, their wrists and ankles bound with lengths of electrical cable from the drum. Then they were bundled into the wall, the large hatch cover replaced. When it was done, Sam knocked on it. 'Keep quiet. We'll get you out when the ship is ours.'

There was no reply.

Meanwhile, a Henerian tech was crouched next to the box of explosives, handling one of the yellowish cubes. 'If they're turning the ship into some kind of flying bomb, then their target has to be the Second Fleet. They'll dock the Lyre right next to the highest-value target they can find, shatter the hull with these explosives, and then use some kind of secondary trigger to set off the power core.'

Sam heard him, but she was looking around the group with a puzzled expression. 'Where's Aren Grant?' she asked them. 'Has anyone seen her?'

A few people exchanged glances, while others shook their heads.

'She was in the hangar with us,' said Anna. 'They took her away for questioning.'

'Nobody's seen her since?'

They hadn't, and Sam wondered why the Mayestrans were still holding her. David would have been a more valuable subjects for interrogation, rather than a mere lecturer. Grant couldn't possibly have recent intel, not after spending so much time recovering from her injuries before being posted to the training base.

Well, there was nothing they could do for Grant at that moment. 'We should get those weapons,' she suggested.

David nodded, and they continued down the corridor until they reached the offshoot leading to the canteen. The door was closed, and inside a dozen troops were lying where they'd fallen, still unconscious. A couple were moving weakly, groaning and clutching their heads, and Anna scooped up a weapon and shot them at point-blank range, the bright flashes of blaster fire knocking them out again. 'What?' she said, as the others looked at her. 'We can't have them raising the alarm.'

The rest of the guns were distributed quickly, and then David outlined the plan of attack. 'Everyone without a weapon stays here,' he said. 'Two more, armed, will stay with them. Barricade the door, but don't do anything rash unless the Mayestrans try to break in.' He indicated the unconscious troops. 'Tie them up, gag them if they come round.'

'What about the rest of us?' asked Piet.

'We'll head for the hangar with the Kestrels.' As the ranking officer David could have made it an order, but they were trainee pilots, not assault troops, and so he added a quick explanation. 'Look, if we hit the *Lyre's* engines, the Mayestrans' plan will be a complete failure. It's the surest way of stopping them.'

'What about capturing Tyler and the other officers?' asked Anna. 'We could overwhelm them and send a signal ahead, warning them about the attack.'

'Too risky. First, we're outnumbered. Second, they're trained in this kind of fighting, and we're not.' He gestured. 'Our best chance is to launch the fighters. Then we're in *our* element.'

'They have Phase IIIs,' Sam pointed out. 'Even if we launch a handful of fighters, we could lose most of them in dogfights.'

David nodded. 'I'm aware of that. Once we reach the ships, I'll decide how many will go for the Lyre's engines and how many will fight off the Phase IIIs.' He glanced at Sam. 'You saw the hangar with the Kestrels. How many personnel would you say?'

'Next to none. Just a handful of ground crew and a couple of petty officers.'

'Do you know the best way to get there? Smaller access corridors, that kind of thing? I want to avoid the main routes if possible.'

Sam nodded. 'We can take a lift down to the lower levels. It's mostly stores down there, and the Mayestrans would have no reason to dig around.'

'Right. Let's move out. And stay sharp, people! We might be the only hope of saving the Second Fleet.'

The smaller group of ten moved out, with David and Sam at the head and Anna and Piet amongst the others. All of them were armed with stun rifles, and as they jogged towards the nearest lift Sam couldn't help feeling they stood a decent chance of success. They might be a rag-tag collection of trainees, with only limited knowledge of close-quarter fighting, but it felt *good* to be charging along that corridor with a clear plan of action.

On the way to the lifts they saw another pair of techs at an open hatchway, installing more explosive charges, and David shot the pair of them without breaking stride.

'Someone's going to find all these Mayestrans lying around the place,' puffed Sam, as they ran on.

'Good. Maybe they'll waste time searching the rest of the ship. We'll have a clear run at the hangar.'

They reached the lift, where David hesitated. Sam could tell he was deciding whether to risk the elevator or take the stairwell, but in the end he chose the lift. They had to descend eight levels, and it would take too long on foot. Plus if some Mayestran tried to enter the lift, the Henerians had enough firepower to blast them right back out again.

Everyone raised their weapons as the lift doors opened, but the interior was empty. They filed in, and Sam pressed the button for one of the lowest decks.

The ride took a handful of seconds, and then the doors opened on a darkened corridor. There was a musty smell, the air a little stale from lack of circulation, and as they trooped out of the lift Sam gestured down the left-hand corridor. They took off again, jogging along with their boots thudding on the metal decking, blast rifles at the ready.

Her plan was to use another elevator at the rear of the ship, which would allow them to access the hangar deck from the far side. She was hoping any Mayestrans in the hangar would not be expecting an attack from that quarter.

Then, once they'd taken the hangar, they could seal the doors and take their pick of the Kestrels. The hangar's force field wouldn't be a problem, as each ship contained a transmitter to grant access. She pictured a flight of Kestrels tearing away from the *Lyre*, before several of them peeled off to target the battleship's engines. Once destroyed, the *Golden Lyre* would become nothing but a hulk, drifting in space until the brass sent a tug to bring her home... or to blow her into space dust where she was. Either way, it would be the end of the line for the veteran battleship, and Sam felt a stab of remorse at the thought.

They jogged on for ten or fifteen minutes, passing storerooms and junctions that led deeper into the maze-like interior of the lower deck. When they finally reached the lifts they were breathing hard.

'Take a few... to catch... your breath,' said David, who was breathing as hard as any of them. 'And remind me to suggest extra... physical training for all sprogs. You lot are a disgrace to the Navy.'

His smile belied the harsh words, and Sam grinned. 'I thought Henerian fighter pilots were discouraged from running, sir?'

'All right, check your weapons, people. We've only got one chance to make this work.'

Sam did as she was told, then hesitated. 'David, can I have a word?'

'Sure.'

They moved some distance from the others, and Sam ignored their curious looks as she spoke in a low voice. 'I can't help thinking of the *Golden Lyre's* crew. Tyler will space the lot as soon as we launch our attack.'

'I know, and I wish I could do something about it.'

'I have an idea.'

'Somehow that doesn't surprise me.' David glanced towards the lift, impatient to get moving. 'All right, you've got thirty seconds.'

'I'm going to hangar one and I'm going to overwhelm the guards. Even if I can't save all the *Lyre's* crew, I might save *some* of them.'

'I can't let you do that.'

Sam took a breath. 'I'm not asking for permission, sir. I'm telling you what I'm going to do.'

He stared at her.

'There'll still be nine of you, which is plenty for your plan,' said Sam. 'Launch the fighters, attack the drives and disable the *Golden Lyre*. Destroy the ship if you must, but I'm going to do what I can for the crew. I know these people. I can't let them die, and nothing you can say will stop me.' Sam gestured at the others. 'Tell them it's your idea if you want, so it doesn't look like I'm weakening your command or disobeying orders, but I'm going to do this.'

'I'm beginning to see why Commander Tosell was eager to get rid of you,' said David calmly.

'After this is over, you can have me court-martialled.'

David shook his head. 'You're crazy for trying this, and I should probably have you shot, but it's worth the attempt.'

They returned to the others, where David explained 'his' unexpected change to their plans. Immediately, Anna and Piet stepped forward. 'Permission to join Sam on the rescue mission, sir?'

'Not you, Anna. I need you flying a kestrel.'

Piet gave them a rueful smile. 'But not me,' he said. 'I just make for a good target.'

David wisely said nothing to that. 'When we reach the hangar deck the two of you will break off from the rest of the party. Try and gain access to hangar one, where they're keeping the Lyre's crew. We don't know how many guards there'll be, but if Tyler is threatening to space the prisoners, I'm guessing any Mayestrans will be on the right side of the airlock. With luck, there might only be a couple of them.'

The lift arrived, and the group of Henerians moved out. It was quiet, tense, and Sam noticed several of them fiddling with their guns. They might only be facing stun weapons, but the consequences of failure would be dire. With the Mayestrans planning on blowing the *Lyre* up, there was little chance they'd be taking all the Henerian prisoners with them before triggering the explosives.

The lift doors opened, and Sam immediately spotted two sentries near the side door leading to the hanger. She got one, the weapon fire leaving a bright streak in her vision, and the second collapsed as he was hit by half a dozen shots.

They left the elevator, and David stopped to clasp her shoulder. 'Good luck, and here's hoping we meet up again afterwards.'

'You can bank on that,' said Sam, and then she and Piet ran down the corridor towards hangar one.

29

As they charged down the corridor, Piet's heavy tread shaking the floor, Sam outlined her plan. 'Once we free the *Lyre's* crew, we'll get them to hangar bay two. Anna and I saw a bunch of Phase IIIs there, but there were troop ships as well. We can take shelter in those.' She glanced at Piet to see how he was taking it. 'Plus if we're sitting in their fighters, they can't launch them to stop the Kestrels. It'll help the others.'

'All this with just the two of us?'

'We have guns and the element of surprise.'

'In that case, the Mayestrans won't stand a chance,' said Piet calmly.

They were skirting the rear of hangar two, and as they reached the small access door Sam paused to glance through the porthole. She saw enemy fighters and transports in rows, looking incongruous and out of place inside the Henerian battleship's hangar. There was more activity than she expected around the ships, with the transports' ramps lowered and personnel moving equipment inside. The fighters' canopies were up too, and several had pilots seated inside, helmets in place as though they were preparing to launch. She felt a chill as she saw them, and she wondered whether the enemy had got wind of the Henerians closing in on hangar three. If so, these ships would slaughter her colleagues in the Kestrels before David had a chance to destroy the *Lyre's* engines.

She glanced over her shoulder, back down the passageway. David needed to be warned, but if she sent Piet she'd be alone against whatever guards might be outside the next hangar, where the *Lyre's* crew were. Well, that couldn't be helped. 'Piet, I need you to go back to the others. Tell them the Phase IIIs are getting ready to launch, and hurry.'

He looked like he was going to argue, then nodded and ran off without a word, his heavy tread fading rapidly. Sam took one last look at the Mayestrans inside the docking bay, then turned and ran further down the corridor, towards hangar one and, hopefully, the remaining crew of the *Golden Lyre*.

◆

Sam slowed as she approached the hangar. She didn't expect many guards, not at the rear of the docking bay, but her rescue attempt would be short-lived if she ran around the corner and came face-to-face with half a dozen armed troops. So, she pressed her back to the wall and moved crabwise, gun across her chest. She placed her feet carefully, keeping her ears open for any sound of conversation, but the background noises from the rest of the ship meant her efforts were almost certainly a waste of time.

Eventually she caught sight of the airlock, and as she leaned away from the wall she saw it was unguarded. She hurried forward, reached it in a dozen paces, then risked a quick glance through the thick porthole.

Relief...that was her first reaction. The remaining crew of the *Golden Lyre* were inside, and they looked okay. She could see about a dozen of them, some sitting on the deck while others were stretched full-length, trying to grab a few moments of rest. There was another airlock on the wall to her left, about forty metres away, linking this hangar with the next. She could see a couple of Mayestrans standing guard, watching the prisoners. They looked alert, and they had their weapons at the ready.

Sam's gaze shifted from the prisoners to the force field at the hangar entrance. That was the danger, because the two guards could step inside the airlock and switch off that force field. The air would vent, and any prisoners who avoided being sucked into space, never to be seen again, would die from suffocation where they sat. She knew her next move could save a dozen lives – or end them – and for the first time in her life Sam understood the pressures of command.

She was still looking through the porthole, working out whether she could get into the hangar and take both the guards out, when something unexpected happened. One of the guards cocked his head, listening to the commset at his shoulder, and then they opened the airlock and left.

Had she been spotted? Sam waited a second or two, hoping the guards weren't about to open the hangar to space, but it remained closed and the guards didn't return. Unable to believe her good luck, she cycled her own airlock and stepped into the hangar.

'Sam? Sam *Willet?*'

She turned to see an older man getting unsteadily to his feet, then smiled at the familiar face of her TacOps instructor. 'Monitor Pretin! It's so good to see you, sir.'

He held her in a tight embrace, then stood back to admire her.

'My, you do look different,' he said. 'No longer the rebellious young woman, I take it?'

'Don't bet on it,' said Sam, with a grin. Then she turned to the other prisoners, and she couldn't help noticing most were the older members of the crew. 'I understand the rest were taken by the Mayestrans?'

'Yes. Commander Hayden, the lieutenants... all of the officers, all the marines and engineers and techs. Everyone of value.'

'Monitor, we both know that isn't true.'

He gestured. 'Some tried to conceal themselves when the enemy came aboard, in order to mount a resistance. The Mayestrans placed a dozen of us in this hangar and threatened to kill us if the others didn't show themselves. They had access to the crew database in the computer, so it was easy to account for everyone. We had no chance, Sam.'

'Yeah, well hopefully we can fight back now.'

He smiled. 'Incidentally, it was such a pleasure to hear the good news about your brother. We all thought he was lost to us.'

Sam nodded her thanks.

Meanwhile, an older man standing nearby had been watching the exchange with growing impatience. From his insignia he was the quartermaster, in charge of the ship's stores, and Sam could see he was itching to get moving. 'Sir, we've got to get out of here,' said the quartermaster urgently. 'Those Mayestrans might come back any minute. Or they could blow the shield and kill us all.'

'Of course, of course.' Pretin nodded towards the airlock Sam had used. 'That way, I think. Sam, I presume the rest of your team are driving the enemy from my ship?'

Sam noticed the possessive with a wry grin, but then she

realised Monitor Pretin was right. He was currently the senior officer aboard the *Lyre*, and therefore it *was* his ship...even if he was only the elderly TacOps instructor. 'Not exactly, sir,' murmured Sam, and she explained the setup as the crew followed Pretin towards the airlock.

'So few of you?' asked Pretin, looking surprised.

'David Richett, the flight leader, is taking a handful of pilots out in the Kestrels. They're going to blow the *Lyre's* main drives.'

'What!'

As the crew passed through the airlock, Sam explained what she'd learned of the Mayestrans' plan. Pretin's face grew redder and redder the more she explained, until he looked like he was going to explode. 'They're turning the *Golden Lyre* into a flying *bomb?*' he thundered. Unfortunately they were passing through the airlock at the time, and several crew standing nearby flinched at the raw outrage in his voice. 'I'll string that Tyler fellow up by his thumbs, you see if I don't!' shouted Pretin, and he turned to the quartermaster. 'Ted, you'd better organise a couple of search parties. One tech to each. Locate these explosives and disarm them.'

'Yes sir,' said the quartermaster, and as they left the airlock he began sorting the crew into small groups.

At that moment they felt a rumble underfoot, the entire hull shaking and swaying.

'What was that?' demanded Pretin.

Sam had a fair idea, and she left the *Lyre's* crew and ran down the corridor to the next hangar. She cupped her hands to the porthole and stared into the bay, and she wasn't surprised to see a number of Phase IIIs rocketing into space with a loud roar from their exhausts. The hangar was a hive of activity, with dozens of Mayestrans making their way across the vast expanse of the bay. Sam saw Tyler and the senior officers amongst them, even as the group hurried up the boarding ramp and vanished into one of the troop ships.

More Phase IIIs departed with a rumble of thunder from their thrusters, rocketing through the force field as they left the bay. As they left, the last of the Mayestrans filed into the troop ships, which lifted off even as the ramps were still closing. Seconds later, the bay was completely empty, and Sam eyed the vast empty space thoughtfully.

Unlikely though it seemed, the Mayestrans had just abandoned the *Golden Lyre*. Now she could send a message to the Second Fleet, warning them of the Mayestran attack. With the *Golden Lyre* back in Henerian hands, it seemed the Mayestran plan had fizzled. For all their bold moves and planning, they'd achieved precisely nothing!

Then, as Sam stood there, she felt the deck heave under her feet. Seconds later there was a tremendous explosion, and the corridor filled with whirling dust and air. At first she thought the Mayestrans had blown the *Lyre* apart, setting off their explosives even as they fled the ship, but she quickly realised the explosions weren't *that* big, and in addition the hull was definitely intact.

Then she heard footsteps, and several of the crew she'd just freed came hurrying towards her. 'What's happening?' she shouted, as they jogged past.

'They've set off charges,' called one of the crew. 'The explosions took out a couple of airlocks, and the atmosphere is venting from the bow section.'

'Where are you going?'

'Control station. We've got to shut the whole section down.'

Sam realised the enemy's intentions right away. The ship's comms, TacOps, the bridge… they were all in the fore section.

If the Mayestrans *had* vented the atmosphere from that part of the ship, nobody would be sending messages to the dockyard, and nobody would be taking the controls of the *Golden Lyre*, either.

There would be spacesuits, of course, but Sam was betting the enemy had thought of that. All they had to do was throw a grenade into each suit locker, or slash the suits and smash all the helmets. They'd probably left other explosives too, booby-trapping airlocks and doorways to prevent anyone passing through. It could take days to undo all the damage, and she reckoned they'd be lucky to have an hour or two.

There was a familiar twisting sensation, and Sam realised they'd jumped again. Immediately afterwards the main drives fired, thrusting the *Golden Lyre* onwards, towards its target.

The Mayestrans hadn't been fleeing, or running from a failure. They'd set things up perfectly, programming the ship towards its final destination before leaving. Worse, they'd made sure the Henerians still trapped on board couldn't do a thing about it!

30

As she stood there in the corridor digesting the full extent of the Mayestran plan, Sam couldn't help feeling a sneaking admiration for the enemy's cunning. First, they'd gone after an older ship, because until recently the *Golden Lyre* had only been used for training, her crew older than average and nearing retirement. They were less likely to put up a desperate fight than a crew of young firebrands out to prove themselves, and as for the *Golden Lyre* herself, her weapons would have been no match for a modern Mayestran cruiser.

Next, instead of killing the crew out of hand, which could have led to pitched battles up and down the ship's corridors as the survivors fought for their lives, the Mayestrans had treated the Henerians well. They'd secured them in the hangar and gone about their business quickly and efficiently.

Then, with a start, Sam realised why the *Golden Lyre* had come to the Handley system in the first place. The attacks on the twin bases! The training base, under Squadron Leader Norton, had been hit before they managed to transmit a warning, but the bigger facility, run by Farren, must have sent out a request for help. The *Lyre* would have picked up that signal and jumped into the system to lend assistance, only to run into the Mayestrans... who'd been waiting for her to show up.

Then the last piece of the puzzle fell into place. After the final dogfight with the enemy, when the Henerians were on the back foot and all but defeated, the Mayestrans had staged that contrived scenario with their pilots flying both Phase IIIs and Kestrels. The Phase IIIs had turned tail and fled, and Phantom flight had invited her, Anna and Aren Grant to follow them to the *Lyre*.

Ever since she'd discovered 'Phantom' flight was actually the enemy, Sam had been wondering why they hadn't just opened fire and blasted the three Henerians from the sky. But now it made sense. The enemy were on a tight schedule, because their plans would be ruined if news of the *Golden Lyre's* capture got out. They couldn't leave survivors behind on planet Handley, because another Henerian ship might happen by. No, they'd staged the 'rescue' to ensure that every Henerian on the planet willingly ran into their welcoming arms.

And now, having scooped up the survivors from the planet, the Mayestrans had given themselves time to rig the *Golden Lyre* for her final journey. The old battleship would self-destruct in the middle of the Second Fleet, and the Mayestrans would strike the biggest blow in the entire history of the war.

It wasn't just a cunning plan, it was masterful. And if it were successful, Sam suspected it could change the course of the war.

Well, she thought, turning away from the airlock, maybe there was still time to halt the Lyre in her tracks. Maybe they could save the Second Fleet. And maybe they could hunt down the fleet of transports and Phase IIIs carrying the Mayestrans to safety, and blast every last one of them into microscopic fragments.

But first she had to find out where David and the rest of the Henerian pilots had got to. Had Piet reached them in time, or had they left the Lyre only to be blown apart by the waiting Phase IIIs?

With with sobering thought, Sam set off at a run for hangar three.

◆

As she ran towards hangar three, Sam realised there might still be a chance. If the Kestrels were still aboard, they could easily lift off and take out the Lyre's engines with no fear of interference from the Mayestrans. With one burst of blaster fire, the enemy's elaborate plan would be stopped.

When she arrived at the hangar, though, she realised the enemy had thought of the danger too. The bay was full of smoke and spot fires, and most of the once-proud Kestrels were nothing but piles of twisted, blackened metal. Piet was there, along with David and the others, and when he saw Sam approaching he came to explain. 'They left small charges aboard every fighter,' he told her. 'It's okay, nobody was hurt, but a few of them got a bit too close.'

'What about those two fighters?' asked Sam, indicating two undamaged Kestrels sitting nearby. 'We can fly those.'

'No, they're rigged to blow if we touch them. We can't fly them until we find engineers to defuse the explosives.'

David was sitting with his back to the wall, his face smudged from the fires. He glanced up as Sam got closer, and gave her a rueful shrug. 'They set us up. Must have guessed we'd try the fighters,' he said, his voice low. 'How about you? Any luck with the crew?'

'I got them out,' said Sam, with a nod. 'Monitor Pretin is in command. He's my old TacOps teacher. The others... there's the quartermaster, a few stores clerks, some elderly techs. Not exactly fighting fit.'

'Ideal hostages, then. Respected by the crew, but not too much danger to the Mayestrans.'

'You don't know Monitor Pretin,' remarked Sam. She brought him up to speed, telling him of the Mayestrans leaving, and the explosion which had taken out the atmosphere in the Lyre's fore section. 'Pretin's organising teams to search for more explosives around the *Golden Lyre*.'

'He should grab those techs we stuck in the maintenance hatch. They might talk if he pressures them.'

'I'll tell him. But the Mayestrans have cut us off from the bridge, and I'm guessing they blew the comms, too. And you probably heard the Lyre's engines firing up.' She nodded towards the rear of the hangar. 'The enemy programmed a course before they left. We must be heading straight towards the dockyard.'

'They won't let us sail right in, not without clearance. They won't let us get close, believe me.'

Sam realised what he meant, because the defences would tear the *Lyre* apart before she could dock. 'The Mayestrans will have thought of that, David. So far, they've been ahead of us every step of the way.'

'So let me get this straight.' David counted on his fingers. 'This entire ship is wired to blow, and it's going to take half the Henerian Navy with it. We can't get to the controls, we can't broadcast a warning, and with only a couple of fighters left, both rigged to explode, we're all going to have a front row seat for the grand finale.'

'That's about it.'

'So tell me, was Pretin happy when you freed him? Because if someone tried to put me in charge of this mess I think I'd quit on the spot.'

Sam grinned. 'He's a tough nut. He'll deal with it.'

'Any idea how long it'll be until we...' he made an exploding gesture with his fingers.

'None at all.'

David nodded, then slowly got to his feet. 'All right, listen up,' he said, raising his voice. 'This is a tricky situation, but we're not done yet. Everyone who's fit for duty, fall in. We're going to offer Monitor Pretin our services.'

Without a word, everyone struggled to their feet and lined up, even those who were still coughing and gasping from inhaled smoke.

'You're a bunch of maniacs, but thanks anyway,' said David, with a grin. 'Now let's go fix this thing!'

— 31 —

It wasn't hard to find Monitor Pretin, because all Sam had to do was follow the crashes and bangs as several of the *Golden Lyre's* crew tried to break through a sealed airlock. It seemed the Mayestrans had done more than blow a few hatches before they left, and apart from venting the air and planting explosives, they'd also taken the time to thoroughly weld several airlock doors together.

Four mechanics were trying to batter their way through the airlock with a large ram, which looked suspiciously like a metal reinforcing column removed from the nearby bulkhead. Repeatedly, they swung it back then drove it forward again, but despite the sickening blows the airlock doors were far too strong.

Pretin had sent several crew members to find a way around the barricade, but they'd just returned with the news that all access to the forward section of the ship had been sealed off.

'Sir, can I speak with you?' Sam asked him.

'Can it wait?'

Then Sam saw movement on the other side of the airlock. For a second she thought one of Pretin's people had got through, but then she spotted a weapon aiming in her direction.

'Look out!' someone shouted, as they saw the same

movement. 'The enemy are on the other side!'

It was true. There was a makeshift barricade further down the corridor, which Sam had taken for a means to slow down the Henerians, but now she realised the barricade was manned, and there were armed troops just the other side. Even if Pretin's people got through the sealed airlock, they'd still have to overcome the enemy before they could alter the ship's course or transmit a warning to the Second Fleet.

'Ted, I want armed personnel in this corridor,' said Pretin. 'Make sure they've got flash grenades, and I want you to set a guard at the other access points too. I don't want any Mayestrans circling round behind us.'

'Yes sir,' said the quartermaster, and he started issuing orders.

'There can't be many of them,' added Pretin. 'They're just a delaying tactic, not a serious force.'

Sam was forced to step aside as a couple of elderly engineers came past hauling a cutting torch on a trolley. While they set it up, everyone else retreated to a safe distance, and then the corridor flashed and flickered with reflected light as the super-heated lance began cutting through the thick metal. The glare was intense, and Sam shielded her eyes and watched the Mayestrans on the far side of the airlock, trying to see how they were reacting. The enemy were vastly outnumbered, and she expected them to turn tail and run for it. Instead, they readied their weapons and held their ground.

Then Pretin took the quartermaster aside. 'This is taking too damn long. At the speed they're going, it's going to be twenty minutes before we get through the door, and there's another after it. Can't we blow the thing?'

'We can't risk explosives, sir. The blast could rupture the bulkheads.'

Suddenly, an idea came to Sam. An idea so crazy, so off-the-wall, and so impractical that she immediately pushed it out of her mind. It was the sort of thing that could have her marched off to the nearest nuthouse... once they'd all finished laughing themselves silly at her expense. On the other hand, she was pretty sure it would get the doors open in no time, and she suspected it would take care of the Mayestrans lurking behind the barrier too... as well as anyone else who happened to be hunkered down for the next hundred metres or so beyond them.

Sam waited another five minutes, during which time the cutting torch managed to carve through another six inches or so of the tough airlock door. Three or four of the *Lyre's* crew had just come back, armed with blast rifles and flash grenades, and Sam could see Pretin's growing impatience at the delay. He wanted the *Lyre* back under his command, and he wanted it now. So, she decided to speak up. 'Sir, I have an idea.'

'Go on.'

'With the right sort of weapon we could shoot the airlock away, sir. Melt it to slag instantly.'

'For goodness sake,' growled Pretin impatiently. 'Don't you think we considered that? No hand gun would touch the airlock doors, Sam. They wouldn't be much of a barricade against a boarding party if the enemy could simply shoot their way through them now, would they?'

'Sir, I wasn't thinking of a *hand* gun exactly,' said Sam.

'Oh, you have to be kidding,' said the quartermaster, as realisation dawned. 'That's not even remotely feasible.'

'What isn't?' demanded Pretin. 'What's the suggestion?'

'She's talking about using a nose gun from one of our Kestrels,' said the quartermaster, in a strangled voice. 'She wants to use a fighter's main armament to blast a hole through the airlock.'

For a second, Pretin looked stunned. He recovered quickly, though. 'Would it work?'

'Work?' cried the quartermaster. 'It'd melt both airlock doors, vaporise those Mayestrans, and probably keep going through bulkheads until it punched a hole right through the Lyre's prow. You'd go down in history as the only commander to shoot his own battleship down... from the inside.'

'We could turn the power down a bit,' suggested Sam.

There was a long silence, broken only by the hiss and spatter of the cutting torch. Then Pretin tapped one of the engineers on the shoulder, jumping back quickly as the torch almost set his uniform on fire. 'If you mounted a gun from a Kestrel and fired it on reduced power, what would happen to those doors?'

'Sir, there wouldn't *be* any doors,' said the engineer, his face red from operating the cutter.

'How about damage to the rest of the ship?'

The engineer looked thoughtful. 'None, if we pulsed the weapon on a low setting. It wouldn't be an explosive blast, sir, just a kind of disintegration.'

Pretin turned to the quartermaster. 'Get it done, Ted.'

'Of course sir. I'll break a gun out of stores immediately,' said the quartermaster smartly, and he signalled to the engineers, who packed the cutting torch up and followed him back down the corridor.

They'd only just left when Sam felt the deck shake, and seconds later there was a distant rumble. Immediately, the ship's main drives cut out, leaving the *Golden Lyre* strangely silent as she drifted through space.

'Will someone find out what's blown up *this* time?' demanded Pretin plaintively.

Moments later, a runner came hurrying up the corridor. 'Sir, an explosive device just took out the control circuits for the main drives. We have no means of propulsion aside from the thrusters.'

At that moment the ship jumped into hyperspace, emerging a split second later after the familiar sensation. The *Golden Lyre* was still racing headlong for the dockyard, since the vacuum of space would never slow the speeding ship. Only now, thanks to the latest explosion, they had no engines to slow down or change their course.

— 32 —

With an engineer and a tech despatched to look over the damaged drive controllers, Monitor Pretin's attention returned to the airlock. The nose gun from the Kestrel fighter was at least two metres long, and it looked huge in the hands of the engineers who were carrying it along the corridor. Another couple of techs followed them, laden with folded trestles, stands and toolboxes.

The stands and trestles were put in place, about thirty metres from the airlock and directly in line. That was about as far as they could get without losing sight of the sealed doors around the curvature of the passageway. Sam knew they'd prefer to be further back, but she guessed Pretin would not be impressed if she suggested ricocheting the blaster shots all the way round the outer wall, even if it meant they could fire the weapon from a safe distance. Her original idea was crazy enough, and adding a wall-of-death element to the shot would probably push him right over the edge.

Once the trestles were ready, the gun was placed on top and clamped down. A thick cable protruded from the rear, and a tech took off a wall panel and busied herself inside, connecting the weapon to the Lyre's main power bus. Once it was wired in, she and two others used handheld devices to re-calibrate the huge blaster, tweaking the settings so it didn't blast a hole clear through the front of the ship.

'Is it ready?' demanded Pretin.

'Yes sir.'

'Get on with it, then.'

The tech tapped her screen, and a beam of red light shot from the weapon's muzzle and played on the airlock door. The heavy metal began to glow immediately, and Sam could see the plexiglass window melting from the sheer amount of energy being applied to it. There was a loud hum from the weapon, and the heat from the glowing door was making the corridor uncomfortably warm.

'More power,' called Pretin.

The tech obeyed, and the hum became something physical. Sam could feel the air being driven from her lungs, and there was an unpleasant vibration deep inside her chest. Meanwhile, the first airlock door gave up the struggle, with half simply dissolving into red-hot slag, and the rest spraying against the second door in a blast of molten metal. The beam hit the second door too, which started to groan and flex as the tortured metal was subjected to immense forces.

'It's going!' shouted Sam, as the door teetered on the point of collapse. The tech cut the beam, but not before it tore right through the second door and blasted down the corridor. The Mayestrans, already warned by the destruction of the first door, barely scrambled free as their barricade was shredded by the beam, and as they rolled on the floor, trying to douse the flames which the hot metal had caused to erupt from their clothing, they were promptly stunned by a barrage of shots from the Henerians.

There was a thunder of boots as the marines charged forward, racing ahead to mop up any further resistance.

Meanwhile, Pretin beamed at Sam. 'That was a capital idea, trainee. Excellent work!' Then, before she could reply, his face fell. 'Commander Hayden will want a report on this. What am I supposed to say?'

The quartermaster cleared his throat. 'Perhaps, sir, you could give the impression that a cutting torch was enough for the job. The use of a Kestrel's main armament could be dismissed as an outlandish rumour.'

'Good idea, Ted. A very good idea indeed.'

◆

After passing through the remains of the airlock doors, still glowing cherry-red, Sam heard shouting and rapid bursts of gunfire as a group of Henerians dealt with the remaining Mayestrans. It didn't take long, as the enemy had been expecting to hold on a lot longer, and the quick breaching of their defences had shattered their morale. That, plus the Henerians were determined to avenge the capture of their ship.

About five minutes after the fighting began, a crew member returned and saluted Pretin, his face red from running. 'Ship secure, sir. There won't be any more trouble from the enemy.'

'Thank you, Wills.' Pretin strode down the passage and the rest of the group hurried to keep up. On the way, Pretin turned to another Henerian following close behind. 'Set up interrogations as soon as possible. I want to know what they were planning.'

'They're out cold for the time being, sir,' Wills pointed out. 'We had no choice but to subdue them.'

'In that case, interrogate them as soon as they're awake.'

'Yes sir.'

'Now, will someone find me a replacement situation room? Thanks to the Mayestrans we can't use the original.'

Ten minutes later they were crowded into a tutorial room, with techs hauling in commsets and terminals and large displays. They started hooking everything up, replicating the ship's original situation room, and while it wasn't as grand, it would serve the same function.

Everyone was present, apart from those trying to get the ship back under control, and the teams locating the explosive charges. Monitor Pretin, temporary commander of the *Golden Lyre*, had already assigned tasks to the dozen or so crew at his disposal, and now he quickly went through the survivors from the bases on Handley, learning their ranks and qualifications. Once he'd finished, he addressed. 'Richett, you're the senior pilot. If we manage to gain access to the bridge I want you at the helm. In the meantime I want you to choose half a dozen gunners for the defensive turrets. The *Scimitar* may be shadowing us, and if they realise we're changing course or upsetting their plans in any way, they might decide to finish us off.'

'Yes sir.' David picked several of those present, a mix of military and civilians, and led them out of the room.

'Mellish,' said Pretin, addressing the political officer. 'I want you to knock up an outline of the enemy's plans. Something concise, please. If we get comms up, I want the outline broadcast as far and wide as possible, on all subspace channels. If we can't stop the *Lyre*, then warning the Second Fleet in advance might be our only chance to save them.'

Mellish nodded, and turned to a nearby terminal to start work.

'Sam, take an engineer to the fighter bay and see whether you can't get those two Kestrels ready. I know the enemy has a dozen Phase IIIs, but I'll be much happier if we can launch a couple of fighters.'

Sam knew what he meant. As long as the Phase IIIs were chasing the Kestrels, they wouldn't be shooting at the *Lyre*.

'Also,' continued Pretin, 'if we fail in our attempts to stop the Lyre, you may have to resort to your original plan, and blow the main drives.'

An engineer raised his hand. 'Sir, can I just say that's not the surgical strike everyone seems to think it is. Taking out the drives could rupture the hull, or destroy the entire ship.'

'I know that, Roy,' said Pretin patiently.

'The Mayestrans didn't just show up on a whim and start fiddling with our systems. This is a well-drilled plan, and they must have spent months going over the tiniest detail.

'Thank you. All of you understand the situation, though. We must stop the Lyre, whatever it takes. We cannot put the Second Fleet in danger, even if it means giving our own lives in the process.'

'Blowing the main drives won't stop the ship in any case,' continued Roy. 'You'd have to take out the jump drives, and they're deep inside the hull. The only way to get at them would be to blast the *Lyre's* guts right out.'

'Great,' muttered someone. 'So if we *do* stop the old girl, the Mayestrans will blow us up. And if we can't stop the *Lyre* in time, we'll have to blow *ourselves* up.'

Pretin frowned. 'We're not defeated yet, son.'

Then he turned to a screen, and started allocating tasks to the rest of those present. Seeing she was no longer needed,

Sam collected the engineer the Monitor had assigned to her, beckoned to Anna, and left the briefing room. On the way out she saw Piet looking in her direction, but she ignored him. With only two fighters, she needed the best pilot she could get her hands on.

They arrived in the hangar a few minutes later, the interior still smelling of charred plastic and stale smoke. Ten of the dozen fighters present had been destroyed by the Mayestrans, but the furthest two were still intact. The engineer, Roy, told Sam to keep her distance, then approached the nearer of the two fighters for a look. 'They didn't have time for anything too elaborate,' he called out. 'Should have this fixed in a jiffy.'

Even so, Sam's heart was in her mouth. One wrong move and the ship would blow up, killing the engineer. He was an older man, and like the others aboard the *Golden Lyre*, she guessed he was serving out the last couple of years aboard the training ship before his retirement. None of them would have expected to become embroiled in a Mayestran plot, and she could only hope the engineer had kept himself current on the latest enemy equipment.

Roy came back, holding a block of explosive in one hand, and a small electronic board with a silver cap on one end in the other. 'She's safe now. Give me a couple of minutes to–'

'This is Monitor Pretin, your commander for the time being.'

Sam glanced up at the overhead speakers.

'Internal communications have been restored, but we're down to one backup server cobbled together from spare parts. Therefore, I'd ask you to restrict use of comms where possible. All working parties, please report in as soon as you complete a task. Pretin out.'

'As I was just saying,' continued the engineer. 'I'll have the second ship ready in a minute or two, and then you can launch.'

'Good,' muttered Anna. 'Time to stomp some Mayestran butt.'

Sam felt the other pilot was being a touch optimistic. The scanners in the Kestrels would reveal the *Scimitar*, if she was in range, and if so, the cruiser and her complement of Phase III fighters would be the ones doing the stomping. Launching the Kestrels would also inform the Mayestrans that their plan was in danger. 'If we spot the enemy cruiser, our only chance is to keep our distance and bring them closer to the *Lyre*, where our turrets might be able to damage her before she realises they're armed.' On that thought, Sam ran to the nearest intercom and called the ready room. 'Sam Willet, in the fighter bay. I have a message for Monitor Pretin.'

'Go ahead.'

'We're about to launch. If the *Scimitar* is still out there, she might close in on the *Lyre* to investigate. Can you advise the commander not to open fire until the last second? You might catch her off guard.'

'Understood, and thanks.'

Sam returned to Anna, who'd just been joined by the engineer. 'They're clear to go,' said Roy. 'We don't have any flight controllers, or, you know, any other fighters, so you can lift off whenever you like.'

'Thanks. You did a great job.'

'I just pulled a few wires out. Beats facing the enemy any day.'

With that sobering thought in mind, Sam and Anna headed for the fighters and prepared to lift off.

33

Sam felt an overwhelming sense of freedom as she rocketed out of the *Golden Lyre's* docking bay. The small fighter was like an extension of her being, reacting instantly to every input. *This* was the reason she'd pressed for a transfer to fighter training and away from the drudge of TacOps, because when she was aboard a large vessel she felt like a tiny cog in the massive Henerian war machine. Here, she was the prime mover.

There was little time to appreciate the nimble fighter's capabilities though. First, she had to find out whether the enemy was still hanging around. With her visor down and the HUD on maximum range, she waited impatiently while the fighter's combat computer scanned the vast area of surrounding space for energy signatures.

Nothing. 'I'm clear, Anna. How about you?'

'I have no contacts, Red Leader.'

Sam remembered the training exercise from the day before, and grinned. 'We can drop the formal call signs. It's not like they're going to confuse us with anyone else.'

'Red Flight, this is Golden Lyre Control. Can you confirm there are no enemy contacts, over?'

'That is correct, Control. Clear in every direction.'

'Message from the commander. We've tapped into the ship's systems, and will now have warning before each jump. You're to dock beforehand to conserve your fuel.'

That made sense, and Sam nodded. The fighters could perform a jump or two, but after that she and Anna would be stranded. It was far better to dock with the *Lyre* and jump along with the bigger ship.

'We've also pinpointed our location on the start chart, and we can confirm the Naval dockyard is our eventual destination.'

'Can you override the controls?'

'Negative, Red Leader. All data is currently read-only.'

Sam had an idea, and she thumbed the mic. 'When you're counting down to the final jump, Anna and I could try and reach the dockyard ahead of you. We can jump first, get within range and transmit a warning.'

'Just a moment.' There was a lengthy delay before the operator came back. 'Commander Pretin agrees with your plan. Please dock at hangar bay three, and be sure to conserve your fuel. Over and out.'

So much for freedom, thought Sam. Still, they'd only have to dock for a while, and then she and Anna could depart on their own mission, racing ahead of the *Golden Lyre*. And perhaps, if she managed to warn the Second Fleet in time, the Navy could send a vessel to transfer all the crew from the inbound battleship.

Sam sat in her fighter, heart pounding. She was docked with the *Golden Lyre*, her fighter at the very entrance to the hangar, engines running and ready to depart at a moment's notice. Anna's ship sat beside hers, and the other pilot was just as eager to get going.

They were both waiting for a signal. The battleship's next-to-last jump was imminent, and the instant it occurred Sam would exit the hangar and use her own jump drive to reach the system containing the dockyard. It would be several minutes before the *Lyre* executed its final jump, arriving soon after the fighters, and those precious minutes were all Sam had to convince the dockyard of the danger, and get them to do something, anything, to save the Second Fleet.

Engineers had been working non-stop to locate and disarm the explosives planted all over the *Lyre* by the Mayestrans, but unfortunately there were just too many of them. No progress had been made on reaching the bridge, either, with entire sections of corridor exposed to the vacuum of space.

The ship couldn't be diverted, and couldn't be stopped, and so warning the dockyard was their only remaining option.

There was a twist as the ship jumped, and Sam was already moving the throttle when the voice rang in her headset.

'Red Flight, go go go!'

Both fighters speared out of the docking bay at full throttle, the wake blasting the deck. They passed through the force field, and the second they were far enough from the Golden Lyre, Sam triggered the jump drive.

'Good luck, Red Flight,' called the Lyre's traffic controller.

Then the jump drive fired, shifting the starfield and leaving Sam disoriented. She recovered quickly, saw the flash as Anna's fighter appeared alongside, then turned her attention to the HUD. There were two or three ships in the system, small green markers indicating friendlies, and a much larger square indicating dockyard Alpha.

'Dockyard control, this is Red Flight out of the Golden Lyre. I have an emergency message for all ships, all personnel.'

There was a pause before the controller responded. *'State your authorisation, Red Flight.'*

Sam gave her ID, quickly and precisely. 'The Golden Lyre was captured by a Mayestran Cruiser. Before releasing her, they rigged explosives. She's–'

'I'm sorry, Red Flight. I have that ID as one Sam Willet, a trainee based on planet Hanley. Can you confirm, over?'

'Yes, that's me. Look, the Lyre will be showing up any second, and she's–'

'Sam Willet, you say you're attached to the Golden Lyre, *but we have that ship on patrol near the frontier. Would you please explain?'*

'There's no bloody time to explain!' shouted Sam. 'The Golden Lyre has been converted into a flying bomb, and she's on the way to your location right now. You have to organise a transport to take the crew off, and you'll need gunners on standby to take her out before she docks amongst the fleet.'

'Trainee, I wouldn't organise a round of drinks on your say-so.' There was a pause. *'I don't know who put you up to this, but–'*

'I'm under direct orders of the Golden Lyre's commander.'

'Captain Hayden sent you?'

'No. Monitor Pretin assumed command after the Mayestrans took Hayden into custody. They've disabled the ship's controls, and–'

'Monitor Pretin. . . the TacOps tutor?'

'He's the ranking officer.' Sam kept her voice level, even though she wanted to reach through the mic and pull the obtuse comms operator's head off. She'd expected surprise when she warned the naval base, maybe shock, but not suspicion and disbelief. 'Look, it's not going to kill you to send a transport, is it? The *Lyre* will emerge from her jump in my location, and you can ask questions while you're taking the crew off.'

'Oh, believe me. If the Lyre appears, we'll ask questions all right. Now clear this channel, please. I have legitimate traffic to deal with.'

'They can't communicate with you,' said Sam desperately. 'Their comms have been cut!'

She would have said more, but at that moment there was an energy flash as the battleship materialised. Relieved, Sam realised that *now* the operator might finally believe her... especially when his calls to the *Lyre* went unanswered. A battleship heading directly towards the dockyard, no response from the crew... surely that would raise eyebrows?

But, as before, the Mayestrans had thought their plan through to the very end.

'This is the Golden Lyre inbound for dockyard Alpha,' said a calm female voice. *'Request docking permission. Repeat, request docking permission.'*

Sam gaped at the huge ship, which dwarfed her tiny fighter. What the hell was going on? For a second she wondered whether the repair teams had taken back control of the ship, but something about the voice was off. It was familiar, but she couldn't place it. Quickly, Sam hit the transmit button. 'Don't listen to her, Control. I'm telling you, the Mayestrans have control of the Golden Lyre!'

'Stay off this channel, Red Flight, or I'll block your comms permanently. Golden Lyre, this is dockyard flight control. Please confirm your authorisation code.'

'Roger Control. Authorisation code follows.'

Sam heard the steady female voice reading out a string of alphanumeric characters, and yet despite her anger at

Control's pig-headed stupidity, she still struggled to identify that voice. Then, with a flash, it came to her. It was Aren Grant, the scarred lecturer from the training base! Nobody had seen her since Sam and Anna had first docked with the *Lyre*, and everyone suspected she'd been dragged away to the Mayestran cruiser, another prisoner to be tortured and put to death. But now, here she was, alive and kicking, and still aboard the *Golden Lyre*! 'Aren, what the hell are you playing at?' demanded Sam.

'Red Flight, this is Control. You had your warning.'

'No wait! You have to listen–' Sam's intercom hissed, and she realised her commset had been blocked at the source. 'Anna? Can you transmit?'

There was no reply.

'Golden Lyre, your orders were to patrol the frontier. Can you explain your presence?'

'Control, we suffered a malfunction in the main drives,' said Grant. *'She's not the youngest ship in the fleet, as I'm sure you're aware.'*

'Roger, Lyre. Cleared for docking bay ninety-six, and I'm glad you made it safely. Over and out.'

'Unbelievable,' muttered Sam. She eyed the huge battleship, which was still heading for the dockyard. Then she glanced to her right, where she saw Anna looking back at her from the cockpit of the second Kestrel. When she saw Sam looking at her, Anna threw her hands up in disgust.

Sam indicated the fighters, then pointed to the battleship. Anna complied, and together both fighters streaked towards the docking bay. Their only hope now was to find Grant, and use her transmitter to warn the dockyard before it was too late.

34

Sam was out of the fighter before the engines had finished spooling down, and the whining roar from the intakes threatened to blow her eardrums as she slid down the cockpit ladder. She ran to the flight deck intercom and jabbed the button repeatedly until someone answered. 'Sit room. Now!'

There was a click. *'Situation Room.'*

'It's Sam Willet. Get me Pretin immediately.'

'He's organising a–'

'NOW!' shouted Sam.

Another click, and seconds later she heard Monitor Pretin's voice. *'Sam?'*

'There's a Mayestran agent somewhere aboard this ship. Aren Grant, from the Hanley training base. She's communicating with the dockyard, and she's just talked them into letting the *Lyre* dock. She must have overridden local comms as well, because I lost touch with you right after take-off.'

'So that's why we couldn't raise you.'

'You've got to find her and neutralise her. I told the dockyard everything, and they didn't believe a word. They're not sending help, and they're not moving the ships out of the way.'

Sam grabbed for support as the battleship lurched. 'What was that?'

'We're altering course. Slowing down,' said Pretin, his voice hollow. *'Sam, it's too late. We're approaching the docking buoy.'*

'I can launch again. We can blast the bridge. I'll take Grant out with the Kestrel's guns!'

'No, Sam. Attack the *Lyre*, and the shipyard defences will tear you to pieces.' She heard Pretin groan. 'We're done for. I'll go down in history as the man who lost the war.'

Even as he spoke, Sam heard a scrape alongside, followed by the unmistakable sound of hull clamps. She turned towards the force field at the hangar entrance, dreading what she might see, and she almost groaned aloud like Pretin had. There were dozens of capital ships surrounding the Golden Lyre, from massive carriers to nimble destroyers and everything in between. Their riding lights gleamed in the darkness of space, and together the ships looked like a massive city laid out before her eyes. The explosion, when it came, would decimate the fleet. Despite her efforts, despite *all* their efforts, it was too late to prevent the catastrophe.

◆

Sam left the docking bay at a run, Anna on her heels. She was heading for the situation room, even though she knew there was nothing she could do. But if there was any last chance to communicate with the dockyard, or to help Monitor Pretin and the others, she wanted to be there.

When she arrived there was pandemonium. One of the screens was displaying a countdown, with barely five minutes left, and Pretin was shouting himself hoarse down a handset. 'I don't care if you have to duct-tape it together. Get someone into a spacesuit and get them into the bridge right now!' He slammed the handset down, then gestured at the countdown on the screen. 'Whose genius idea was that?'

'People wanted to know how much time they had left,' muttered a tech defensively. 'We all do.'

Sam approached Pretin. 'Sir, the Kestrels can take four people to safety. Two pilots and two others. Maybe... you could draw names? It might take their mind off the end.'

'No, we're staying until the last second. I still have people hunting down explosives, and they're telling me they might have found enough already to make a difference.'

Sam felt a surge of hope. 'You mean the explosion won't destroy the core?'

'That's exactly what I mean.' Monitor Pretin raised his voice. 'We're going to seal the airlocks leading to this section. It's already been cleared, so we know there aren't any explosives in this area. When the rest go off the ship may de-pressurise in certain sections, but my teams are confident they've found enough devices to avert a total catastrophe.'

There was a palpable feeling of relief, although Sam couldn't help noticing Pretin had given them a more positive-sounding update than the one he'd given her in private.

'Three minutes,' called someone.

Pretin gestured at two crew members. 'Take six people each. Check all the airlocks again.'

The two saluted, and left with a dozen others at a run.

'To think I always wanted to command my own ship,' muttered Pretin. 'I swear I've aged ten years in the past hour.'

'Sir, we should probably move the fighters,' said Sam.

'You're right. Knowing the top brass, they'll probably bill me for them.' Pretin gestured at the door. 'Take Anna and stand clear of the ship. Tell the guards at the airlocks I authorised your passage.'

'Sir, I'm not running away,' said Sam firmly. 'I'd rather you picked someone else.'

He seemed about to argue, then nodded. 'All pilots present, please raise your hands.' He glanced around the room, then pointed to Piet and David. 'You and you. Take the Kestrels to safety.'

'I'm staying right here sir,' said Piet.

'These are my trainees,' said David. 'I'm not abandoning them.'

'If I ordered you to go, would it make any difference?'

'No sir.'

'One minute,' called the tech, whose gaze hadn't left the big screen.

'It seems you're too late anyway,' said Pretin conversationally.

There was a buzz from the intercom, followed by an excited voice. *'Sir, I'm calling from the bridge. I'm sorry, but the Mayestran agent blasted the subspace transmitter before we could get to her. There's no way to communicate outside the ship, sir. I'm sorry.'*

'You did your best, son. Thanks.' Then Pretin turned to Sam. 'You know, I'd like to hear about your brother's rescue. I hear it was quite an adventure.'

Sam stared at him, then realised what he was up to. With under a minute left until the explosion, anything was better then staring at that countdown. 'Well, sir, you recall I was sent to the Coriolis for Lim's memorial service?'

'Of course, of course.'

'Well, it was like this...'

Sam launched into the tale, recounting her attack on the Mayestran flagship. She felt detached from her body, as though she were floating above the room, looking down on the occupants. The seconds ticked by, and as the clock neared zero she saw the crew gripping each others hands, staring at the screen, mouthing what might be their last words. Even Pretin stop pretending to listen to her as the time ran out.

'Ten,' said the tech. 'Nine. Eight. Seven...'

35

'Three. Two. *One.*'

For a moment nothing happened, until Sam heard a series of small explosions in the distance. They weren't very loud, and the force of the blasts barely shook the deck underfoot.

Then... silence.

'Sounds like someone forgot to light the fuses,' remarked a woman standing nearby.

There was a ripple of laughter, and then, unbelievably, a call came over the intercom. *'The hull is intact, sir. We've made it!'*

There was a massive cheer as everyone heard the news. People were slapping each other on the back, beaming all over their faces, and Sam felt the relief like a shot of hard liquor. The Mayestrans had screwed up somehow, or maybe the *Lyre's* crew really had disabled enough of the explosive devices to save the ship... and the fleet. Either way, they'd come through the ordeal unscathed.

'All right, that's enough!' called Pretin, who'd been cheering with the rest of them. 'Ted, put together those working parties. I want access to the bridge, and I want comms up. There's still plenty to do, people!'

At that moment an engineer entered the situation room. He looked tired, and Sam realised he must have spent the past hour or two running all over the ship looking for the explosives.

'Sir,' said the man. 'I need to speak with you.'

'Out with it,' said Pretin.

The man held up a small yellow block. 'This is one of the charges.' He saw the commander's expression. 'Don't worry, it's safe. But the thing is, it's not powerful enough.'

'I know. We barely heard the explosions.'

'That's not what I meant, sir.' The engineer turned the cube over. 'It's not pure. It's been doctored with some kind of inert substance.'

There was a hush in the situation room.

'You mean it was sabotaged?' demanded Pretin.

'No sir. It was made like this.'

'But that means...' Pretin took the explosive and examined it. 'They *weren't* trying to blow the *Lyre* apart?'

The engineer shook his head. 'That stuff would barely part your hair.' He eyed Pretin's bald pate and blanched. 'I mean–'

'Yes, yes,' said Pretin, gesturing impatiently. 'But if that's the case, what was the point of this entire exercise? What were the Mayestrans hoping to achieve, if they weren't trying to blow the *Lyre* apart and damage the fleet?'

'That's not the only thing, sir. My people finally gained access to the core chamber, and there's no sign of tampering. Even if these explosives had managed to split the hull open, the core wouldn't have ruptured.'

'How'd you like that,' someone called out. 'The Mayestrans were let down by their own incompetence.'

Pretin shook his head. 'I've been fighting this enemy my entire life. I refuse to believe the Mayestrans would go to these lengths only to fall at the last hurdle. There's something else. We're missing their coup de grace.'

207

'Sir, a dockyard vessel is approaching hangar three.'

Pretin grabbed a handset. 'I'm coming down. Don't let them leave until I speak with them, you hear?'

'Yes sir.'

Pretin had barely finished speaking when the lights went out with a bang. In the sudden darkness, vicious bolts of lightning flashed across the situation room, felling half a dozen of the crew unlucky enough to be standing in the way.

'Down!' shouted Sam, throwing herself to the deck. She covered her head with her hands and squeezed her eyes shut as the powerful discharges flickered and flashed around the room, shattering screens, blowing up electronic terminals, and melting wiring.

Suddenly, Sam felt herself floating, and with a shock she realised the gravity generators had gone out. Looking around, she saw helpless crew members tumbling in mid-air, many struggling in vain to regain the deck. Even as she watched, lightning passed through several of them, and they jerked uncontrollably before floating away, as still as corpses.

Finally, the electrical storm died down, until everything was silent. Silent, that is, apart from the groans and coughs of the wounded, and the spark and crackle of fried electronics.

Soft emergency lighting came on, barely enough to see by, and Sam felt a gentle tug towards the deck as the gravity generators came back in low-power mode. Her feet touched the deck and she moved towards the nearest casualty, only to take a great flying leap which had her fending off from the far wall. All around the situation room, she saw others struggling to adjust to the low gravity, while at their feet unconscious crew members lay huddled on the deck.

Sam managed to reach the nearest casualty, and she saw it was Anna. The sleeve of her flight suit had been slashed open by the discharge, and her forearm was red and raw. 'Leave me, I'm fine,' said the pilot, gritting her teeth. 'Check the others first.'

Sam did so, and she encountered Monitor Pretin next. He was lying on his side, eyes closed and face deathly white, and for a second she thought he was dead. She found a pulse though, and she saw his arm move as he started to regain consciousness. 'Lie still, sir. Wait for a medic.'

Pretin gripped her hand. 'Wh-what happened?'

'There was a massive power surge.'

'Mayestrans? Got to stop them. Might be more...more...' His voice faded, and Sam felt Pretin's grip relax as he lost consciousness once more.

Then someone crouched beside Sam, eased her aside. 'I'll look after him. You should take some of the crew and get the power back on.'

'David's in charge. He's the senior officer now.'

'Richett, the flight leader? He's out cold. Took a blast in the chest.' The man looked up at her. 'There was a shuttle docking in the bay. Maybe you could ask them to take our casualties off? We could use a team to help with the walking wounded, too.'

Sam barely heard him. She was looking across the darkened room to a figure lying motionless on the deck. It was David, and a couple of people were crouched beside him, tending to his wounds. She wanted to help, to see how he was, but with her basic first aid she knew she'd only get in the way. Instead, she decided to follow the advice she'd been give. 'Listen up,' she said, raising her voice. 'Anyone who doesn't need medical assistance, please clear this area. Any techs or engineers, with me. We need to find out what caused this, and maybe get the power back up if it's safe.'

Three others joined her, Piet amongst them. 'I may not be an engineer or a tech,' he said, 'but you may need someone to open all the airlock doors by hand.'

They left the situation room and almost ran into someone coming the other way. It was one of the engineers, coming to report, and he followed Sam's group back down the passageway, recounting what he knew. 'Something drew an immense amount of power, and I'm guessing it was an EM generator.'

'EM?'

'Electro-magnetic. Whatever it was, it sent out a massive pulse, tripping all our circuits. I've got someone checking the main distribution panel, but I could use some more help.'

Sam indicated the techs accompanying her and Piet. 'They can go with you. But before you get the power back on, make sure it's not going to trigger another pulse.'

'Yes sir.'

The three crew members departed at a run, and Sam turned to Piet. 'We're going to the hangar. Before the pulse, a shuttle was coming in to dock. We need to warn them about the Mayestrans so they can get a message to the dockyard...and the fleet.'

Piet snorted. 'If that EM pulse was as big as the engineer said it was, I think the entire fleet will be alerted by now.'

'Oh *shit*.' Sam stopped dead. 'They weren't trying to blow the *Golden Lyre* apart at all. That was just a diversion to keep us busy!'

'It certainly worked,' remarked Piet.

'Yeah, but don't you see? They must have hidden this pulse generator on board, and it was timed to go off when we reached the shipyard.'

'Explosions or EM pulses, what's the difference?' asked Piet, with a shrug. 'It's still an attack.'

Sam pointed a shaking finger at the bulkhead. 'The Second Fleet is out there, all around us. What if that huge electrical pulse tripped the circuits on every vessel? What if the dockyard defences, the fighters, the gun batteries... what if they're all disabled right now?' She saw Piet's expression as realisation dawned. 'Exactly. Our fleet is completely helpless. Now imagine a dozen Phase IIIs and a Mayestran cruiser let loose amongst them. It'll be total carnage.'

'They'll destroy every last vessel,' breathed Piet. 'The fleet, the dockyard... there'll be nothing left.'

'Right, whereas blowing up the *Lyre* might have damaged two or three ships at best.' Now that the full extent of the Mayestran plan was revealed, Sam realised just how clever it was. From the start, the Mayestrans had foreseen their enemy's response to each new threat, and at every turn the Henerians had blundered straight into the trap. Now the jaws had finally snapped shut, and the result was going to be an incalculable loss of lives and ships.

'So how are we going to stop them?' asked Piet.

Sam almost laughed at his confidence, but she knew it was a serious question. 'Piet, we have two Kestrels against the entire Mayestran strike force... and that's assuming our fighters haven't been fried by the pulse.'

'They weren't powered up when the pulse hit,' Piet pointed out. 'A tech might be able to fire them up. Reboot them, maybe.'

And then what? Sam wanted to yell at him. *What can two trainee pilots possibly achieve against such overwhelming numbers?*

36

Sam and Piet passed through the first airlock, struggling to open and close the heavy doors. Slowly, they'd manage to get a big enough gap to pass through, and then they had to fight just as hard to close the doors again.

'We could leave them open,' suggested Piet.

'No, too risky. A hull breach in the next section could kill everyone in the situation room.'

Once they were finally clear of the airlock, they took the corridor to the nearest stairwell, covering five metres at a time thanks to the low gravity. Sam decided there was no point even trying the lifts, not with the reduced power.

They bounded down the stairs, heading for the hangar deck. On the way they passed a porthole, and Sam paused to look out onto space. To her surprise there was no sign of the fleet. In fact, she couldn't see anything at all.

'Where are our ships?' asked Piet.

Sam cupped her hands to the porthole, shading her eyes from the dim light behind her. As her eyes adjusted to the darkness she began to pick out the brightest stars, and slowly the rest of the rich starfield came into view...apart from numerous patches of total darkness. She realised these were the outlines of the friendly ships comprising the Second Fleet, and they were as lifeless and as dead as the Golden Lyre. Even as she watched, one of them flickered with electrical energy, a ripple of blue lightning that passed from one end to the other, encircling the entire hull. 'They're all helpless,' she breathed.

'What was that?' demanded Piet, pointing into the distance.

Sam saw it too – a yellow flash, tiny and remote. It happened again, and with a sick feeling she saw flickering tracers of blaster cannon. 'The Mayestrans are attacking,' she said urgently. 'They're hitting our ships and we can't fight back.'

There was another yellow flash as a ship was hit, and Piet turned and ran down the next flight of stairs with Sam hot on his heels. In low gravity they were forced to haul themselves downwards using the balustrade, and at each turn in the staircase they swung around wildly before throwing themselves down the next flight.

By the time they reached the hangar deck they were out of breath. The thought of the helpless fleet spurred them on, though, and they burst into the corridor and sprinted for the hangar. The airlock stood open, and Piet darted inside and prepared to use his strength on the second set of doors, only for Sam to grab his arms. 'No! Check the force field is up!'

They peered through the misted porthole, and to Sam's relief the sparkling blue force field still covered the hangar entrance. As a critical system, she guessed it was prioritised above everything else. 'Okay, let's go.'

Sam closed the doors behind them while Piet opened the doors leading to the hangar, and then they ran past the ruined fighters to reach the two remaining Kestrels. A couple of elderly techs were busy with each fighter, and Sam groaned as she saw the open access panels below the cockpit.

'We thought you might be needing these,' said one of the

techs, a grey-haired man of around sixty. 'Give us a few moments and we'll have them reset and ready to go.

'We don't have any time. We need them now!' Sam gestured at the hangar entrance, where the one-sided battle could be seen in the distance. 'Our people are getting slaughtered out there.'

'Unless you want to push these things into battle, you'll just have to wait.' The tech turned his back on her and resumed his work on the fighter's internals.

Sam was desperate to join the fight, but she could tell the techs were working as quickly as possible. On the way to the hangar she had no clue whether the fighters would even be useable, so she accepted the delay with as much patience as she could muster.

'You might as well get in,' called the tech over his shoulder. 'We've been doing this job for forty years, and you're not going to make things any quicker by breathing down our necks.'

Sam dragged herself up the ladder with a single pull, and she settled in the fighter's cockpit, putting the helmet on and connecting herself into the flight systems. Across the way she saw Piet doing the same, his face set and expressionless. Sam understood how he felt, because they both knew this was a one-way flight. They could put up a show of resistance, maybe hold the Mayestrans off for a few minutes, but the outcome was inevitable. She just hoped that all over the fleet, other ground crew were desperately trying to ready and launch their own fighters.

There was a huge flash in the distance, and Sam looked up to see a spreading cloud of debris shot through with twisting streamers of flame. One of the fleet's bigger ships had just been ripped apart by a massive explosion, the first victim of the Mayestrans' sneak attack. The light reflected off the hulls of dozens of nearby ships, and she wondered how long it would be before the fleet could rally its defences and fight back.

'Okay, you're set!' called the nearest tech. 'Good luck out there.'

Sam gestured her thanks, then activated the flight systems and closed the canopy. She saw the console lighting up, the displays initially filled with diagnostic logs before they showed the familiar dials and instruments. Then, crossing her fingers, she lit up the main drives.

There was a steady roar, and Sam activated her mic. 'Piet, I'll take point. Follow me out, over.'

'Copy Red Leader. All systems go.'

Sam lifted off and eased away from the landing pad, conscious of the tech sheltering behind a low wall. Blast for the exit, and her wash might have thrown him across the hangar. When she judged she'd gone far enough though, she opened the throttles and the Kestrel rocketed through the force field. '*Golden Lyre* defences to all ships,' she transmitted. 'Does anyone read, over?'

There was no reply, and Sam gripped the flight stick, her eyes scanning the HUD inside her visor. For now it was just her and Piet against the entire Mayestran force.

37

Even as she turned her ship towards the distant battle, Sam knew it was going to be hopeless. She knew there were Phase IIIs ahead, because she could see their gunfire and the fiery red splashes as they hit their targets, but the enemy cruiser was suppressing their signals, meaning she couldn't see the fighters on her HUD. Occasionally there'd be a flicker, but nothing she could hunt down and destroy.

For an action like this she needed tactical operations – TacOps – to back her up, to cut through the whirling cloud of fighters and assign targets, and to watch her back and to keep her as safe as possible. She herself had once been a trainee in TacOps, and she knew how vital it was in a battle involving capital ships. The scanner aboard a cruiser or a battleship was far more powerful than the compact unit in her own fighter, and could counteract enemy jamming and fake signals in order to guide friendly fighters.

Unfortunately, with comms down and terminal screens dead right across the fleet, there was nobody to guide her, and no friendly voice in her ear to warn of Phase IIIs on her tail. She would be fighting blind, all but helpless.

Briefly, Sam considered a do-or-die charge directly at the Mayestran cruiser, but that was pointless. The enemy would see her coming, and their guns would shred her and Piet before either Kestrel got close.

A searing beam of light cut across her vision, close now, and she realised the enemy cruiser had fired its main guns. She saw a Henerian destroyer almost cut in two by the blast, a huge glowing cavity appearing in its flanks as if by magic. How many had just lost their lives, she wondered.

'Red Leader, this is the Golden Lyre. Do you copy?'

Sam jumped as the voice rang in her ears, loud and confident. Then she grinned, because it was none other than Monitor Pretin. 'Copy you loud and clear, Lyre.'

'TacOps is now operational, Sam. Transmitting vectors towards a suitable target.'

Sam's spirits soared at the news. Sure, she and Piet were still facing inevitable death, but now there was a chance they could take a few of the enemy fighters with them. 'You just made my day, Monitor.'

'Don't be too hasty with the thanks,' said Pretin drily. *'I may teach this subject in class, but it's years since I directed a live battle.'*

'Sooner you than anyone else, sir.' Quickly, Sam adjusted course until she was on the vector Pretin had sent her. Despite his self-deprecating words, her old tutor was a wily fox with decades of experience. Time and again he'd demonstrated moves in class which had left the students scratching their heads, or looking completely foolish. More than one had accusing him of rigging the training battles in his favour... only to lose to their tutor by double the margin in the next match-up. 'Piet, close up on my six. We need to hit them hard, before they know what's going on.'

'Got that, Sam.'

The second fighter got closer, until Sam was satisfied. Then Pretin sent her a course adjustment, and she saw the target's

217

heading and speed on her HUD. The enemy fighter was attacking a destroyer, its blaster shots like repeated pinpricks against the much larger vessel. But, as Sam knew, enough such pinpricks could eventually tear apart a whole planet, never mind a defenceless ship.

She closed with the target, and as the distance narrowed she spotted the fighter through her cockpit. It was a Phase III, and it was turning sharply to unleash another burst on the helpless destroyer. Sam saw the flicker of its guns as it opened fire, and then, as it swam across her sights, she opened up. A murderous stream of blaster fire closed the distance to her target in the blink of an eye, and then the graceful enemy ship was torn to fragments, the pilot given no chance to react. There was a brief detonation as the fuel tank went up, and Sam roared away on a tangent to avoid the debris from her kill. 'Splash one,' she said curtly.

'Next target on your HUD,' replied Pretin.

Sam turned towards the enemy, only to receive a gentle reminder.

'Follow the vectors, Sam. I sent them for a reason.'

Sam saw the waypoints on her HUD, leading her around the far side of a cruiser. The enemy fighter, her target, was on the near side, and she understood the tactic immediately. By using the bigger ship for cover she'd slot in right behind the Phase III, just as they were turning away from their latest pass on the cruiser. Tucked into their blind spot, she could take them completely by surprise.

Tearing along the cruiser's underbelly, so close she could almost reach out and touch the smooth hull, Sam felt the sensation of raw speed and power as something visceral. Her senses were alive, her entire body focused on finding and killing the enemy. Of course, the Mayestrans would soon realise what was happening, especially if their fighters kept winking out, but then they'd be forced to hunt her and Piet down in the maze of capital ships, and that would only buy the defenders more precious time. It wasn't about winning the battle, it was all about holding on long enough for the Second Fleet to rise from the canvas and start fighting back.

'*Closing on target,*' said Monitor Pretin. '*Stay focused now, and prepare to engage.*'

'*Golden Lyre, this is Dockyard Control,*' said a female voice, breaking in. '*Our TacOps is now operational, and we'd ask you to—*'

'*Stay out of this, Control,*' said Monitor Pretin sharply. '*Those are* my *people out there.*'

'*We have seniority, Lyre. I'm ordering you to—*'

'*Will you get off the air this instant!*' roared Pretin, more incensed than Sam had ever heard him. In fact, she couldn't recall him raising his voice to anyone, and the sound of his anger was scarier than a whole squadron of Phase IIIs.

'*Very well. You have TacOps,*' said the operator, sounding miffed.

'*Interfering bloody pencil pushers,*' growled Pretin, and Sam wondered whether he'd transmitted the comment on purpose. But then she spotted the Phase III, and her focus returned to the battle. She lined up on the target, and was about to open fire when the pilot must have sensed the danger. The ship darted sideways, and her burst of fire shot past harmlessly. Cursing, she brought the nose of her Kestrel round... just as Piet opened up on the enemy. His shooting was dead-on, and she saw the ripple of flashes as his blaster fire travelled from the Phase III's nose all the way to its tail, penetrating the hull, smashing through the canopy and ending the pilot where he sat. The ship disintegrated, trailing a cloud of smaller particles, but there was no time to waste on their latest victim, because Pretin was already vectoring her towards the next attacker.

'Good one, Piet. Nice shooting.'

'It was about time I hit something,' said the other pilot. *'Normally they hit me first.'*

Sam eyed the HUD and frowned. This time there were two fighters, and they were harrying a destroyer in concert. She raced towards the confrontation and saw spot fires gleamed from the larger vessel where the enemy attacks were hitting home. Even as Sam watched she saw an explosion from one of the destroyer's rear-mounted drive clusters, the blast hurling spinning fragments of hull into space. Once, during a lecture, Sam had asked Aren Grant what the chances were of running into a piece of debris during combat. Grant had replied that she had nothing to worry about, because space was big... really, *really* big.

She wondered what had caused Grant to betray the Henerians, then put the tutor out of her mind. The debrief, the questions, would come later, after the battle. Then Sam remembered the odds against her and Piet, and she smiled grimly. Others would have to worry about Grant, not her.

They lined up on the two fighters, and as before their approach was noted by the enemy. For a few seconds there was a deadly chase, the enemy splitting up and hurling their ships around in space, trying to avoid the pursuers. For their part, Sam and Piet stuck to their respective targets, anticipating and following every move. Gunfire flickered in both directions, as the Phase III turned in its own length to bring its nose to bear on Sam's fighter, but she flew sideways to avoid the stream of blaster fire. Her own gun was firing, and she twitched the Kestrel's nose to the right, catching the Phase III with a glancing shot that blasted it directly below the canopy. She saw a flash light up the cockpit interior, the pilot already dead, and then a larger explosion as the fighter went up. Then she eyed her HUD, looking for Piet. He was engaged in a desperate battle with the second fighter, the two of them circling and firing as each tried to kill the other.

The fight was taking place right next to a destroyer, the huge slab-sided hull reflecting frantic blaster fire. Sam gauged their course, then picked her target and roared in, guns blazing. Her shots caught the enemy pilot unawares, concentrating as he was on Piet's ship, and Sam's lips tightened as the Phase III shook and flashed under her withering burst.

The pilot managed to roll his stricken ship away, evading the rest of her deadly cone of fire. Sam applied a delicate touch to the controls, bringing the Kestrel's nose round, and her second burst blasted the rear thrusters right off the Phase III. Without directional control, the ship flipped over and over, spinning through space until it slammed into the destroyer's armoured hull, which was about as unyielding as a sheer rock face. The Phase III split open with a vivid flash, leaving a dark scorchmark and very little else.

'Thanks Sam,' called Piet. 'He was getting the better of me.'

'Any hits?'

'Negative. All good.'

'Red Flight, TacOps here. The enemy are onto you, and they're forming up.'

Sam knew the surprise couldn't last, and here was the proof. The easy kills were over, and now she and Piet were about to become the hunted.

'Follow my vector to avoid the first flight,' said Pretin, his voice calm. 'We have no defensive weapons, so if they get close to the Lyre we're done for.'

Sam tracked the heading on the HUD, and saw that Pretin

was directing them on a long, curved course which would take them outside the area occupied by the fleet before bringing them back in range of... the *Golden Lyre*. That made absolutely no sense, given his warning about the ship's defences, but she wasn't about to disobey his orders. No, she didn't want him yelling at *her*, thank you very much. So, she turned onto the new course and opened up the throttles, roaring away from the pitched battles going on behind her. It felt like running away, especially when she saw five red dots on her HUD turn to follow. They'd catch up with her and Piet just as they reached the *Golden Lyre*, and two against five would make for a brief, pointless struggle.

Then those five fighters would turn their guns on the *Lyre*.

As she rocketed towards the old battleship with Piet in close company, Sam wondered what Pretin was playing at, because from what she could tell he'd just signed the *Golden Lyre's* death warrant.

38

Sam and Piet roared towards the *Golden Lyre's* position, weaving like crazy. All thoughts of maintaining a neat formation had gone out the window as the Mayestran fighters fell on them, and blaster fire criss-crossed the area of space immediately surrounding Sam's cockpit as the enemy did their best to take her out.

She pulled every trick she'd learned in her brief stints as a combat pilot, plus a few she'd learned from her brother during his infrequent visits over the years. Piet, with far less training, was struggling to survive, his fighter already having survived some very near misses.

All the while Sam followed Monitor Pretor's waypoints, flying the proscribed course as best she could with the enemy on her tail. 'Piet, go to thrust mode three. We've got to get ahead.'

'*Confirmed, Red Leader,*' said Piet, sounding rushed. And no wonder, because the enemy had his range and he was hanging on by a thread.

Sam remembered David telling his training flight about the special mode, that the emergency power was for use in life-threatening emergencies only. She'd laughed at that, because what part of fighter combat *wasn't* life-threatening? Sure, there was a risk the engines might blow, but there was a certainty the Mayestrans would get them if they couldn't increase the range.

Both of them activated the extra boost, and Sam winced as the engine note rose to a tortured howl. It felt like the fighter was shaking itself to pieces around her, but the HUD showed they were definitely outpacing the Phase IIIs. Then she saw the red lights flashing all over her console. 'Okay, cut the extra boost,' she told Piet.

The burst of extra speed had given them some breathing space, and now that the Kestrels were travelling faster, the Mayestrans would never catch them. There was no drag in space and Sam's ship wouldn't slow again until she reversed the thrusters. Unfortunately, the enemy was still in gunnery range for the time being, and shots were still coming uncomfortably close.

To help Piet out, Sam flipped her fighter over until the nose was facing backwards, past Piet's cockpit. Travelling in reverse, but still moving in her original direction, she opened fire. Her shots lanced past Piet's ship, illuminating his canopy and fuselage, and she saw the enemy scatter as the bolts blasted through their formation. She knew they'd be back on her tail soon enough, but a glance at the final waypoint told her the manoeuvre might just have bought them the time they needed. 'Piet, course adjust. Transmitting now.'

The two fighters moved as one, firing their side thrusters as they approached the waypoint. It took longer to adjust course than expected, thanks to their extreme speed, but once they were on the new vector Sam saw the Golden Lyre ahead. Unfortunately, the direction change had also burned off forward momentum, and the Phase IIIs were catching them. Somehow, the enemy pilots had anticipated her course change, and they'd started theirs sooner, with the result that they were now cutting across the arc of Sam's course. From what she could tell, the five enemy fighters and the two Kestrels would all arrive in the Golden Lyre's vicinity at the exact same time.

'*Shit, we're screwed,*' growled Piet, as he came to the same conclusion.

Sam looked around, but there was no escape. Any change in direction now would just slow her down even more, and no shooting, however fancy, could take out five enemy ships before they could blast her. 'Piet, flip around. Fire at them long range.'

Both fighters turned to face the enemy, and Sam fired burst after burst at the unseen Phase IIIs. It was more defiance than anything, because at that range there was zero chance of a hit. 'TacOps, this is Red Leader. Coming in hot, five bandits in pursuit.'

'*Copy Red Leader,*' said Pretin. '*Stand by.*'

Stand *by*? Sam bit off a sharp retort as she heard the useless instruction. Not only was he flanneling her, but Monitor Pretin sounded as calm as a schoolteacher checking attendance. She wanted to shout at him, to get him to understand the hopeless situation he'd thrust her and Piet into, but something held her back. As long as the Phase IIIs were chasing her, they weren't blasting away at the fleet. Pretin could be sacrificing her and Piet to save many more lives, and in that context she knew it made sense.

'*TacOps, this is Kestrel six-eight. Permission to join red flight?*'

Sam didn't wait for Pretin to speak. The new voice was male and sounded close, and she needed all the help she could get. 'Sure, six-eight. With five bogies on intercept we can use you for sure.'

'Welcome, six-eight,' said Pretin calmly. 'You are designated Red Three. Join the flight and await further orders.'

'Roger that,' said the newcomer.

'Where did you come from, Three?' demanded Sam.

'The light cruiser Pallax. They're working like crazy to launch more fighters, but for now it's just me.' He hesitated. 'Say, how did you get your birds up so fast? Are your hangers shielded or something?'

Sam glanced to her left. Somewhere out there, five Phase IIIs were on an intercept course, and it seemed like a strange time to hold a conversation. Then again, what else was she meant to do? 'Not shielded, no. The Golden Lyre is a training ship, and the crew is...' she was going to say ancient, but Monitor Pretin would be listening. 'They're all close to retirement, but after years in the service they sure know their stuff.'

'Red Flight, cease chatter,' said Monitor Pretin sharply.

Despite his tone, Sam thought she detected a hint of a grin in his voice. Or maybe it was an artifact from the enemy jamming. 'Roger TacOps.'

Without warning, streamers of blaster fire came out of the darkness to her left. They went wide, but some came uncomfortably close as the enemy adjusted their aim. Sam shifted her fighter upwards, anticipating the next burst, and she wasn't overly surprised when it passed right through her previous position. The fighters accompanying her had followed the move, and all three powered on through empty space, unharmed. 'They're just getting the range,' commented Sam. Ahead, she could now make out the Golden Lyre as a bright speck in space, while to her right the unseen Second Fleet was even now battling to launch more fighters, power up their disabled gun batteries, and finally put up a fight.

The Lyre grew rapidly, and Sam felt a lump in her throat as

she roared towards the grand old ship. It had been her first posting, and she didn't want it to be her last.

More flashes came out of the darkness to the left, and Sam ordered her flight to fire back. All three Kestrels spat streams of bolts at the enemy fighters, and Sam hoped just one of the tiny specks got through.

'Red Flight, immediate turn right. Power mode three, execute!'

Sam didn't hesitate. She threw the fighter round and hit the boost, holding on tight as the cockpit seemed to whirl around her. The engines snarled and she gripped the flight stick, hunching down as she imagined the enemy fighters lining her up for a final, withering shot from their guns.

Then came flashes of light, glaring beams which all but blinded her. The endless night of deep space was suddenly turned to daylight by rampaging gunfire. There were even brighter flashes too, and Sam imagined the shots tearing Piet and the unknown pilot flying Red Three to pieces, their final breaths consisting of nothing but vacuum, fire, metal fragments.

Sam felt a sudden anger, and she swore under her breath. She wasn't going to die running away, she was going to face her enemy like a true fighter pilot. Flipping her ship around, she prepared to unleash one final burst before the Phase IIIs got her... and then she froze.

The scene that met her eyes was so unexpected, she was unable to react. Instead of seeing the spreading fragments of Piet and Red Three's fighters, she was looking at the huge fireballs which were all that remained of a pair of pursuing Phase IIIs. The streams of blaster fire criss-crossing space weren't coming from the enemy, they were coming from the *Golden Lyre!* Even as she watched, the gunners found their mark, and a third Phase III was shredded by the powerful weapons. Somehow, the Lyre's crew had got their defensive turrets up, and Pretin's odd waypoints had been a ruse to bring as many Mayestran fighters into close proximity with the old battleship, ensuring the hail of fire would catch them by surprise.

Three of the five had already been blasted, and their pilots would take that surprise to their graves. The other two, aware of the terrible danger, were doing everything they could to get away. Unfortunately, by pursuing Sam and Piet at top speed, they'd committed themselves to a course that would take them directly past the Golden Lyre. No matter how much thrust they deployed, or where they pointed their fighters, the laws of of physics meant they were doomed.

She saw one of the fighters trying to escape by lifting his nose and firing his engines at full power. This had the effect of slowly adjusting his course, so that he continued to fly towards the Lyre while slowly, slowly moving up and away. The gun turrets tracked him easily, and the pilot died in the burning explosion which claimed his once-proud fighter.

The other pilot flipped his fighter over and tried to bring it to a stop, in order to boost directly away from the Lyre. That was an even worse choice than the first pilot's, because all this manoeuvre achieved was to make the Phase III fly directly towards the Lyre's guns, the blaze of its exhaust giving the gunners the perfect aiming spot. At that range they couldn't miss, and the Phase III just... vanished.

'Nice work, TacOps,' said Sam, and she realised her voice was shaking.

'No chatter,' said Pretin. Then he relented. 'Thank you all, Red Flight. You followed your instructions to the letter.'

'Don't thank me,' said Red Three. 'I only showed up for the end.'

39

As Sam turned towards the *Golden Lyre* she saw the ship was ablaze with light. The power was on, the defences were up and now, hopefully, the battleship could join the fight against the Mayestran cruiser and the remaining Phase IIIs. The enemy would know that their fighters had been lost, and Sam hoped they were shocked by the stiff resistance the 'helpless' Henerians were putting up.

Having accounted for at least eight fighters, she calculated the enemy might have no more than four more at their disposal. Once the Henerians launched a few more Kestrels, the attacking cruiser would have no choice but to flee.

'*Red Flight,*' said Pretin, '*turn to the indicated heading and prepare to offer close support. We're going to stop that cruiser.*'

Sam obeyed, and out the corner of her eye she saw the immense flare as the *Golden Lyre's* main drives fired. Smaller attitude thrusters adjusted her course, and soon the huge battleship was powering towards the enemy's position. The three Kestrels took point, ready to ward off any incoming attackers... although Sam could still picture the battleship's defences ripping apart the Phase IIIs, and she wasn't sure the escort was entirely necessary. Still, it felt good. In fact, it felt like she was taking a professional boxer to school in order to settle a playground grudge. The Mayestran cruiser might be newer and faster, had already beaten the *Lyre* into submission once, but Sam reckoned the show of force and the looming threat of the entire Second Fleet would have the enemy jumping to safety in no time.

'TacOps, how did you get your defences up so quickly?' asked Red Three. *'The rest of the fleet are still looking around for torches.'*

Monitor Pretin chuckled. *'As Sam told you, the Lyre has a much older crew than usual. When you've spent as long as we have in this game, you learn a few tricks they don't teach you in the academy.'*

'But–'

'Red Three, that Mayestran cruiser is attacking our ships while you're busy asking questions. Please be silent and stand by for further orders.'

The *Lyre* turned onto her new heading in a big, lumbering arc, and then Sam's flight of three Kestrels formed up to provide cover. They flew in convoy, heading past the rest of the fleet as they made for the distant flashes and explosions of the ongoing battle. On the way Sam noticed several other ships in the fleet coming to life at last, although the only evidence was a handful of riding lights.

'TacOps, Kestrels six-four and six-five reporting for duty.'

'Roger, Kestrels four and five,' said Pretin. *'You're attached to Red Flight. Keep the same designations.'*

Sam glanced left then right, and spotted the new arrivals joining her flight. 'Welcome aboard, Red Four and Red Five. We've got some trade ahead, but we'll try and leave some for you.'

'Copy that. Sorry we're late to the party. It took a while to get ready, over.'

'Better late than never,' remarked Sam.

'Just point me in the right direction and I'll blast that enemy cruiser into scrap.'

'Negative Red Four,' said Sam quickly. 'They've got dozens of our people on board.'

'Shit. That's going to make life difficult.'

Silently, Sam agreed with him. It was bad enough taking on the enemy raider with one old battleship and a handful of fighters, but worse still that they couldn't just blast away at will. They'd have to go for the defences, perhaps try and disable the engines... although as one of the Golden Lyre's engineers had pointed out earlier, that was a huge risk.

'Red Flight, this is TacOps. I want to remind you that the first priority is to defend the Second Fleet. If there's no other option, that cruiser will have to be destroyed... whatever the cost. Those are your orders, on my authority.'

Sam flew on in silence. Monitor Pretin had the most to lose in the coming encounter, because almost the entire crew of the *Golden Lyre* was aboard the enemy ship. All of the elderly tutor's colleagues, his friends, and his senior officers... all their lives were in the balance, and she couldn't begin to imagine what it had taken for Pretin to give the kill order. 'Copy, TacOps. Let's hope it doesn't come to that.'

They were approaching the cruiser now, the ship represented by a large red circle in Sam's HUD. There were half a dozen enemy fighters too, all of them having broken off their attacks to protect the capital ship. *Surely they know it's over,* thought Sam. *Why don't they just leave?*

The answer was alongside her, in the shape of the *Golden Lyre*. Old, battered, and with nothing more than a makeshift crew, the Mayestrans saw her as easy meat. Take out the *Lyre* and the Kestrels flying in close support, and the enemy cruiser could resume its attacks on the rest of the fleet. How many additional capital ships would they take out before they finally fled the scene? Four? Five? Even one more was too many.

'Red Flight, we're going to hit the cruiser's main guns,' she transmitted. 'It's the only way to save the fleet.' It felt odd to be giving orders when some of the other Kestrel pilots were no doubt seasoned officers with years of experience, but Sam had been leading the defence from the very start, and she guessed Monitor Pretin didn't want to get everyone's rank and service history in the middle of a fight. They could sort out the chain of command once the cruiser had been stopped in its tracks. For that matter, the elderly TacOps tutor had suddenly found himself commanding a battleship, and the other pilots probably outranked him too.

Suddenly, a burst of heavy gunfire spat out of the darkness ahead, flashing between Red Flight's ships. Sam was leading the pilots straight in, and her instinct was to fly a tangent to make her ships a little harder to hit. Unfortunately, that would leave the *Golden Lyre* defenceless against any Phase IIIs the enemy might send against the battleship, and so she had no choice but to fly a steady course. Well, *she* did, at least. 'Red Four and Five. Break off and approach the carrier from either side. Try and draw their fire, but don't make yourselves an easy target.'

'Copy that.'

Two Kestrels split from the flight, tearing away into the darkness. Sam saw the glow of their exhausts fading as they sped away, and she hoped the enemy would confuse the single ships with a much larger attacking force. She knew the *Lyre* would be jamming the enemy's scanners for all she was worth, and with luck the ghost-like images on the Mayestran's TacOps screens might look like flights of fighters instead of two lone wolves.

There was a flash of light as the Golden Lyre fired her one remaining turret, the other having been destroyed when she was captured. The searing beams of fire stretched into the distance, and there was a muted flash as they hit their target. Then came the answering fire, four heavy beams worth, and Sam winced as one of the beams tore along the *Lyre's* flank, ripping open her hull.

'*Red Flight, leave us,*' said Pretin urgently. '*Don't worry about defending us from their fighters. Go and get their turrets, Sam!*'

40

Sam gave the order, and the flight of three Kestrels launched off the mark, leaving the *Lyre* standing in their wake. Smaller tracer fire started to track them, whizzing past with a series of blinding flashes, but the fighters were nimble targets and the enemy gunners were firing at shadows.

As they approached the cruiser, Sam saw it was flying with its broadside towards her. It was a large, sleek vessel, modern and deadly, and as she approached she saw the main guns firing a fresh salvo at the Golden Lyre. 'Red Two and Three, take the for'ard gun turret. I'll go for the rear.'

'*Watch out for fighters Sam,*' called Piet. '*You'll be swamped if they spot you.*'

'Worry about your own target,' replied Sam, as they sped towards the cruiser. The gunfire was heavier now, and she was shifting her fighter around with quick movements on the controls. 'Red Four, do you copy?'

'*I hear you, Red Leader.*'

'Join my six. Red Five, I want you to give those smaller batteries something to think about.' Even as she said it, Sam wondered whether she was sending the unknown pilot to his death. Each of the rapid-fire batteries was capable of shredding a Kestrel at short range, and he'd be facing half a dozen of them... alone. She was about to countermand her order when he heard his voice in her headset.

'Red Five going in.'

Another blast of fire from the *Golden Lyre* flashed by, narrowly missing her ship. Sam saw the shots graze the cruiser's hull, just above the jutting prow, and she squinted as a whole section disintegrated in a fiery explosion. When the glare disappeared, there was a ragged, semi-circular crater where two of the smaller gun batteries had been. It was a risky move, hitting the cruiser like that, and she hoped the *Lyre's* crew weren't being held in that very spot.

Then she forgot the Lyre and the captured crew, and turned her attention to the attack. They were so close that the cruiser's gunners could pick them out against the starfield, and a dozen turrets were spitting death at the incoming Kestrels. The shots came close, too close, and Sam knew it was only a matter of time before one or more of the fighters were hit. Then, ahead and below, she saw a lone Kestrel streaking along the cruiser's hull, blaster fire tearing from the nose guns. The fighter was strafing one turret after another, catching the gunners unawares as they were busy shooting at the four Kestrels on an intercept course. Then one of the turrets swung around to meet the threat, getting off a quick burst, and Sam saw Red Five ripped apart before her eyes.

She felt a stab of fury, and all her insticts screamed at her to follow Red Five in, blasting those smaller turrets into slag and reducing the gunners to a few handfuls of ash. But she knew the larger batteries were the priority, and with an effort she reined in her anger and targeted the big gun turret at the rear of the ship. Even as she flew towards it, the turret fired on the *Lyre* once more, the big gun barrels recoiling as they hurled the massive energy blast towards the battleship. A return blast from the *Lyre* missed the turret by a whisker, instead burning a molten furrow across the cruiser's foredeck. Even as she dived on the gun battery, Sam could see a cloud of vapour pouring from the scar, shot through with electrical sparks and thousands of glittering fragments. Then she lined up her sight right between the big barrels, and squeezed the trigger. Flashes and explosions rippled across the heavy armour, and she saw one of the barrels spinning away as her shots tore it out at the roots. The second split open, spewing jets of flame, and then the armoured turret blew up. Just before Sam pulled out of her dive she saw half a dozen tiny figures cartwheeling into space, jerking uncontrollably as the hard vacuum sucked the life from their bodies.

Then a series of shots flashed across her cockpit, and she felt a massive impact from the rear of her ship. A two-tone buzzer sounded, and as the cockpit filled with smoke she saw a dozen warning lights blinking on the console. Her starboard engine had taken a direct hit, destroying it, and her first action was to shut down the fuel supply. Then she applied full power to the remaining engine and weaved for all she was worth, hoping to put the gunners off as she headed for safety.

'*Red Leader, are you all right?*' called Red Four, sounding concerned.

'I'm down to one engine, but the other's holding. How did the second turret go?'

'*With a bang,*' said Piet, breaking in. '*Red Three didn't make it, though.*'

Sam felt a rush of relief, tinged with regret. If they'd taken out both turrets, the cruiser would be helpless against the *Golden Lyre*. But she'd also lost a fellow pilot, the second during the attack, and she felt it keenly. He'd seemed a friendly type, cheerful and good-natured, and now he was gone.

'They're running for it,' said Piet. 'They're trying to get away!'

'Piet, look out!' shouted Sam, as she saw movement on her HUD. 'The fighters!'

The Phase IIIs had held off until the last second, fearful of attacking the Kestrels in the blazing confusion of fire from the cruiser's guns. But now they pounced with a vengeance, and it was six against three. Make that two and a half, amended Sam, remembering her own damaged craft. On the HUD, she saw half the enemy fighters coming after her, the rest heading to engage Piet and Red Four. Meanwhile, the cruiser had altered course, and was heading for the safety of deep space. If the *Lyre* opened fire now, her shots could hit the engines… and go right through the hull, tearing along the cruiser's interior and killing everything in their path.

'*TacOps to Red Flight. Withdraw to my location, and we'll suppress those fighters.*'

By 'suppress' Pretin meant 'blast out of the sky', and Sam was fine with that. They could deal with the cruiser later. Unfortunately, Piet had other ideas. '*Red Leader, I'm going after the cruiser. Good luck, all.*'

'Piet, no!'

It was too late. Sam could see his ship in the distance, streaking towards the cruiser with two Phase IIIs on his tail. The cruiser couldn't fire at him for fear of hitting their own ships, but she doubted he'd get halfway there before the enemy fighters took him out. Then she saw Red Four turn to follow, bringing his own attendant Phase IIIs with him, and the four sets of ships all tore towards the cruiser line astern, each group firing at the one ahead.

'Oh, sod it,' muttered Sam, and she put her controls over to follow them in. Her wounded fighter reacted sluggishly, but as soon as the Phase IIIs tailing Red Four swam into her sights she opened up, giving them burst after burst of gunfire to think about. She knew she had several of the enemy on her tail as well, and she braced for the withering hail of blaster fire which she was certain was going to rip her apart at any second.

But instead of bothering with her, the Phase IIIs on her tail rocketed past, pursuing Piet. They'd sensed the greater danger, and it certainly wasn't Sam limping into battle in the wounded wreck of a Kestrel.

Sam thought Piet might be going for the smaller turrets again, or the main drives, but instead he flew straight over the ship, from the stern all the way to the bow. And, as he flew over the bridge, from which the senior officers would be leading the battle, he flipped his ship around and opened up with everything he had.

Blaster fire tore into to the front of the superstructure, tearing holes right through the bridge and ripping through the armour-plating at the rear. Piet's ship was still travelling backwards, fast, and as he whipped past the ship's prow he strafed the length of the deck, destroying cable ducts and sensors and communications arrays. Explosion after explosion followed his ship, hurling debris high into space, and the pursuing Phase IIIs were forced to take evasive action as they encountered the cloud of whirling metal. One was too late, and she saw it disintegrate as it ran into the spreading field of debris. Space might be big, thought Sam, but you could still fill it up if you had enough shrapnel.

Then she watched in horror as a pair of Phase IIIs caught up with Piet, their shots tearing his fighter apart until only a tumbling section of hull remained.

41

'TacOps, this is Squadron Leader Fredricks. I have a dozen birds ready for action if you please.'

Sam had just seen Piet killed before her eyes, and she barely heard the calm female voice through her headset.

'I have you on screen, squadron leader,' said Pretin. 'Your designation is Green flight, over.'

'Copy that. Targets in sight, engaging now.'

The remaining Mayestran Phase IIIs turned tail and fled, abandoning the cruiser in their attempts to get away. The cruiser had stopped firing after Piet's brave, stupid, costly attack on the bridge, and was now drifting in space nearby, lifeless. But Sam had eyes only for the wreckage of Piet's fighter. She could just make out the section of cockpit, the nose destroyed, the canopy shattered, and as she nudged her ship closer she saw Piet's legs protruding from the fore section, waving gently. Sickened, she turned away, and then to her surprise she heard a weak voice in her headset.

'I told you I made a good target.'

'Piet?' Stunned, Sam turned to stare at the cockpit. As she did so, a helmeted face popped up over the edge, and Piet managed to wave his gloved hand. 'How the hell did you survive that?'

'Simple. They shot away all the bits I wasn't sitting in,' said Piet.

'Well, hang in there and I'll pick you up.'

Sam got closer and closer, and when she was within reach, the tip of her winglet almost brushing the gently-turning remains of Piet's cockpit, she checked her helmet was sealed before opening her fighter's canopy. The air misted and vanished instantly, and then she saw Piet slowly climbing out of the wreckage of his ship. He managed to stick a hand out and grip Sam's wingtip, pushing off from the cockpit at the same time. The momentum flipped him right over, and he thudded into the surface of the wing with a blow that Sam felt right through the padded seat. Then, recovering, he dragged himself into her fighter and crouched behind her seat.

The canopy came down, and once it was sealed Sam contacted TacOps. 'Red Leader requesting docking. One engine gone, sir, and I don't think I can do much more.'

'Come aboard when ready, Sam,' said Monitor Pretin. *'Incidentally, you'll be happy to hear the enemy cruiser just surrendered. We've done it. We saved the fleet.'*

Sam breathed a sigh of relief, then turned her damaged fighter and headed towards the *Golden Lyre*. All the way there, she noticed explosions going off behind her as the Kestrels dealt with the remaining Phase IIIs, and then the distant flashes died out and she knew the battle had been won.

◆

Sam landed in the familiar surroundings of the Lyre's second docking bay, where she climbed down from the cockpit of her fighter. Piet clambered down after her, his flight suit scorched where the explosion and blaster shots had left their mark.

Nearby there was a fleet shuttle, doors open and the interior empty. Sam remembered it had been approaching the Lyre when the EM pulse went off, and she was glad to see it had landed safely. Then she heard a thunder of footsteps, and she turned to see Monitor Pretin, Anna and several others hurrying towards them. David was there too, following behind, his face pale.

There was a big smile on Pretin's face, and he embraced Sam before giving Piet the once-over. 'Son, have you thought about joining the infantry? You'd save the Navy a fortune.'

'I'm sorry about the fighter, sir.'

Pretin grabbed his hand and shook it enthusiastically. 'Who cares about a single fighter? You captured a cruiser. They'll give you a medal for this!'

'Unless you've got a more famous brother,' murmured David.

Sam gave him a grin, then reeled as Anna clapped her on the shoulder. 'Good job, Sam. Wish I could have been there.'

'How's the arm?'

'It'll heal.'

Sam turned to Pretin. 'Sir, is there any news on Aren Grant? Was she really a Mayestran agent?'

A shadow crossed Monitor Pretin's face. 'She's still unconscious, but believe me, there'll be some questions when she awakens.' He nodded towards the shuttle. 'By the way, the dockyard authorities sent someone to interview you before all of this kicked off, but she's far more interested in Grant now.'

'Question me? Why?'

'When you flew here ahead of the *Golden Lyre* and warned

them the enemy was launching an attack, they didn't believe you, correct?'

Sam recalled the frustrating exchange she'd had with dockyard control when she first arrived in her fighter. 'You could say that.'

'Well, they wanted to charge you with inciting panic, sowing fear, and damaging morale. They were on the way here to arrest you when the EM pulse went off.'

Sam almost laughed. 'Talk about solid proof.'

'Indeed. They spent a terrifying hour trapped in the shuttle, with no power and very little air to breathe. And now, I suspect Aren Grant will suffer the brunt of the investigator's anger.'

'Incoming ships,' shouted someone. 'Clear the bay for incoming shuttles!'

The small group retreated to the rear of the hangar, and they had a perfect view as half a dozen boxy Mayestran shuttles flew through the force field. 'Feels liked a damned invasion,' muttered Pretin, as the pristine white ships settled on their landing legs.

Then there was an excited shout. 'I just got confirmation. It's the rest of the *Lyre's* crew!'

It was true. The nearest shuttle opened its doors, and Commander Hayden strolled down the ramp to the flight deck. He was flanked by two lieutenants, and all three eyed the crowd until they spotted Monitor Pretin. Then Hayden advanced, his face set. 'What have you done to my *ship?*' he demanded.

Pretin was still reaching for an answer when Hayden's face was split by a huge grin, and he took the older man in a tight embrace, slapping him on the shoulder. 'Excellent work,' he cried. 'Truly excellent. Couldn't have asked for a better man.'

The lieutenants saluted Pretin as well, and then Hayden

thanked Sam, Piet and the rest for their efforts. 'You won out against impossible odds. Nobody will forget this day, least of all the Mayestrans.'

Then the senior officers retired to discuss the battle, and the repairs needed to bring the *Golden Lyre* back up to full strength. Meanwhile, crew had been streaming out of the shuttles, and there were joyous reunions as shipmates greeted their comrades. Sam watched the scene, feeling pleased at the outcome. Then, as she eyed the returning prisoners, she realised someone was missing.

Where was Roger Mellish?

42

'Have you seen Mellish?' Sam asked David. 'I can't spot him anywhere.'

David eyed the crowd, then shrugged. 'He's a political officer. They've probably got him quizzing the enemy officers.'

'They'd need a medium for that,' said Sam, as she recalled the way Piet had blown the cruiser's bridge wide open. She was still eyeing the returning crew, but she couldn't see Mellish. 'I hope the Mayestrans didn't...'

'He'll be fine,' said David shortly. 'His kind always make it through.'

'What do you mean?'

'Smooth talking. Charming. You know the sort.'

With a shock, Sam realised David was jealous. There was no time to dwell on it, though, because at that moment Monitor Pretin caught her attention. 'Sam, Commander Hayden has agreed to a tour of the enemy cruiser. The Mayestran crew has been secured, and this could be our one and only chance to inspect an enemy vessel up close.'

He looked excited, and Sam decided this wasn't the time to tell him that she'd already seen the insides of a Mayestran flagship... right before she blew it, and the entire crew, apart. 'That would be most interesting, sir.'

'Piet, Anna, David,' said Pretin, turning to the others. 'Will you come too? After this, the enemy cruiser will be taken apart and examined rivet by rivet, so it's now or never.'

They all agreed, and Pretin gestured towards the nearest shuttle. 'Then let us proceed.'

They entered the shuttle, which had an unfamiliar layout and a scent which Sam couldn't quite put her finger on. It was like a new-car smell, but alien somehow.

'They use similar construction materials to us,' said Pretin. 'Similar, but not identical. Odd, isn't it?'

Sam agreed, then took a seat and buckled up. The shuttle lifted off without fuss, and she had a last view of the Lyre's hangar as the nose swung around. The pilot, a female officer, handled the controls with ease, and before long they were crossing the void between the battleship and the enemy cruiser. Sam could see the signs of battle damage everywhere she looked, and she was amazed either ship had survived.

Traffic was busy as they approached the cruiser, and it looked like every commander in the Henerian fleet had sent a team to study the Mayestran vessel. Sam guessed many of them were hoping to identify a flaw or a weakness which they could exploit the next time they ran into the same type of ship. Either that, or it was just plain curiosity.

As they got closer they joined a couple of Henerian shuttles, and before long they passed through the cruiser's force field and set down in a busy hangar. There were Henerians everywhere, many of them carrying data terminals and files pillaged from the ship back to their shuttles. Others carried armfuls of trophies – everything from propaganda posters to military items to regular, everyday items.

'Someone's going to have to put a stop to this,' muttered Pretin. 'We're going to lose much of value.'

Once, Sam had watched a video of predators tearing a much larger beast apart. This had the same feel. 'Sir, we should try and find Mellish.'

'Who's that?'

'He's the political officer from the training base. The Mayestrans brought him aboard, and nobody's seen him since.'

'Let me ask.' Pretin collared a sentry, who was doing little more than watching the wholesale looting. 'Son, do you know where the prisoners are being held?'

'Next hangar, but they've already been searched. You're better off heading further into the ship.'

Pretin turned away, and the small group of Henerians pushed their way through the crowds until they reached the rear doors. Here, they entered into a passageway, following the signs to the second docking bay. There was a sentry at the door, but he saluted and stepped aside as Pretin explained who they were. Then they passed through into the hangar itself, where they saw about three dozen sorry-looking Mayestrans organised in rows. They were sitting on the deck with their hands secured behind their backs, and many of them looked like they'd been roughed up. As Pretin, Sam and the others entered, there were several wary looks. The rest kept their heads down.

'I'm looking for one of our people,' called Sam. 'Roger Mellish, a civilian. You brought him aboard when you abandoned the *Golden Lyre*.'

There was no reply, and before Sam could stop her, Anna strode to the nearest captive. She grabbed his arm and hauled him to his feet. 'Speak, you maggot, or I'll–'

'Anna!' snapped Pretin. 'Release him this instant!'

Reluctantly, Anna obeyed, giving the man a stony look as he sank to the deck.

Then Sam spotted someone amongst the prisoners. It was a woman dressed in a black uniform, and Sam's eyes narrowed as she recognised her face. The last time she'd seen this particular Mayestran, the woman had ordered the execution of the captives on planet Handley.

'Don't worry, I've already passed her name on to the authorities.'

Sam spun around and saw Mellish in the doorway. He looked tired, but he managed a weak grin. 'I see you've come to watch the circus.'

'Are you okay? Did they hurt you?'

'Things were pretty grim for a while, but they're a lot better now this lot have been defeated.' He searched her face, then glanced at Piet. 'I hear you two had a big hand in this victory. Who'd have thought, eh?'

'Come on,' said Pretin. 'I'm keen to inspect the enemy TacOps setup. I've heard rumours it's similar to ours, but I want to see it with my own eyes.'

He was as excited as a child in a candy store, but Sam could see Mellish was all-in, and David was out on his feet as well. As for her, the thought of battling crowds of souvenir-hunters left her cold. 'Sir, would it be all right if we returned to the *Lyre*? We're all exhausted.'

'Yes, yes, of course. Take the shuttle, and let them know I'll be back as soon as possible.'

'Yes sir.' Relieved, Sam led the others to the shuttle bay, where things seemed even more chaotic than before. All she wanted now was a quiet, peaceful room, something hot to drink, and a comfy bed for a solid eight hours of sleep. They found the shuttle that had brought them, which stuck out like a sore thumb amongst the Henerian vessels, then instructed the pilot to take them home.

'I was worried they'd shot you,' Sam told Mellish.

'They were still at the questioning part when you blasted the bridge.'

'That was Piet.'

Mellish eyed the male pilot. 'So you finally hit something, eh?'

'To be fair, it was a pretty big target,' admitted Piet.

'Well, it caused absolutely chaos on board, I can tell you. Half of them wanted to surrender, and the other half wanted to activate the self-destruct. Fortunately they were shouted down.'

Sam started. 'Nobody actually *got* to the self-destruct, did they?'

'No chance.' Mellish jerked his thumb at Piet. 'It takes two officers, and he took care of those.'

They docked with the Golden Lyre, and after the frantic scenes in the Scimitar's hangar, the docking bay seemed empty and peaceful. Sam led the way to the rear doors, and she was just about to open them when she saw someone coming through the airlock from the other side. It was a messenger, and he was looking for Monitor Pretin.

'He stayed aboard the cruiser,' Sam told him. 'Was it anything important?'

'Not really. The prisoner, Aren Grant... she's coming round. Monitor Pretin wanted to know.'

'Ok. You might want to send a message to the cruiser, but I wouldn't expect him back in a hurry. He'll be up to his elbows in the Mayestran TacOps setup by now.'

The messenger saluted, and they all passed through the airlock together. 'Where to?' asked David.

'Food,' said Anna.

'Then sleep,' said Sam. 'I'm out on my feet.'

'You guys go ahead,' said Mellish. 'I've got to file a report.'

'Ah, yes,' muttered David. 'Keeping us all safe with the mighty pen.'

Mellish faced him. 'Do you have a problem with me?'

'More than one, sunshine,' said David, bristling.

'Oh, shut up, the pair of you,' snapped Sam. 'I'm tired, I'm hungry and I'm not putting up with this shit. We're alive, aren't we? We defeated a major enemy attack, saved the Second Fleet and captured a cruiser. This is not the time for bickering.'

The two men eyed each other, then David gave a snort and turned away. Mellish watched him go, then shrugged and headed for the lift.

'What's the matter with you?' demanded Sam, as she caught up with David. 'He's doing his bit for the war, even if he's not firing a gun or piloting a fighter.'

'There's something about him,' muttered David. 'He sets my teeth on edge.'

Sam was silent. She suspected the two of them were involved in some petty battle over her, and if either of them thought she was going to be claimed like a Mayestran souvenir, they had another thought coming. She had half a mind to buy Piet a drink, just to send the other two idiots a message... then decided that would only make matters worse.

They reached the nearest canteen, where they found a couple of dozen crew members getting refreshments. There was a jovial atmosphere, and Sam heard snatches of conversation as she took a table with the others.

'...they reckon her guns are twice as powerful as ours...'

'...flew straight in and...bam!'

'...supposed to be some kind of traitor...'

The words jumbled in Sam's mind, her tired brain struggling to process them. But one word kept repeating, over and over, jangling and insistent: *traitor!*

Sam thought of Aren Grant, presumably confined to sick bay, restrained to a bunk. *What made a loyal Henerian change sides?* She'd never found out the cause of Grant's terrible scars, and she wondered whether the enemy had captured her, fragile and badly injured. They'd done the same to Sam's brother, after all, but she'd managed to free him before the Mayestrans truly went to work on his mind. What if Grant had been subjected to months of brainwashing? Was that all it took to switch sides and betray your own people?

Traitor!

A memory surfaced unexpectedly. It featured Aren Grant, back at the training base, and she was sitting at the bar in the mess. Mellish was with her, and they were chatting animatedly, discussing some aspect of the war. They'd left together soon afterwards, and Sam had assumed they were an item. Either that, or they were seeking comfort in each other's arms.

And yet, Mellish had shown no emotion when the messenger had told them Grant was coming round. He hadn't asked after her, or shown the slightest interest. For a political officer who was meant to keep his finger on the pulse, that seemed a little...odd.

Traitor!

'Oh shit,' muttered Sam.

'Coffee not to your liking?' asked Anna.

'I just had a bad feeling.'

'Yep, that's the coffee all right.'

'No, it's about Mellish.'

David snorted. 'Your description still applies.'

'Does anyone know where Grant is being held?' asked Sam.

'Sick bay, I should think. Why, do you want a lecture on the superiority of the Mayestran empire?'

'Let's go.'

'But I haven't finished!' protested Anna, gesturing at her plate.

'Now!'

43

As she hurried towards the sick bay with Anna, David and Piet on her tail, Sam hoped she was wrong. The others kept plying her with questions, but she ignored them. If she told them what she suspected, and it turned out to be pure fantasy, they'd never let her forget it.

They rounded a corner and stopped. Ahead, a marine was lying in the corridor, motionless. They ran up to him, and David crouched to check him. 'He's dead!' he whispered. 'Shot at close range. His gun's missing too.'

Inside, they found a blood-chilling scene. A couple of nurses were slumped over their desks, shot where they'd been sitting. A medic was huddled on the floor, still clutching a clipboard, and two patients had been shot nearby. Someone had gone through blasting the lot of them, and Sam had a pretty good idea who. 'It was Mellish,' she muttered. 'He's with the Mayestrans.'

'Are you kidding me?' demanded David. 'That devious little prick did all this?'

Sam wasn't sure what had annoyed him more... the fact Mellish was a traitor, or that he was more than capable of using a gun after all.

Meanwhile, Anna had been checking the nearest casualty,

and then she checked another before looking up in surprise. 'They've been shot with a stun weapon. They're still alive.'

'We've got to find Grant,' said Sam quickly. 'There might still be time.'

'Why, what's he going to do?'

'He'll try and silence her, that's what. He'll kill her so she can't be interrogated, then escape or take his own life.'

'I'll happily put him down, if that's what he wants,' vowed David.

They ran through the next two rooms, where they found more scenes of chaos. Then they hauled open a door and froze. Mellish was standing on the far side of Grant's bed, with a small blaster levelled at the woman's head. She was conscious, just, and her eyes were fixed on the gaping muzzle. Both her hands were restrained with cuffs, and she could do nothing to defend herself. Nearby, the guard's blast rifle was leaning against the bed.

As the four of them burst in, Mellish summed up the situation at a glance. Then he brought the pistol up, covering them all. Sam expected him to fire, to shoot them all down so he could finish the job, but he must have known it was hopeless. He'd get one or two if they charged him, but the others would be on him before he could get them all. So, it was an impasse. 'What were you trying to achieve?' Sam asked him calmly. 'You would never have got away with this. It's over.'

'I just need to silence her and be on my way.' Mellish gestured with the gun. 'Step back please. You're crowding me.'

'I'm not going anywhere,' growled David.

With his free hand, Mellish reached down and picked up the blast rifle, which he levelled at the four of them. Now there were two guns facing them, and Sam realised the odds were definitely in Mellish's favour. 'I don't want to shoot you all, but I will.' He gestured at Sam with the pistol. 'Over here, please.'

'Why?'

'I'm getting out of here, and you'll make the perfect hostage. Nobody will shoot at me if there's a chance of hitting little miss perfect.'

Sam knew she had no choice, and she decided to play for time. Someone would happen across the carnage in the sick bay before too long, and once they raised the alarm Mellish would never get away. 'Okay, everyone relax. Nobody has to get shot here.' She glanced at the others. David looked fit to burst, Anna was itching for a fight and Piet looked like he would rip the bed in two to get at Mellish. 'I mean it. Take it easy and do what he says.' *Until the right moment,* she thought, and she hoped the others caught her meaning. Slowly, hands raised, she approached the bed, where Mellish put his arm around her, blast rifle still clutched in one hand. Then he pressed the smaller pistol to her neck. The muzzle was cool against her skin, and she wondered whether she'd have the slightest inkling that he'd fired before it was too late.

Then Mellish levelled the blast rifle, and he shot Anna before anyone knew what was happening. He got Piet next, the pilot still frozen in shock, and that left the injured David until last. David was unable to move as fast as the others, something Mellish was well aware of, but the wounded pilot tried his best to jump clear anyway. The shot caught him in mid-air, sending him crashing into the doorframe, and Mellish drew in a sharp breath as David slumped to the floor, unconscious. 'Ooh, that's got to hurt.'

'You didn't have to shoot them,' muttered Sam.

254

'We both know I did.' Mellish looked down at Grant, who was still drifting in and out of consciousness and barely seemed to know what was going on. Sam saw his predicament immediately, because if he took the pistol from her neck to shoot the woman in the bed, Sam would be free to fight back. And the blast rifle was gripped in his other hand, so all he could do was render Grant unconscious.

'Let her live,' said Sam quietly. 'Leave her be, and I'll help you escape.'

He looked at her in surprise. 'Why would you do such a thing?'

Sam tried to keep her expression neutral, because she was just trying to keep him talking to buy herself some time. 'Call it a trade. You go free, but we get some info out of Grant. I can live with that.'

'The top brass won't see it that way. You'll be crucified.'

'They don't have a gun to their heads, do they?'

'Fair point.' Mellish eyed Grant for a moment or two, then shrugged. 'All right, it's a deal. Let's go.'

'Where?'

'The *Scimitar*. I have unfinished business over there.' Mellish led her to the sickbay entrance, grabbing a white lab coat on the way. He motioned Sam against the wall while he slung the blast rifle over his shoulder and donned the lab coat, covering the bulky weapon. Then he gestured for her to get close again. As she approached she debated whether to launch herself at him, to try and take him down before he could shoot her. His finger was on the trigger though, and she could tell he was prepared for any sudden moves.

So, they left the sickbay together, with the pistol pointing at her from a pocket in Mellish's lab coat. 'Where to?' she asked him.

'Hangar bay two.'

They reached the main passageway and turned for the hangar. Along the way they passed several members of the crew, but Sam was careful not to attract their attention. She knew that Mellish would gun them down if they tried to interfere, and she didn't want their deaths on her hands.

They'd made it all the way to the hangar's main airlock when a siren began to sound. Someone must have visited the sickbay, seen the chaos and raised the alarm.

'All personnel, we have one or more intruders on board. The ship is now in lockdown, and you will remain where you are until the threat has been neutralised.'

'Too bloody late,' growled Mellish, and he gestured for Sam to operate the airlock. They passed through into the hangar, which contained half a dozen Mayestran shuttles and a handful of ground crew and techs. They looked around as Mellish entered, and Sam hoped desperately they wouldn't challenge him. In the confines of the hangar, with next to no cover, it would be a bloodbath.

Nobody stopped them, and they continued towards the nearest shuttle. The doors stood open, and Sam could see right into the passenger cabin with its two rows of seats. She'd already discarded several plans as unworkable, but now she saw an out. It was obvious Mellish was going to force her to fly the thing, and all she had to do was crash it into the hangar entrance on the way out. The shuttle's dampers wouldn't cope with that kind of impact, and Mellish would be hurled against the front of the ship. She'd brace before the impact, wait for him to slam into the controls, then take the gun away and subdue him. It was risky, but definitely worth a shot.

Then she spotted a pair of marines, both armed. 'You two,' called one of them. 'Hold there please!'

Mellish tensed. The shuttle was only ten metres away, and she knew instinctively that he was going to run. She wrenched his arm free and dropped to the deck. 'Mayestran agent!' she shouted. 'Take him!'

Mellish swore at her, then turned and bounded for the shuttle. The marines brought their weapons up and fired after him, but they were forty metres away, caught by surprise, and Mellish was moving fast. Some shots sprayed the deck at Mellish's feet, while others slammed into the shuttle and still more ricocheted off the hangar walls to pass harmlessly through the big force field at the entrance.

Two steps, three, and Mellish dived into the shuttle, shots going wild all around him. Then the doors closed, and Sam saw him appear in the cockpit. The marines were still firing, but their shots splashed harmlessly off the shuttle, and they lowered their weapons and ran to her. 'What's going on?' one of them asked.

'It's all right, he's trapped. Fetch a bigger gun, and he'll have to surrender.'

In the meantime, Mellish had taken the pilot's chair, and with a sinking feeling she saw him preparing the shuttle for flight. 'Warn the defensive batteries,' she told the second marine. 'If he lifts off, they'll have to take him out.'

'But they're not manned. We stood everyone down after the battle.'

The shuttle's engine fired with a roar, and Sam watched it lift off and turn for the entrance. 'All right. Call the enemy cruiser. Let them know they've got a Mayestran inbound. He might try to talk his way through and go for the self-destruct.' Sam remembered Mellish telling her the self-destruct needed two officers to activate, but now she realised that was probably another lie. He might not be able to save himself, but if he used the crowds of souvenir hunters for cover he could blow up the cruiser and everyone on board. How many high-ranking officers were poking around the Mayestran vessel at that very moment? From what she'd seen, most of the fleet had sent shuttles full of personnel to the cruiser. If Mellish took them all out it would be an incalculable loss.

The shuttle roared out of the bay, the noise drowning out her very thoughts. Then she got up and ran for the airlock.

'Hey, I need you for questioning!' shouted the marine.

'Sam Willet, fighter pilot. You can question me when I get back.' Sam ran on, and she felt an itch between her shoulder blades as she cycled the airlock. If the marine shot her now, hundreds might die.

Then the airlock door opened, and she ran to the next hangar, dodging several people on the way. The air stank of burning from the destroyed fighters, but she saw what she needed directly ahead. 'Emergency launch!' she shouted to the ground crew. 'A Mayestran agent just took off in a shuttle. He's got to be stopped.'

The only fighter was her own, and one engine was just a smoking ruin where the enemy had blasted her in the recent dogfight. Mellish must have known that when he took the shuttle, and was assuming he could lose himself in the other traffic before Sam could organise a pursuit.

'This thing's not going anywhere,' said a mechanic, stepping in front of her.

'It's not your decision. Get out of the way.'

'You'll get yourself killed!'

'If I don't stop the shuttle, hundreds might die.'

The mechanic saw she meant in, and he followed the others into cover, hiding behind a low wall designed for the purpose.

'I still say you're crazy!' he shouted, as Sam shot up the ladder to the cockpit.

She sat in the seat, one hand activating the flight systems while the other struggled with the electrical and data connections to her suit. Then she realised there was no helmet.

'Sod it,' she muttered, and she closed the canopy. The shuttle wouldn't be hard to find, and it wasn't like TacOps would be there to guide her. The one remaining engine fired, the sound much louder than normal without her helmet to muffle the noise, and she winced as she realised she'd have to put up with it. She checked the landing pad was clear then lifted off, the engine note becoming something physical, with waves of sound hammering at her unprotected ears.

Sam ignored the noise and focused on the hangar exit, launching the fighter out of the *Lyre's* docking bay with a push on the throttle. The Kestrel tore into space, and she spotted the enemy cruiser a couple of kilometres away, surrounded by the specks of shuttles arriving and departing.

Then she saw Mellish. He was going flat out, with flame jetting from the exhausts as he tried to put distance between himself and the *Golden Lyre*. Even on one engine Sam was catching him fast, her throttle at barely twenty percent, and as she got closer she armed her weapons. She didn't intend to shoot him down, just put a warning shot across his nose. In fact, she planned to corral him until help arrived, at which point they'd take him into custody. After all, it wasn't like he could fight back.

She drew alongside, then turned her fighter's nose until the guns were pointing directly into the shuttle's cockpit. She could see Mellish inside, and she almost laughed when she saw his jaw drop in surprise. Then he hunched over the controls, and the shuttle accelerated further.

Sam angled to the left and fired a burst. The flashes lit up the shuttle's interior, bathing it in stark light, but Mellish didn't change course.

Now Sam realised her plan wasn't quite perfect. Firing across someone's nose wasn't particularly effective if they chose to ignore the threat. Mellish was betting she wouldn't blast him out of space, and at this stage she knew he was right.

The shuttle's engine was still blazing away, and Sam glanced to her left, towards the *Scimitar*. They were getting closer and closer, and if Mellish didn't slow soon he was going to run right into the thing. Sam could see the force field at the entrance to the docking bay, and she imagined all the people crowded inside. Then, slowly, she turned to gaze at the shuttle.

With dawning horror, she realised what Mellish was planning. He wasn't going to sneak aboard the cruiser to use the self-destruct... he was going to slam the shuttle into the *Scimitar's* docking bay at full speed.

44

Sam pictured the destruction if Mellish succeeded, and the blood ran cold in her veins. He'd kill dozens, maybe hundreds, in the initial blast and there was a good chance the explosion would damage the cruiser's hull, too, venting atmosphere.

Desperate to stop him, Sam fired another burst across the shuttle's nose, this time even closer, but again Mellish ignored her. She knew she should blast him there and then, but shooting an unarmed target wasn't her idea of warfare. It would be murder, pure and simple.

The problem was, she was running out of time. If she destroyed the shuttle now, the fragments would fan out, with maybe a handful hitting the cruiser. But if she waited until the last minute, the wreckage hitting the cruiser could do as much damage as the intact shuttle.

'*Golden Lyre to Red Leader. Your launch was unauthorised. Please return to the hangar immediately.*'

'I can't do that, Lyre. I'm pursuing a Mayestran agent who's trying to flee in a shuttle. He's heading towards the enemy cruiser, and I think he means to ram her.'

'*Can you stop him?*'

'I tried, but he's ignoring my warning shots.'

'*That's not what I meant, Red Leader.*'

'Are you ordering me to destroy the shuttle?'

There was a pause. *'Confirmed. Take the shot.'*

With a heavy heart, Sam roared away from the shuttle before coming round in a tight arc. As the tiny vessel swam into her gunsight she reminded herself that Mellish had killed the guard outside the sickbay. He'd sided with the enemy, passing on information which had probably cost the deaths of dozens. And now he was planning to kill many more.

Feeling sick to her stomach, she squeezed the trigger, and the shuttle rocked under the concentrated fire from her guns. There was a brief flash, and then a fading cloud of particles. 'Target destroyed,' she said, her voice low.

'Thank you, Sam. Return to base for debrief.'

With a stony expression, Sam turned her fighter towards the *Golden Lyre.*

◆

Sam set the damaged fighter down on the landing pad, then sat in the pilot's chair staring into the distance, her eyes unfocussed. It was one thing to battle enemy fighters, but blowing up the shuttle had been another matter entirely. She could still see the helpless craft falling apart under her guns, and she knew she'd never get the image out of her head.

She just couldn't understand what Mellish had been trying to achieve. He must have known it was hopeless, trying to get away, and even his attempt to silence Aren Grant had proved a failure. Any intel Mellish might have gathered, intel he was hoping to pass to the Mayestrans, would have been destroyed along with him.

To Sam, they weren't the actions of a trained enemy agent, they were just...pointless.

She sat there in the cockpit, thinking it over from the beginning. Assuming Mellish's actions had a genuine purpose, what had he really achieved? He'd met with Grant, and then he'd created a brief diversion as he tried to get away. That's what it boiled down to.

Could it be something to do with Grant? Mellish had been standing over her when Sam and the others found him in the sickbay, but he hadn't killed her despite having plenty of time to do so. What if he'd passed her a data cube containing all his intel on the Henerians, in the hope that she'd somehow get it back to the Mayestrans?

But why? Grant had already been captured, and nobody suspected Mellish. He could have fled long before she revealed he was a traitor under questioning, delivering the data to the enemy himself. There was no need for him to seek Grant out at all.

Unless Grant could do something Mellish couldn't. That was the only reason Sam could think of for the political officer to sacrifice himself. He'd been giving Grant a chance to complete a mission of her own.

Sam recalled the scene in the sickbay. Aren Grant had been lying in bed, barely conscious, her wrists secured. What if she'd been fully alert, and only pretending to be dazed? What if Mellish had already loosened the restraints before Sam and the others showed up? As soon as he and Sam left the sick bay, Grant could have leapt out of bed, grabbed a gun and gone...where?

There were only two likely destinations Sam could think

of. Grant could have made for the nearest hangar, to try and escape in a shuttle. Or, she could have headed for the Golden Lyre's power core, to blow up the wounded old battleship, and with her the captured cruiser and any other Second Fleet ships nearby. It would be a final, devastating blow just as the Henerians were celebrating their hard-fought victory.

Frowning, she toggled the mic. 'Golden Lyre, this is Sam Willet. Can you confirm you have Aren Grant in custody?'

'Negative, Sam. She escaped the sick bay and we're hunting her now.' There was a pause. *'How the hell did you guess?'*

'Mellish must have freed her. I suggest you check the power core right away, because I think she's planning to blow the whole ship.'

'We're ahead of you there. If that's where she's heading, she won't get through.'

'Copy that.' Sam released the mic and sat back, relieved. Luckily, it looked like Grant's final roll of the dice was going to be about as successful as Mellish's.

Then she felt the cockpit shake. It was a tremble at first, settling down to a steady rumble.

'Lyre, what the hell is that?'

'Grant's on the bridge! She's taken out the officer of the watch and the helm and barricaded herself in!'

The rumbling increased, and through the force field Sam noticed the enemy cruiser slipping to the right. But it wasn't the cruiser moving, it was the *Golden Lyre,* and she was turning directly towards the enemy ship. 'She's going to ram the cruiser!' shouted Sam. It was all too clear now... the Mayestrans weren't going to let one of their newest ships fall into Henerian hands, and she guessed Grant might have even prepared for this moment when the pilot had flown the *Lyre* to the dockyard earlier. Grant had been alone in the bridge for an hour or more after it had been cut off from the rest of the ship, and she would have set up her final desperate plan then.

The huge battleship was still turning, not yet moving forward, but Sam knew that once the main drives fired it would all be over. Even a brief burst would be enough to get the huge ship moving, and once that happened it wouldn't stop until it ploughed into the enemy cruiser. Not unless the crew gained access to the bridge, overpowered Grant and hit full reverse thrust... and they only had seconds to do it.

Sam knew what she had to do, and she fired up the fighter's one remaining engine, her hands flying over the controls. She checked the landing pad, then lifted off and steered directly for the forcefield. 'Lyre, this is Red Leader. I'm departing the hangar, and will circle round to the rear of the ship. If you can't get into the bridge, I'll shoot the main drives out.'

'Copy that. Stand by.'

Sam flew out of the hanger and turned left, bringing the bulk of the battleship into view through her canopy. She could see the ship's bridge high above, and then she glanced along the hull, towards the engine cluster at the rear. Even as she watched, she saw a massive flare of light as the drives fired. Then, out the corner of her eye, she saw a bright flash of light from the bridge. 'Lyre, did you gain entry?'

'Wait, reports coming in now.' The controller came back to her, his voice sounding shaky. 'She... detonated a grenade, Sam. Took herself out, and half the bridge with it.'

'Can you cut the engines?'

'No chance. It's... it's a complete mess.'

The huge battleship was starting to move, and Sam knew there was only one thing left to try, risky though it was. She brought the damaged fighter round in a turn, until the huge, flaring exhausts filled her cockpit, then opened fire.

Blaster shots lanced from the nose of her fighter, slamming into the Lyre's engines, tearing the exhaust ports apart before digging deeper, into the drives themselves. There were several explosions, with huge jets of exhaust firing in all directions as the out-of-control engines, and then a rippling blast that had Sam turning sharply and blasting away to safety. She flew until she'd reached a safe distance, then turned her ship to see whether she needed to fire on the battleship again.

There was no need. The rear of the ship was a blackened, twisted mess, with jetting flames and explosions flaring between the molten beams and buckled armour plating. Air was venting from cracks in the hull, and as Sam eyed the damage she knew the Golden Lyre would never fly again. 'Lyre, this is Red Leader. Is everyone all right?'

'Damage reports like you wouldn't believe, but they're sealing off the aft section now. We'll live, over.'

Sam glanced towards the Mayestran cruiser, which was lying directly across the path of the drifting hulk. A few more seconds of thrust and the battleship would have been hurtling towards the enemy ship, but she'd managed to take out the main drives in the nick of time. As it was, the *Golden Lyre* was barely moving, and she guessed it would take an hour or more to cross the distance. Plenty of time for the repair crews to fire up the reverse thrusters in the fore section, bringing the stricken battleship to a halt.

Still reeling from the explosion she'd caused, Sam turned the Kestrel and headed for the nearest docking bay.

◆

Sam was still shutting down the fighter's one remaining engine when she heard a knock on the plexiglass canopy, and she turned to see Piet smiling at her through the glass. She operated the controls, opening the hood, and he clambered back down the ladder to give her room.

Once on the ground, she saw David and Anna nearby. 'I hear you got Mellish,' said Anna.

Sam nodded.

'I never did like that guy,' muttered David. Then he nodded towards the exit. 'Come on, we've got a meal to finish.'

'And coffee,' said Anna.

Sam smiled. 'Yeah, but you're buying. And after that, I'm going to sleep for a week!'

On the way out of the hangar, Piet fell in beside her. 'Did you *have* to shoot down a battleship?' he complained, in a bantering tone. 'They were still congratulating me for stopping that cruiser, and then you go and top my effort in a fighter with a missing engine!'

The rest laughed out loud, and as they headed for the canteen they recounted their recent battles in excited voices. Sam strode beside them, smiling to herself, because while the war against the Mayestrans would never be easy, with comrades like these it was certainly going to be more bearable.

If you enjoyed this book, please leave a brief review at your online bookseller of choice. Thanks!

About the Author

Simon Haynes was born in England and grew up in Spain. His family moved to Australia when he was 16.

In addition to novels, Simon writes computer software. In fact, he writes computer software to help him write novels faster, which leaves him more time to improve his writing software. And write novels faster. (www.spacejock.com/yWriter.html)

Simon's goal is to write fifteen novels before someone takes his keyboard away.

Update 2018: goal achieved and I still have my keyboard!
New goal: write thirty novels.

Simon's website is spacejock.com.au

Stay in touch!

Author's newsletter:
spacejock.com.au/ML.html

facebook.com/halspacejock
twitter.com/spacejock

Acknowledgements

Rich, Gabrielle, Ray, Neil. Frauke, Val, Gin, Tim, Ian (in advance),
thanks for the awesome help and support!

The Hal Spacejock series
by Simon Haynes

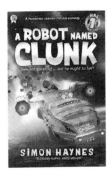

1. A ROBOT NAMED CLUNK

Deep in debt and with his life on the line, Hal takes on a dodgy cargo job ... and an equally dodgy co-pilot.

2. SECOND COURSE

When Hal finds an alien teleporter network he does the sensible thing and pushes Clunk the robot in first.

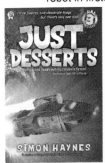

3. JUST DESSERTS

Gun-crazed mercenaries have Hal in their sights, and a secret agent is pulling the strings. One wrong step and three planets go to war!

4. NO FREE LUNCH

Everyone thinks Peace Force trainee Harriet Walsh is paranoid and deluded, but Hal stands at her side. That would be the handcuffs.

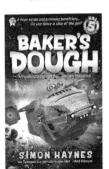

5. BAKER'S DOUGH

When you stand to inherit a fortune, good body-guards are essential. If you're really desperate, call Hal and Clunk. Baker's Dough features intense rivalry, sublime double-crosses and more greed than a free buffet.

6. SAFE ART

Valuable artworks and a tight deadline ... you'd be mad to hire Hal for that one, but who said the art world was sane?

7. BIG BANG

A house clearance job sounds like easy money, but rising floodwaters, an unstable landscape and a surprise find are going to make life very difficult for Hal and Clunk.

8. DOUBLE TROUBLE

Hal Spacejock dons a flash suit, hypershades and a curly earpiece for a stint as a secret agent, while a pair of Clunk's most rusted friends invite him to a 'unique business opportunity'.

9. MAX DAMAGE

Hal and Clunk answer a distress call, and they discover a fellow pilot stranded deep inside an asteroid field. Clunk is busy at the controls so Hal dons a spacesuit and sets off on a heroic rescue mission.

10. Cold Boots

The Spacers' Guild needs a new president, and Hal Spacejock is determined to cast his vote... even though he's not a member.

Meanwhile, Hal's latest cargo job belongs to someone else, his shiny new ship is losing money hand over fist, and doing a good favour could turn out to be the biggest mistake of his life.

Ebook and Trade Paperback

The Secret War Series

Set in the Hal Spacejock universe

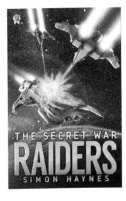

Everyone is touched by the war, and Sam Willet is no exception.

Sam wants to train as a fighter pilot, but instead she's assigned to Tactical Operations.
It's vital work, but it's still a desk job, far from the front line.

Then, terrible news: Sam's older brother is killed in combat.

Sam is given leave to attend his memorial service, but she's barely boarded the transport
when the enemy launches a surprise attack, striking far behind friendly lines as they try to
take the entire sector.

Desperately short of pilots, the Commander asks Sam to step up.

Now, at last, she has the chance to prove herself.

But will that chance end in death... or glory?

Ebook and Trade Paperback

The Harriet Walsh series

Harriet's boss is a huge robot with failing batteries, the patrol car is driving her up the wall and her first big case will probably kill her.

So why did she join the Peace Force?

When an intergalactic crime-fighting organisation offers Harriet Walsh a job, she's convinced it's a mistake. She dislikes puzzles, has never read a detective mystery, and hates wearing uniforms. It makes no sense ... why would the Peace Force choose her?

Who cares? Harriet needs the money, and as long as they keep paying her, she's happy to go along with the training.

She'd better dig out some of those detective mysteries though, because she's about to embark on her first real mission ...

The Peace Force has a new recruit, and she's driving everyone crazy.

From disobeying orders to handling unauthorised cases, nothing is off-limits. Worse, Harriet Walsh is forced to team up with the newbie, because the recruit's shady past has just caught up with her.

Meanwhile, a dignitary wants to complain about rogue officers working out of the station. She insists on meeting the station's commanding officer ... and they don't have one.

All up, it's another typical day in the Peace Force!

Dismolle is supposed to be a peaceful retirement planet. So what's with all the gunfire?

A criminal gang has moved into Chirless, planet Dismolle's second major city. Elderly residents are fed up with all the loud music, noisy cars and late night parties, not to mention the hold-ups, muggings and the occasional gunfight.

There's no Peace Force in Chirless, so they call on Harriet Walsh of the Dismolle City branch for help. That puts Harriet right in the firing line, and now she's supposed to round up an entire gang with only her training pistol and a few old allies as backup.

And her allies aren't just old, they're positively ancient!

Ebook and Trade Paperback

The Hal Junior Series
Set in the Hal Spacejock universe
Spot the crossover characters, references and in-jokes!

Hal Junior lives aboard a futuristic space station. His mum is chief scientist, his dad cleans air filters and his best mate is Stephen 'Stinky' Binn. As for Hal ... he's a bit of a trouble magnet. He means well, but his wild schemes and crazy plans never turn out as expected!

Hal Junior: The Secret Signal features mayhem and laughs, daring and intrigue ... plus a home-made space cannon!

200 pages, illustrated, ISBN 978-1-877034-07-7

"A thoroughly enjoyable read for 10-year-olds and adults alike"
The West Australian

'I've heard of food going off
   ... but this is ridiculous!'

Space Station Oberon is expecting an important visitor, and everyone is on their best behaviour. Even Hal Junior is doing his best to stay out of trouble!

From multi-coloured smoke bombs to exploding space rations, Hal Junior proves ... ***trouble is what he's best at!***

200 pages, illustrated, ISBN 978-1-877034-25-1

Imagine a whole week of fishing, swimming, sleeping in tents and running wild!

Unfortunately, the boys crash land in the middle of a forest, and there's little chance of rescue. Is this the end of the camping trip ... or the start of a thrilling new adventure?

200 pages, illustrated, ISBN 978-1-877034-24-4

Space Station Oberon is on high alert, because a comet is about to whizz past the nearby planet of Gyris. All the scientists are preparing for the exciting event, and all the kids are planning on watching.

All the kids except Hal Junior, who's been given detention...

165 pages, illustrated, ISBN 978-1-877034-38-1

Ebook and Trade Paperback

New from Simon Haynes
The Dragon & Chips Trilogy

"Laugh after laugh, dark in places but the humour punches through. One of the best books I've read in 2018 so far. Amazing, 5*"

Welcome to the Old Kingdom!

It's a wonderful time to visit! There's lots to do and plenty to see!

What are you waiting for? Dive into the Old Kingdom right now!

Clunk, an elderly robot, does exactly that. He's just plunged into the sea off the coast of the Old Kingdom, and if he knew what was coming next he'd sit down on the ocean floor and wait for rescue.

Dragged from the ocean, coughing up seaweed, salty water and stray pieces of jellyfish, he's taken to the nearby city of Chatter's Reach, where he's given a sword and told to fight the Queen's Champion, Sur Loyne.

As if that wasn't bad enough, the Old Kingdom still thinks the wheel is a pretty nifty idea, and Clunk's chances of finding spare parts - or his missing memory modules - are nil.

Still, Clunk is an optimist, and it's not long before he's embarking on a quest to find his way home.

Unfortunately it's going to be a very tough ask, given the lack of charging points in the medieval kingdom...

Ebook and Trade Paperback

Printed in Great Britain
by Amazon